CAVANAUGH STAKEOUT

Marie Ferrarella

HARLEQUIN®ROMANTIC SUSPENSE

Recycling programs
for this product may
not exist in your area.

ISBN-13: 978-1-335-66223-1

Cavanaugh Stakeout

Copyright © 2019 by Marie Rydzynski-Ferrarella

Printed in U.S.A.

The time for inner reflection, for wondering and wavering, had passed.

Because Finn was kissing her.

Nik felt her head swimming. And then she could feel Finn smile against her lips, his lips warming her.

Seducing her.

"Why are you smiling?" she asked.

"Because that was exactly the way I imagined it would be," he confessed.

And then the reality of what he had just done hit him. Finn sobered, realizing that she might misunderstand what had just happened. "Sorry. That wasn't the reason I wanted to see you to your door. But I would be lying if I said that it wasn't to have a few more minutes with you."

Reviewing their relatively short association, she looked at him skeptically. "I thought you couldn't wait to get rid of me."

"In the beginning," he conceded. "But I have to admit that you have a way of getting to a guy. And I have to say that you are pulling your own weight."

"You sure know how to turn a girl's head with sweet talk."

* * *

If you're on Twitter, tell us what you think of Harlequin Romantic Suspense! #harlequinromsuspense

Dear Reader,

Welcome back to the ever-growing Cavanaugh clan. When Seamus, the eternally young patriarch of the family, is mugged and left for dead one night in the parking lot of one of the buildings his security company oversees, his spirit is crushed and all but drained from him. The rest of the family rallies around him. They all want to find the person responsible for hurting Seamus, but that proves to be far more complicated than it might seem.

Detective Finley Cavanaugh from the robbery division heads up the investigation because Seamus's car was stolen. But it quickly becomes a homicide investigation when bodies of women start piling up, beginning with the one whose blood was found in the trunk of Seamus's stolen vehicle. To complicate matters, as a favor for a friend searching for her missing daughter, insurance investigator Nikola Kowalski begins looking into Seamus's case. It seems that the missing daughter's fingerprint has turned up on the back of Seamus's rearview mirror. Try as he might, Finn can't get the annoyingly inquisitive Nik to back off. And soon, almost against his will, he realizes that he doesn't want to. Meanwhile, more and more young women are having their lives snuffed out while Finn and Nik find themselves going around in circles, following clues that lead nowhere.

As always, I thank you for taking the time to pick up and read one of my books. I sincerely hope it entertains you, and from the bottom of my heart, I wish you someone to love who loves you back.

All my best,

Marie Ferrarella

USA TODAY bestselling and RITA® Award–winning author **Marie Ferrarella** has written more than two hundred and fifty books for Harlequin, some under the name Marie Nicole. Her romances are beloved by fans worldwide. Visit her website, marieferrarella.com.

Books by Marie Ferrarella

Harlequin Romantic Suspense

Cavanaugh Justice

Visit the Author Profile page at Harlequin.com for more titles.

To
Charlie.
Just When I Think My Heart
Can't Be Any Fuller,
You Do Something Wonderful
And Make It Grow
A Complete Size Larger.

Prologue

He hated the expression "feeling your age." More than that, the onetime robbery detective hated the fact that getting in behind the wheel of his dark blue sedan was now a two-step, sometimes three-step, procedure that involved lowering himself into his seat, then physically picking up and lifting his left leg in order to maneuver it into position inside the vehicle.

Not that he would ever actually admit as much to anyone. After all, he was Seamus Cavanaugh, the eighty-one-year-old patriarch of the Cavanaugh clan, a family known and respected for its many members within the law-enforcement community.

Cavanaughs didn't complain, not when it came to things they had no control over.

Like time.

That sort of thing came under the heading of resigned acceptance.

If his sons ever suspected how often various parts of his body ached and gave him trouble, there would be no end to their trying to talk him into permanently retiring from the security firm that he had founded.

A laugh rumbled deep within his chest. *As if that would ever happen.*

He had tried retirement once and had concluded that retirement, even retirement in comfort, was for the birds—definitely not for him. He liked being active, even if that activity came with a price, like painful knees, aching shoulders and a back that insisted on periodically acting up.

To him the alternative was to slowly wither away and then finally die.

No, thank you, Seamus thought, shifting so that he could get comfortable—if that was even possible— behind the wheel before he started up the engine. The hell with retirement. He *needed* to be vital. That was why he was out here in one of the industrial-complex areas within Aurora's neighboring cities long after dark. He was doing an unexpected final check on one of the buildings his security firm protected. There'd been an attempted break-in on the building a little more than a week ago and he just wanted to be sure there were no repeat occurrences in the making despite the fact that the alarms and cameras on the premises had been silent.

Thanks to his grandchildren, grandnieces and grand- nephews, he knew how easily systems could be bypassed or hacked into. The expert IT crew he employed at his firm was considered to be the best in the business, but Seamus was still old-fashioned. As far as he was con- cerned, nothing beat a hands-on approach.

So he had deliberately gone through all the safety pro- tocols within the building, then driven around the building's perimeter just to put any apprehensions to bed. Now that he had, he was ready to head home and have that well-loved nightcap he'd been promising himself. His cardiologist, Dr. Benvenuti, a specialist who had treated him for years, frowned on his habit, but his doctor only looked at his year of birth. He did not take into account the patriarch's spirit.

His age didn't define him, Seamus thought rebelliously. He was still young at heart, still had a spring in his step, even though, he was willing to grudgingly admit, that spring had gotten just a wee bit rusty of late.

It was going to rain, Seamus thought now, as he was ready to leave. His shoulder, the one he had gotten shot in in the line of duty almost four decades ago, ached the way it always did just before it rained. Fortunately for him, rain was *not* a regular occurrence where he now lived, in California.

Preoccupied with his aching shoulder, Seamus wasn't aware of what was happening until it was too late.

One second he had just started to fasten his seat belt—his door was still open because he needed space to wrestle with the belt—the next, someone had come up to his car, aimed a gun at him and growled, "I need your car, old man. Get out!"

Seamus didn't know which bothered him more—the fact that someone was trying to steal his car, or being referred to as an "old man." Having a gun aimed at him notwithstanding, his response was automatic.

"The hell I will!" Seamus growled.

The would-be car thief's expression registered surprise, then darkened. "Wrong answer, old man," he snapped.

It was the car thief's turn to be stunned. Seamus didn't

willingly hand over his car keys or his car. Instead, he angrily demanded, "Who the hell do you think you are?"

Still partially hidden by shadows, the tall, well-built, dark-haired man's face went from handsome to foreboding. Despite himself, Seamus felt a chill go up his spine. Out of the corner of his eye, Seamus thought he saw another figure move, but he couldn't be sure. He was completely focused on the car thief.

"I'm the man who's going to be driving that car of yours. You're two steps away from death, old man, and trust me, you won't be needing it," the car thief informed him.

"But I'm not dead yet," Seamus countered as he shot out a hand to grab the other man's wrist.

With his other hand, Seamus reached for the weapon he carried in his pocket. Although he no longer belonged to any branch of the police department, Seamus had a permit to carry a concealed weapon and he went regularly to the firing range to continue honing his already considerable skills.

"Wrong move, old man," the other man snarled.

Using leverage, the car thief pulled hard, yanking Seamus out of his car. Seamus put up a fight, but he was at least two decades older than his opponent and it acted against him.

The tug-of-war was short-lived, and Seamus wound up smashing his forehead against the concrete, cutting his temple as he landed facedown in the parking lot.

Seamus had put up more of a fight than the car thief expected. A barrage of heated curses were heaped on Seamus head.

Gaining possession of Seamus's gun, the car thief laughed in satisfied triumph. "How did you think this was going to turn out, old man?" he demanded, uttering another round of curses. Then, drawing in a deep breath as if to fortify himself for what he was about to do next, the car thief shot at Seamus with the weapon he was holding.

Fighting to remain conscious, Seamus thought he heard a woman's scream, but that might have just been the buzzing noise in his head. He couldn't tell.

"That's what you get when you mess with your betters, old man," the robber crowed. He began to bend down to check if he had killed the old man who had had the audacity to try to overpower him. He also wanted to grab the watch that had caught his eye. But as he reached for it, he froze.

The sound of an approaching car had him abandoning the watch. Instead, he focused on his own survival. Another string of curses erupted from his lips, as he damned Seamus's soul to hell after his insides had been ripped out and eaten by rabid wolves.

Seamus couldn't make out the words. His gut instinct said they were meant for him. Darkness was closing in around him, sealing him away, which was just as well. He couldn't endure the excruciating pounding in his head any longer.

Just before he slipped into the smothering embrace of a dark world, Seamus thought he heard the sound of two doors being shut.

And then there was the sound of a car—his car?— driving away.

After that, mercifully, there was nothing.

Chapter 1

Former police chief Andrew Cavanaugh immediately thought the worst whenever a phone rang, the shrill noise elbowing its way into his sound sleep, especially whenever it happened after midnight. It was at that time more than any other that icy fear would grip his heart even before he was fully awake. Because of the nature of his job and the jobs held down by so much of his family, half-formed dire scenarios would flood his mind the instant the phone began to ring.

Andrew was groping around on the nightstand, searching for his phone before his eyes were even open or his brain was fully engaged.

His wife, Rose, shared the very same feelings. And fears.

"Who is it, Andrew?" she asked, turning toward him in their queen-size bed.

Andrew didn't answer her. Fully awake now, he focused on listening to what the voice on the other end of the call was telling him.

The intense look on his face had Rose grasping his forearm, as if that would somehow help her assimilate what the caller was saying to him. Or, at the very least, allow her to share with him whatever burden those words might be creating.

What she was hearing from Andrew's side of the conversation only fueled her dread.

"When?" Andrew asked, his usually genial face a mask of concern. "How bad? Is he—?" Rose saw her husband exhale a shaky breath, dragging his hand through his hair. For a split second, the man everyone leaned on so heavily looked almost lost. "What hospital?"

By now Rose's adrenaline had escalated to an exceptionally high level. She quickly got out of bed and, rather than throw on a robe, automatically began to get dressed. Quickly.

The second she was finished, she was laying out her husband's clothing. She knew Andrew inside and out. She knew that the moment he hung up, they would be on their way to whatever hospital the person that this call was about was in.

With children, brothers and sisters-in-law, as well as an entire extended collection of family members, almost all involved in some capacity of law enforcement, there were many potential candidates for whom that path might have very well ended tonight—or had come very close to ending.

There was no other reason why a call would have suddenly shattered their night this way, or why her husband looked so distressed.

Without knowing whom this call was about or what the actual damage was, all Rose could do was pray as she moved quickly to get Andrew's clothes ready for him. It was her form of "busywork," something to keep her occupied so that her mind wouldn't go to that awful place that it was wont to go thanks to this middle-of-the-night call.

It just went with the territory because she was the former police chief's wife. A peaceful night's sleep wasn't always part of the equation.

Rose had laid out all of Andrew's clothing as well as his shoes and had just pulled out a pair of socks when her husband hung up the phone.

The moment that he did, she whirled around to face him.

"Who?" she asked breathlessly.

Throwing off the rest of the covers, Andrew's bare feet hit the cold floor. The change in temperature hardly registered. His mind was racing, unearthing a dozen memories at once. But mainly Andrew was praying. Praying every bit as hard as he had when he had gone looking for his missing wife all those years ago when her car had driven off the road, into the lake.

It had taken him years to find Rose again, but he had, he reminded himself. Finding her when she'd been suffering from amnesia had been, admittedly, an incredible long shot, but he had never given up looking, despite the odds. And, in the end, he had found her.

This was going to be another kind of long shot, but just like before, he had every hope that it was going to work out.

It just had to.

Rose caught hold of her husband's arm, pulling him and his attention back from wherever it had drifted to and toward her.

Startled, Andrew blinked, as if suddenly remembering that his wife was there.

"Who is it?" Rose asked point-blank.

The answer hurt, and it took him a second to actually form the words to tell her.

"It's Dad," Andrew answered, shrugging into his pullover sweater.

Of all the names that had gone rushing through Rose's anguished, feverish brain, her father-in-law's name hadn't been among them.

Armed with this piece of information, Rose's mind went in an entirely different direction.

"Heart attack?" she guessed quietly as she watched Andrew slip on his shoes.

Grabbing his wallet from the nightstand and putting his cell phone into his pocket, Andrew shook his head. "It wasn't a heart attack."

"Then what?" Rose asked, confused.

Andrew drew in a deep breath, as if to insulate himself from the fears that went with what he was about to say.

"As near as the patrolmen who found him can tell," Andrew said, "Dad was the victim of a mugging. At least that's the working theory. His car is missing, and he was found lying facedown in the North Tustin Industrial parking lot."

Horror flashed across Rose's face. The next moment, she managed to regain control over her emotions.

"But Seamus is all right, isn't he, Andrew?" she asked, willing her husband to give her a positive reply.

Andrew avoided making eye contact with his wife. "He's breathing," he answered, heading toward the stairs. He loved having Rose with him under any circumstances, but he wanted to spare her this. His father was a strong man, but age had a way of eroding strength. Andrew had no idea what he was in for.

"Dad hasn't regained consciousness since they found

him." Sailing down the staircase's seventeen steps, he was at the front door in seconds. "I'm going to the hospital," he told her.

Rose was just a beat behind him. "Not without me you're not."

He turned toward her. "There's no point if he's still unconscious. Maybe you should just stay here, hold down the fort," Andrew gently suggested.

The stubborn look he knew and loved so well came into Rose's eyes. "The fort can hold itself down. I'm not letting you face this alone, Andrew Cavanaugh," she informed him in no uncertain terms.

This was one of the many reasons he loved her, but even so—or maybe because of it—he didn't feel right about dragging her with him like this, Andrew thought. "People are going to be calling here, asking questions about what happened."

He wasn't telling her anything she hadn't already considered. "I'm sure they will. Don't worry about it, we have call forwarding. They'll find us," Rose assured him. "After all these years of marriage, that old man is as much my father as he is yours and I'm not about to stay here like a good little soldier, twiddling my thumbs and waiting for word that he's all right—*and he will be all right*," she told her husband in a no-nonsense voice. "Now, let's just stop wasting time debating this and let's go," Rose ordered.

Andrew's heart swelled with affection as well as gratitude. Sparing himself one moment, he caught his wife up in his arms and kissed her.

Hard.

The next second, he let her go again. "If I haven't mentioned this to you lately, I love you, Rose McGee Cavanaugh."

Rose briefly touched his face and smiled at Andrew, all the love she felt for this man who was her entire universe shining in her eyes.

"I know," she replied. "Now, let's get moving!" she urged again, pulling open the front door.

"Yes, ma'am," Andrew answered, utterly grateful that this was the woman who was sharing his life.

Rose had always managed to give him hope.

Rose sat in the passenger seat of the vehicle she had surprised him with last Christmas as they sped off to the hospital. To ensure that they would get there as quickly as possible, Andrew had placed his police lights on the roof. Though he didn't believe in abusing any of the privileges that were at his disposal, this situation negated his natural impulse for caution.

While the lights on his roof flashed and the siren blared, Rose was busy calling various members of their family to tell them that the man who was responsible for starting the family was very possibly fighting for his life in the hospital. Rose knew that nobody would want to be left out of the loop under the guise of being "spared" the news until morning. Everyone loved and respected the crotchety patriarch and would have been distraught if they weren't able to be on the premises, pulling for Seamus and adding their prayers to the rest.

This was the sort of thing that transcended everything else. This was about family.

Despite the hour, Aurora Memorial Hospital's parking lot was teeming with vehicles. Andrew gunned his SUV up and down the aisle, searching for a place to park. As he searched, he spared Rose a glance. "How does it feel being a modern-day Paul Revere?"

"I would have preferred just inviting people to one of your parties instead of telling them to come to the hospital because Seamus has been the victim of some psychopathic thief," Rose answered grimly. She reached for her husband's hand and squeezed it. "He's going to be all right," she promised, her voice thick with emotion. The words were meant to hearten her as much as they were to encourage her husband.

"Of course he is," Andrew agreed in a voice that was as emotional as his wife's. "Dad's too ornery to just give up and…retreat," he said, finally finding a word he could use without having his voice break.

"There," Rose said suddenly, pointing over to the side. "There's a space."

"Good eye," Andrew said, temporarily taking refuge in the minutia of ordinary banter.

He angled his vehicle into the rather tight space and was out of the driver's side in a matter of seconds. He heard the passenger door slamming shut and paused, waiting for Rose to join him.

"Don't wait for me," his wife said, waving him toward the ER entrance. "Just go!"

Nodding, Andrew made his way to the rear ER doors quickly. How many times had he been here over the course of his career and then some? Far too many to count, he thought. Once, years back, he'd even been brought here himself.

It never got any easier, he decided.

It took Rose two beats to catch up and be at his side.

"You move fast for an old man," she told him, trying to tease Andrew and lighten the huge weight that she knew had to be weighing down on him.

"Not that old," Andrew replied.

Just then the young woman behind the registration

desk turned toward them. A look of mild recognition crossed her face.

The next moment the pieces of the puzzle were falling into place. "You're here about Seamus Cavanaugh, aren't you?"

Under ordinary circumstances, Andrew might have said something light in response, but these were not ordinary circumstances. They were scarier than he could ever remember them being. His father had been beaten, possibly shot. Add to that the man had age working against him. Despite trying to keep a positive attitude, this was not the best of scenarios.

Andrew got down to business immediately. "Yes, we are. How is he?"

"Grandpa's a hearty warhorse, Dad. You know that," his oldest daughter, Callie, said as she hurried up to join him.

She was not alone. Behind her was her husband, Benton Montgomery, as well as her two brothers, Shaw and Clay, and her sisters, Teri and Rayn, along with each of their spouses.

Hugging her father, she said, "When Mom called to tell me what happened, I got the word out. Most of the family's either already here or on their way."

Rose smiled at her husband when he turned toward her. "I thought it wouldn't hurt to have a first floor full of Cavanaughs praying for Seamus's recovery. God can't ignore this many like-minded people all asking for the same favor."

Though he tried to mask it, the breath he released was shaky. "Well, that would explain the crowded parking lot. Let's hope you're right," Andrew said to his wife. It was obvious to Rose that he was afraid to be too confident about the outcome.

"I'm always right," Rose informed him with a confidence she really didn't feel. She looked around the immediate area. "Anyone know where your granddad's doctor is?" she asked the ever-growing sea of people.

Dax Cavanaugh spoke up first. "He was here a minute ago," he told his aunt.

Brian Cavanaugh, Aurora's chief of detectives, came up behind his son and put his hand on Dax's shoulder as he addressed his sister-in-law. "I'll have him paged, Rose." Turning, Brian spotted an official-looking nurse and headed straight for her. When he saw that she was about to turn away, he called out to get her attention. "Ms.? Excuse me, Ms.!" Brian sped up his pace.

Marsha Williams, whose newly bestowed official title was head nurse of the ER, stopped in her tracks and slowly turned around. The pasted-on friendly smile quickly turned into a wary expression. Before she could stop herself, she murmured, "Oh, lord, they warned me about this."

Brian cocked his silvery head. "Who warned you about what?" he asked in an amicable voice.

"The last head nurse. Rachel Rubin. She told me that sooner or later—most likely sooner—there would be a flood of you people in here because one of your own was hurt in the line of duty and that you wouldn't leave until you were absolutely sure that the law-enforcement person was going to pull through." She had a tablet with her and scrolled through it now, checking on new admissions and recent patients who had been brought into the ER. "But no one like that was brought in."

"Try again, dear," Brian's wife, Lila, instructed the head nurse. There was no mistaking the authority beneath the friendly voice. For the woman's benefit, the recently retired detective began to fill her in. "Seamus Cavanaugh was brought in unconscious less than—"

Recognition entered the head nurse's eyes as they came to rest on a recent entry.

"Oh, here he is," the woman declared. Marsha raised her head. "Dr. Iverson is overseeing his case," she reported.

"And what's the name of the doctor who's actually *doing* something for my grandfather?" Detective Troy Cavanaugh asked, a note of impatience in his voice.

Marsha Williams's somewhat high-handed attitude receded. "I'll go get the doctor," she replied, moving away.

Having quietly slipped into the circle gathered around the woman, Andrew smiled at the head nurse. "Thank you," he said in a subdued, civil-sounding voice.

The former chief of police turned toward the rest of his family as the nurse hurried away to find the missing physician.

"Anyone have any more information on what happened than what we already know?" Andrew asked the various members of the family around him.

"Sounds like a mugging gone bad," his younger brother Sean answered. Several other heads nodded. "Not much to go on yet," Sean concluded.

"Who found him?" Brian asked, throwing out the question to anyone who could answer it.

"A guy walking his dog," his daughter, Riley, volunteered. "He called a patrolman."

"Who was the detective who was first on the scene?" Andrew asked.

"That would be me," Detective Finley Cavanaugh said, raising his hand as he stepped forward to the front of what was quickly becoming a very large crowd. "I caught the case and I was hoping to have a few words with your father, Uncle Andrew."

"So are we, Finn," Andrew replied with feeling. "So are we." He looked around, hoping to see the ER doctor cutting through the growing gathering of his relatives.

Rose tugged on her husband's arm. When he looked quizzically in her direction, she pointed toward a rather young-looking man in hospital scrubs quickly walking toward them.

"Looks like maybe the doctor's finally going to tell us what's happening," she said.

Dr. Joshua Logan had recently transferred to Aurora from a hospital located on the opposite coast. He was still getting acclimated to the mild weather. His easygoing manner belied that he was a top-notch emergency-room physician.

Dr. Logan quickly assessed the crowd, then introduced himself. "The good news," he continued after shaking the hands of the people nearest him, "is that there doesn't seem to be any internal bleeding or a skull fracture."

"And the bad news?" Andrew asked since the doctor's tone clearly indicated that there was a downside as well.

"I'm afraid that your father's pride was badly wounded."

Chapter 2

"Wait," Andrew responded suddenly as the doctor's words registered. "Does that mean that my father's conscious now?" There was no missing the eager hope resonating in his voice.

"He was for a few minutes," Dr. Logan qualified. "But when I told your father that I wanted to keep him here overnight for observation, he started to become very agitated. I thought that it was best if I gave him a sedative."

Brian wanted the ER doctor to realize that their father wasn't just being difficult. "The problem is our father doesn't really like being in a hospital," he explained.

Dr. Logan nodded, curtailing the need for any further explanation. "I completely sympathize, but I still want to keep your father for twenty-four hours, just to make sure he's all right before I discharge him." His expression turned serious. "Your father *did* sustain a severe blow to his head," he told the family gathered around him. "I'm sure none of you want any unpleasant surprises suddenly coming up if he goes home too soon."

"Do what you need to do, Doc," Andrew told the emergency physician, speaking on behalf of the entire family. "We want to be sure to keep that annoying old man around for a lot more years to come."

Dr. Logan seemed to take Andrew's words seriously. "Well, barring any more unforeseen incidents like this one, I'd say that you should probably get your wish. Except for being banged around and getting a number of cuts and bruises, your father appears to have a very strong constitution."

Andrew blew out a breath. "That's definitely reassuring. When can we see him?" the former chief of police asked.

While hearing everything that Dr. Logan had just said was definitely making him feel more hopeful, Andrew still felt a very strong need to see his father with his own eyes before he could begin to rest easy.

"Tomorrow morning," Dr. Logan replied automatically.

As the ER physician turned on his heel to leave, Rose quickly moved directly into the man's path.

"Doctor, please," she said, then looked toward her husband.

Logan read between the lines. The woman's meaning was clear. "All right. But just one of you," he asserted, raising his voice so that it carried in order for everyone to hear. "And just for five minutes, is that clear? If Mr. Cavanaugh should come to, I don't want him getting any more agitated."

"Understood," Andrew responded solemnly.

Logan nodded. "All right then. You'll find him in the third bed." Since all the beds were hidden behind individual curtains, the ER physician offered, "I'll take you to him."

Andrew hesitated, looking back at his two younger brothers, silently asking if either of them wanted to go in his place.

But no one contested the decision. "You're the head of the family," Brian told him.

"Go on in before the doctor changes his mind," Sean urged.

With a grateful nod, Andrew quickly followed Dr. Logan out of the area.

They went down a long corridor and then the doctor abruptly stopped.

"He's right in here," Logan said, parting the curtain just enough to give Andrew a glimpse inside the interior. "Remember, five minutes," the doctor cautioned again and then left in order to give Andrew some privacy with his father.

Drawing closer, Andrew very gently took his father's hand in his. For the very first time that he could remember, his father's ordinarily strong hands somehow looked and felt almost fragile. They weren't the powerful hands he recalled, that seemed capable of lifting up and holding anything.

Hands that seemed almost inconceivably strong and incredibly capable.

Andrew squeezed his father's hand, but Seamus didn't squeeze back.

When he thought of what might have happened, Andrew felt tears spring to his eyes. He blinked hard to keep them from falling. This wasn't the time to fall apart, he thought.

"You gave us one hell of a scare, old man," Andrew whispered thickly to the unconscious man in the hospital bed. The sight of a bandage wrapped around his father's head, all but covering his right eye, hurt to look at. What if the damage had been worse? "What did those lowlifes do to you?" Andrew asked, trying to control his mounting anger. "And why were you even there at this time of night? You have people for that," he insisted almost angrily. This didn't make sense and it didn't have to happen. "Young people," Andrew stressed. "Haven't you learned how to delegate yet?"

Andrew sighed, answering his own question. "Of course you haven't. You're a Cavanaugh and you feel you have something to prove—to yourself if not to the rest of us."

There was no answer forthcoming from his father even though Andrew would have given *anything* to have heard his father's voice as the older man attempted to explain his actions.

But he just continued being unconscious.

"I sure hope you can tell us who did this when you come to, because you know that you've got every single member of the family dying to make that person pay for hurting you."

For a second, he could have sworn he saw his father's eyes flutter. But then they were still and his father continued sleeping.

"Chief?" Logan said respectfully, peering in between the curtains.

Andrew knew that his time was up. "I've got to go, Dad." He leaned over his father's bed and pressed a kiss to the older man's forehead. "I'm happy you're still with us. Happier than you'll probably ever know."

Andrew went to retrieve his father's cell phone from the plastic bag where his clothes and possessions had been placed. Finding it, the former chief of police stepped away from the hospital bed and reentered the corridor.

Despite the fact that his father was unconscious and couldn't help provide any leads, it was time to get this investigation started. In his experience, there was always someone, whether they knew it or not, who had seen *something*.

The trick was to find that someone.

With renewed purpose, Andrew went back out to where the rest of his family was waiting. He looked around for Brenda, one of Brian's daughters-in-law. Brenda was the head of the IT section in the crime-scene investigation lab. He needed the young woman's expertise at the moment.

Spotting her next to her husband, Dax, Andrew headed over to them. Brenda and Dax were instantly alert the second he approached them.

"How is he?" Dax asked before his wife could.

"Still unconscious. He looks pretty banged-up," Andrew admitted. "But he's a tough old bird. He'll be issuing orders by morning," Andrew said confidently.

Murmurs of "That's great" and "Thank God" echoed throughout the area.

Andrew held out the phone he had taken to Brenda. "This is my father's phone," he told her. "Pull whatever you can off it so we can retrace his steps before he was attacked."

Brenda immediately took possession of the cell phone, wrapping it in her handkerchief to avoid smudging any possible fingerprints that might be on it and *didn't* belong to anyone in the family.

"Right away, sir," she promised.

"Once the chief of police, always the chief of police," Brian commented to his older brother with a smile.

"Look," Andrew began, "I know that technically I don't have the authority to ask anyone to do anything, but—"

"Sure you do," Shaw, the current chief of police and Andrew's son, said, interrupting his father. "Don't worry, Dad. We'll find the SOB who did this to Grandpa," he promised. "There'll be so many of us out there combing the area, we're going to wind up tripping over one another. But we'll find him."

Andrew looked over toward Finley, who had been keeping silent, but Andrew could guess what was going on in the young man's mind.

"Finn was the one who was first on the scene," he reminded the others. "That makes him the lead detective on this."

"Once I realized who the victim was, I knew that there would be no shortage of help with the investigation." Moving toward the center of the group, the tall, good-looking, dark-haired young man's green eyes swept over the people standing closest to him.

Finley Cavanaugh belonged to the other branch of the family, the branch that Andrew had uncovered when he went to search for Seamus's younger brother, Murdoch. Murdoch and Seamus had been separated at a very young age when their parents divorced, splitting the family in two and going their separate ways.

Things didn't always have fairy-tale resolutions, despite the best intentions. Murdoch died before the two brothers could be reunited. Even so, Murdoch's four children and their families slowly migrated to Aurora and eventually became, to a great extent, part of the city's police department. Some had already become police detectives before they transferred, while others were eager to prove themselves in this new venue.

All were happy to become part of a larger whole.

And now they found themselves united in a less joyous undertaking: trying to find and bring to justice the cold-blooded carjacker and would-be killer who had done this to one of their own.

"This isn't a matter of territory and I'm not about to try to pull rank here," Finn told the group. "We all want to get whoever did this to Seamus and then left him to die in a deserted parking lot," he said, his voice growing cold and steely.

Several voices resounded in the group, agreeing with what Finn had just said.

Riley shivered. "If that man hadn't been walking his dog when he was…" Her voice trailed off, as she was unable to finish her thought.

"But he was out in the right place at the right time," Brian told his daughter. "Focus on that." Wanting to say something further to Finn along those lines, Brian turned toward the young detective. But the man was no longer there.

Seeing the perplexed look on Brian's face, Sean asked, "Who are you looking for?"

"Finn. He was just here," Brian said, still looking around to find Finn. He hadn't seen the young detective leave.

"Looks like he wanted to get started looking for the person—or persons—who did this to Dad," Sean said, supplying his take on the matter.

Brian nodded. "He's got the right idea." He raised his voice to address them all. "Let's put all our resources together and see if we can make short work of this. Those of you who have them, talk to your CIs." He glanced at the members whom his order applied to. "I want answers, people. Was this a random mugging or was Seamus targeted? If it's the latter, find out why he was targeted and by whom," the chief of detectives stressed. "We have got one of the finest police departments in the country," he reminded the people gathered around him. "Let's put that to good use."

Everyone knew that wasn't a suggestion—that was a quietly issued order.

"Well, that certainly didn't take long," Sean commented to Finn several hours later as he and two other members of his crime-scene investigation team carefully circled around the abandoned, badly battered vehicle that had been tracked down. The car had been discovered less than ten miles away from the parking lot where Seamus had been found.

Finn had been the one who had found the car, after beginning his search the moment he had left the hospital. As soon as he had verified that the vehicle was the one that had belonged to Seamus, he had immediately placed a call to Sean.

Sean and his team were out there within twenty minutes, snapping photographs and documenting anything that could even remotely be considered evidence.

"When do you think I'll be able to run prints?" Finn asked Sean. "Provided you find them," he qualified.

"When we find them, you'll be the first to know," Sean assured him. He looked thoughtfully at the smashed-up vehicle. "You know, for a carjacker, this guy was certainly very careful not to leave any incriminating fingerprints around," he observed.

"No matter how careful, there's always a slipup," Finn told the older man, trying to smother the impatience that was mounting within him.

"I hope you're right," Sean replied. "By the way,

thanks for the heads-up when your men came across this," he said to Finn.

"My dad always said that if you want the best results, make sure you go with the best," Finn answered, never taking his eyes off the members of the CSI team as they systematically worked in and around the vehicle. He kept his fingers crossed.

"I'm sorry I never got to meet your father," Sean told Donnal Cavanaugh's son.

Finn paused for just a moment, recalling his father. "You would have liked him," he told Sean. "Come to think of it, he was a lot like you," he decided. The next moment, he cleared his throat. "I'd better stay out of your way," he told Sean. "You've got my number if you find any prints."

"Like I said," Sean told him, getting back to work as Finn began to walk to his own car, "you'll be the first one I call."

Finn picked up his phone the second that he heard it ring. He didn't bother checking the caller ID—he just naturally assumed that it was Sean on the other end of the line.

"Did you find any fingerprints?" he asked immediately.

"It was the cleanest car I've ever dusted," Sean admitted.

He knew going in that it was only a slim chance that the crime-scene investigators would find a print, but even so, Finn felt deflated. "So then the answer's no?" he asked, disappointed.

Instead of a confirmation, Sean began, "Except—"

Instantly alert, Finn interrupted the head of the crime-scene lab. "Except what?"

"Except that whoever stole that car from my father didn't stop to think when they went to adjust the rearview mirror. They wiped down every surface except for that one." He could hear Finn all but champing at the bit, so he put him out of his misery. "We found just one partial fingerprint on the back of the rearview mirror."

"Do you have any idea who the print belongs to?" Finn asked. If anyone would have asked him for a description of himself, Finn would have said that, in general, he was usually a patient man. But at the same time, there was something about waiting that really got to him. Especially when he was involved like this.

"Not yet," Sean answered. "But we will. We've got Valri running the print, looking for a match. If whoever stole the car is in the system in any manner, shape or form, I guarantee that she'll find them. Valri's the best all-around computer tech that we have," Sean said.

Finn still saw a slight problem with that. "What if the person's not in the system?"

"Well, then we're no worse off than we were before," Sean answered. "But remember, there are a lot more people in the system now than there used to be. People need to be fingerprinted for any number of reasons these days. Keep a positive thought," he told his nephew cheerfully.

Finn pressed his lips together. "Right," he murmured.

"Oh, and, Finn?" Sean said just as Finn was about to hang up.

"Yes?"

"There was one more thing." Sean paused and it was for effect, something he didn't usually do, but given the nature of this case, he felt he could be forgiven this one time.

"Yes?" Finn asked again.

"We found blood in the trunk."

"Blood?" Finn repeated, stunned.

"Yes. It looks like there was a body transported in the trunk," Sean said.

"Talk about burying the lead!" Finn cried. Pulling himself together, he asked, "Do you know who the blood belongs to?"

"Not yet," Sean answered. "We'll call you about that, too," he promised.

"I will be waiting," Finn said, trying not to sound as impatient as he felt.

More than an hour later, the phone rang again. Finn had just gotten up from his desk and was about to leave the robbery division's squad room. The moment he heard his phone, he hurried back and yanked up the receiver. "Finn Cavanaugh."

"You know that positive thought I told you to keep earlier?"

Finn recognized Sean's voice immediately. Hope sprang up in his chest. "Yes?"

"We found a match to that print," Sean told Finn. "Or rather, Valri did."

Sometimes things really did work themselves out, Finn thought. "Who does the print belong to?"

"It belongs to a Marilyn Palmer," Sean answered. "There was only one arrest down in her file. Nothing too spectacular. She was part of some sort of group staging a college protest a few years ago. She spent the night in jail, then was released to her mother. As near as Valri could tell, there have been no repeat performances since that date."

"Until she stole Seamus's car," Finn reminded Sean grimly, "and carted off a body in the trunk."

"Right, until then," Sean agreed.

"Have you matched that blood yet?" Finn asked.

"No luck so far, but we're working on it," Sean said. "Now, if you have a pen, I'll give you Marilyn Palmer's address."

"All right, shoot," Finn said to the head of the CSI day unit, ready to copy down any and all information that Sean had for him.

Finally, Finn thought in relief, they were beginning to get somewhere.

Chapter 3

"Hey, Finn," Detective Joe Harley, Finn's occasional partner, called out as he stuck his head into the robbery squad room. "There's a woman out here who's looking for you. She says she wants to talk." Harley grinned at him. "Looks like you finally got lucky."

Finn was already on his feet. Armed with the address that Sean had just given him, he was just about to leave the precinct. He wanted to talk to the twenty-year-old who had just become his prime suspect. Unless this was really important, he didn't have the time to waste on someone coming in to report something that she only *thought* was missing but in reality had just been misplaced. It didn't matter how attractive she was. His focus was on something far more important.

"You talk to her, Harley," he told the other detective.

But the ten-year veteran he sometimes teamed up with shook his head.

"Believe me—" Harley glanced over his shoulder toward the hallway "—I'd like to, but she said she only wants to speak to the person in charge of the investigation concerning the stolen car found in Merryweather Park…and that would be you."

Finn immediately snapped to attention. Maybe this woman *did* have something significant to tell him after all. "All right, Harley, show the lady in," Finn instructed.

Harley pretended to salute as he sighed and retreated. "Y'know, some guys just have all the luck," he muttered under his breath.

Finn wasn't sure just how to take that—until the detective returned less than a minute later. Walking beside Harley was a statuesque blonde with a knockout figure that could, in his opinion, bring strong men to their knees and make them salivate, as impossible fantasies began to dance in their heads.

However, despite her other attributes, it was the woman's clear-water blue eyes that instantly caught Finn's attention. He knew it wasn't possible, but her eyes looked as if they could see right through a man, and like the fictional superheroine with her golden lasso, would allow nothing but the truth to fall from his lips.

Getting a hold of himself, Finn managed to regain the use of his tongue just as she came up to him. He put his hand out as he introduced himself. "I'm Detective Finn Cavan—"

The woman slipped her hand into his and Finn could have sworn that there was a momentary spark of electricity shooting up his arm. He dismissed it as adrenaline, with everything that was going on.

"I know who you are, Detective Cavanaugh," the woman said, cutting him off as she smiled warmly at him.

"Well, that puts you one up on me," Finn told her. He

didn't like being caught at a disadvantage. "Detective Harley didn't tell me your name."

"Well, that's easily solved. I'm Nikola Kowalski. Nik, to my friends," she added, putting her other hand over his as she shook it.

Because she seemed so friendly, something within Finn backed off. He didn't trust people outside the family who were this outgoing. They usually had some sort of a hidden agenda. Women who looked as exceptionally attractive as this one did were usually the type to use their looks to disarm people.

Finn's voice grew distant as he asked, "Do you know something about the car that was just recovered, Ms. Kowalski?"

Nik picked up on his cool, reserved voice immediately. He was attempting to maintain distance between them. Too bad. She preferred a warmer, friendlier attitude, but she didn't need him to be all warm and toasty in order for her to do this.

"If you're going to go the formal route," she said, referring to his using her surname. "The *w* is pronounced like a *v*," she informed him. "But 'Nik' is a lot easier," she stressed.

He guessed right. The woman who looked as if she had just stepped off the cover of a swimsuit magazine intended to use her feminine wiles to pump information out of him. But he had no intention of being pumped.

"We're getting off-topic," Finn told her. "What do you know about the car that was found?"

That hadn't become public knowledge yet. The details about his grandfather's brother being savagely attacked and left for dead were being kept tightly under wraps. If she knew about it, then she had to be involved somehow. He looked at her with heightened interest.

She saw the spark in his eyes and wasn't quite sure what to make of it. He hadn't acted as if he was interested in her a moment ago. But she did answer his question just to move this along.

"Well, for starters," she told the steely-eyed detective in front of her, "I am fairly certain that Marilyn Palmer didn't steal it."

Considering that he had only been given the woman's name a few minutes ago, Finn's suspicion that the blonde talking to him was somehow involved increased tenfold. His eyes narrowed as he scrutinized her.

"How would you even know that we thought that?" he challenged. Not waiting for an answer, he decided to approach this squarely and asked, "Are you mixed up in this in some way?"

"Only as a Good Samaritan," she told him.

"You're going to have to elaborate on that, Ms. Ko-*val*-ski," he said, deliberately stretching out her name.

Nik winced a little at his belabored pronunciation of her last name. It was right even though, at the same time, it somehow felt wrong. Despite that, she wasn't insulted. "'Nik,' please," she corrected. She had a temper, but it took a lot to arouse it. She decided to just keep it in check. She had a hunch that she would get further that way. "Maybe I should have told you that I'm an insurance investigator."

His expression didn't change, other than to allow some of the impatience he was feeling to seep in. "I still fail to see the connection here," Finn told her between slightly clenched teeth. "It's far, far too early for any insurance claim to have been filed."

She had a habit of jumping ahead and burying the headline. Nik took a breath and started again.

"Marilyn's mother is a friend of mine. She came to me

with her concerns. She's afraid that her daughter might be in over her head, running around with someone she feels might be taking advantage of her and getting her into some sort of trouble." Her friend hadn't given her any names yet, but when she heard through her sources about the carjacking, Nik immediately thought that might be a place to start.

He thought of the way Seamus had looked when he'd been called to the crime scene. He'd been on the ground, unconscious, deathly pale, with the gash in his head bleeding profusely.

"I'd say that it looks like she passed the 'running' part and is now smack-dab embedded in a very specific kind of 'trouble.' Where is she?" Finn asked.

"I have no idea," Nik answered honestly. "I'm trying to track her down."

He didn't believe her. "You could be charged with obstructing an investigation, not to mention vehicular theft after the fact."

Rather than having intimidated her, Finn was surprised to hear the woman laugh. He hadn't said anything remotely funny. When he looked at her, puzzled, she said, "I bet you say that to all the girls, Detective."

As far as he was concerned, this was *not* a laughing matter. "Only the ones I arrest," he responded darkly. "I want you to know that if you're withholding evidence, you're on very thin ice—"

She stopped him right there. "The only 'evidence' I have is her name, which you already know," she reminded him. "And I'm in the process of trying to find out the name of this 'mystery' bad influence her mother is worried about, if her mother got that part right—and there is still a very real possibility that she didn't."

"Ms. Ko-val-ski—" Finn began again, his patience running really short.

"Nik," she corrected again.

"*Why* are you here?" he demanded, his voice rising along with his temper.

"Well, the simple answer is I thought we could pool our resources and work together since we're both looking for Marilyn, albeit for different reasons," she answered.

"Pool our resources," Finn repeated in somewhat stunned disbelief.

"Uh-huh." Because he was looking at her as if he expected her to clarify what she meant by that, she said, "You tell me what you know and I'll tell you what I know. It seems more efficient that way."

He was *not* about to work with an amateur, gorgeous or not. If she had anything he could use in his investigation, he intended to hear her out, but he wasn't about to give her any information. As far as he was concerned, she was in the same class as the press and he made it a rule to always stay clear of the press.

"All right," Finn replied, tilting his head. "You first."

She wanted to tell him that she wanted *him* to go first, but she had a feeling that he would just dig in his heels. She could tell that he wasn't the type to be receptive to that kind of a suggestion. She supposed that she needed to get this serious, distant man to trust her. The only way to do that was to be agreeable to his terms.

"From what I've been told, Marilyn has always been a good girl," she began, only to abruptly stop. "You don't need to roll your eyes like that, Detective. There *are* still good kids left in the world."

In his experience, that was the sort of thing people said when the exact opposite was true. But for now, he let it ride.

"Go on," Finn said, doing his best to put a lid on his skepticism, at least for the moment. *Anything* to hurry this along, although he was losing his patience at what felt like the speed of light.

"According to her mother," Nik continued, "Marilyn has been acting strangely lately. My friend—Kim—thinks that her daughter has run off with this guy who she feels is a bad influence on her."

"You already said that," he reminded her flatly. "This 'bad influence,' does he have a name?"

She didn't care for his condescending manner, but for now she went along with it. "*Everyone* has a name, Detective," Nik responded with a smile.

"Then let me rephrase that," Finn said evenly. "Does this bad influence have a name that you're familiar with?"

"Not yet, but I'm trying to locate her friends, who don't seem to be around, either," she said.

How convenient, he thought sarcastically. "All right, do you have a description of this so-called bad influence?"

"No," she told him. She hated being unable to answer his questions. As he indicated he was going to leave the squad room, she quickly said, "But I'm working on it." Even as she said the words, she knew how lame that sounded.

Finn nodded shortly, dismissing her. "Come back when you have something substantial."

The truth was he could probably get the description himself if this "bad influence" was in Seamus's car with her as she drove away. Valri was already reviewing all the traffic-cam videos in the immediate area of the mugging, trying to spot Seamus's car in all the recorded footage. Added to that, he had several members of his team collecting any and all surveillance videos caught on the cameras that were recording activity in the industrial center at what he approximated was the time of the mugging. However, giving the woman an assignment seemed the best way to get her to leave, he thought.

However, as he began to walk away, she placed herself directly in his path and announced, "Your turn!"

"My turn what?" Finn asked. There was an edge in his voice.

"Well, I told you what I know and you agreed to pool our resources, so now it's your turn to tell me what *you* know," she explained in a cheerful voice, which he found exceedingly irritating.

"You agreed," he pointed out, his voice as dark as hers was light. He saw a fire enter her eyes that, under different circumstances, he might have even found intriguing.

But these weren't different circumstances. This was about finding who had done this to his grandfather's brother, and until he accomplished that, nothing else was going to take center stage for him.

"But," he said evenly, "in the spirit of 'sharing,' I'll tell you that Seamus Cavanaugh was mugged and left to die in the North Tustin Industrial parking lot while the person who did this to him drove away in Seamus's vehicle."

When he said that, the words tasted incredibly bitter in his mouth. The idea of someone doing something like that to an old man, let alone a member of his family, galled him beyond words.

"I already know that," Nik pointed out. Finn wasn't about to share anything, she realized.

"Well, then I guess you're all caught up," Finn told her. He looked toward the doorway and began walking. "Now, if you'll excuse me—"

To his annoyed surprise, she fell into step with him. When he glared at her, she responded, "Where are we going?"

"*I'm* going down to the crime lab," he growled. "I don't know where *you're* going."

"That's simple," Nik answered, still keeping her voice light. "I'm going with you."

Okay, time to put an end to this. He stopped dead in his tracks. Looking down at her, he told her sternly, "Oh, no, you're not."

The man was very uptight and extremely territorial, she thought. Nik decided to rephrase her words to sound less objectionable to him. "I thought I'd throw my lot in with you—temporarily, of course."

This woman was harder to get rid of than a strip of paper covered in superglue, he thought. "There is no 'of course,' Ms. Kowalski," he informed her.

"Ko-val-ski," Nik corrected, resigned to the fact that she wasn't going to get him to use her first name. At least not yet.

Finn threw up his hands. "Whatever." And then he fixed her with a penetrating look. "Let me make this perfectly clear for you. We are *not* 'working' together," he told her. "I'm a professional and you're not."

Undaunted, she pointed out, "We're both investigators."

"Only in the broadest definition of the word," he responded, this time gritting his teeth together. She was taking up precious time with this game of hers, he thought.

"Here," she said, taking out her business card and holding it out to him. When he didn't take it, she deliberately took his hand and pressed the card into it. "Believe it or not, I am very good at what I do and you *might* want to change your mind down the line," she told him.

As Nik walked away, Finn looked down at the card in his hand. "I really doubt it," he murmured.

* * *

"So, do you have anything for me?" Finn asked Valri as he entered the computer lab.

The petite woman glanced up at him from the monitor she had been reviewing now for hours.

"What I have is a huge headache right between my eyes," Valri told him, massaging the bridge of her nose in an effort to chase away her headache. It didn't work. "I think I'm going to be seeing Granddad's car in my sleep for the next six months. However..." She shrugged as she indicated the monitor.

"So, nothing yet?" Finn asked, frustrated.

Valri's mouth curved ever so slightly. "That's what I like about you. You catch on fast." She sighed, turning back to the monitor. "I'll give you a call if I do find anything."

"Sometimes it feels like two steps forward, one step back," he murmured. Locating all these surveillance tapes had been the two steps forward. But not finding anything on them felt like a giant step back.

"No time to talk about your dance lessons, Finn. I have a car to find," Valri told him as she resumed her search.

"Then I'll leave you to it," he said. "I'll check with Ramirez and Collins, the two detectives I have canvassing the area. Maybe they came up with something useful."

"There's always hope," Valri said, already blocking out his presence.

Other than the dog walker who had placed the 911 call that had brought out the paramedics, Finn and the other detectives and patrol officers working on the case weren't able to find anyone who could add anything to the slim amount of information they already had.

The worst part of working a case, Finn decided, was that helpless feeling that took over when he ran into a wall.

Back at his desk, Finn closed his eyes and tried to think. There had to be something he was overlooking, a way he could get this case moving, he thought in frustration.

He sighed. After spending a day spinning his wheels and going nowhere, he decided that he needed to go somewhere for a few hours to unwind so he could think. For him, as for so many other law-enforcement agents, that meant either attending one of Uncle Andrew's parties, or going to Malone's, the local saloon that was so popular with the police department.

Since Andrew was currently involved keeping vigil over his father at the hospital—Seamus was still lapsing in and out of consciousness—that left Malone's.

It was misting when he drove up to the popular saloon, a rare occurrence in its own right. It hardly *ever* rained outside of the rainy season. Finn couldn't help wondering if this misting was some sort of an omen.

As a rule, Finn wasn't superstitious, but there was a part of him that he admitted was open to things that he didn't fully understand.

Walking into Malone's, he looked around. For once the place wasn't packed to the gills the way it usually was. Instead of taking a booth, Finn decided to make himself comfortable at the counter. He slid onto the barstool that was closest to him.

Because Malone's was currently only half-full at this point, the patrons there provided just the right level of noise to allow him to completely submerge his thoughts. Finn promised himself that for the next half hour or so, he was not going to think about anything at all.

Looking all the way down the bar, he spotted Devin Wilson, the bartender who was tending bar tonight, and he waved at the stocky man. To Finn's surprise, Devin made his way over toward him. He was holding a large, frosty mug in his hand.

He placed the mug in front of Finn.

"I didn't order anything yet," Finn pointed out. He didn't always have the same drink and Devin wasn't in the habit of second-guessing his patrons.

"No, you didn't," the retired police officer, who was one of the owners of the bar, agreed. And then he smiled. "But she did," he told Finn, pointing toward the other end of the bar.

Finn looked to where Devin had indicated and saw the woman who had turned herself into his own personal royal pain raising her own glass toward him in a silent toast.

He frowned.

It was that annoying investigator woman.

Chapter 4

Glaring down the bar at the woman who Devin had pointed out, Finn made his way over to her. Without thinking, he automatically brought the glass with him.

Once he reached her, Finn asked her point-blank in a low voice, "Are you stalking me?"

Granted Malone's was open to the general public, but it was a known fact that this was where law-enforcement officers gathered. By definition, that meant that this was supposed to be a haven for cops, not the place where he could be confronted by someone from the outside.

Finn watched as the woman's lips curved. She obviously saw some humor in this, but he certainly didn't, he thought.

"Well, considering that I was already here when you walked in, if anything, I could ask *you* that question." Nik cocked her head as she looked up at the detective innocently. "So, are you stalking me, Detective Cavanaugh?"

Finn gritted his teeth. "You know the answer to that."

"Let's just say, for the sake of argument, that I don't," she answered. "Why don't you pull up a stool and we'll talk about it?" Nik gestured toward the empty stool next to hers. "Or about any subject you want, really. It doesn't have to be about our mutual interest," she told him.

Dark eyebrows drew together over the bridge of his nose. "We don't have a mutual interest," Finn informed her.

"Well, now, that's not entirely true and you know it," Nik pointed out sweetly. She paused then, fascinated as she studied his face. "Are you aware that your eyes shoot sparks when you hear something that annoys you?"

Finn laughed dryly as he assured her with feeling, "Oh, lady, I'm tired and frustrated and I am *way* past being annoyed."

Nik shook her head. "You know, harboring feelings like that is *really* bad for your health, Detective," she began, "if you want my advice—"

"I don't," he interrupted sharply.

Rather than back off, Nik continued as if he hadn't said a thing, "I'd say that you should think about doing something about that."

"Oh, I'm definitely thinking about it," Finn assured her. "But unfortunately, what I'm thinking is against the law."

Nik grinned as she lifted her glass to him, making another silent toast. "It's reassuring to know you have a sense of humor," she said.

There wasn't even a hint of humor evident in Finn's voice as he told her, "I wasn't trying to be funny, Ko-*val*-ski."

Nik nodded, as if she was evaluating his response to her. "Good deadpan, too," she commented. Taking another sip of her drink, she waited until it wound down into her system, giving Finn enough time to relax a little—if that was even possible. "So, have you had time to think over my proposition?"

Just then, Miles Crawford, a detective with almost twenty years on the job, came up to the bar to get another refill. It was obviously not his first refill of the evening.

Crawford stumbled a little as he leaned against the counter and fixed Nik with a look. "If he doesn't take you up on it, I'm free," he told her.

Finn scowled at him. "Why don't you try that again when you *haven't* had a few too many, Crawford?" he suggested.

Crawford turned his head, then waited as his surroundings came back into focus. "Sorry, didn't mean to tread on your territory," he said, addressing Finn. "You Cavanaughs always do get the best pickings."

That was *not* the impression he was trying to project. The scowl on Finn's face intensified. "Nobody's picking anybody and you owe the lady here an apology," he informed Crawford.

"Yeah, yeah." Crawford waved his hand at Finn. Leaning into Nik, he said, "Sorry you wound up with him." Pushing his empty mug to the very edge of the counter, the older detective raised his voice and called out, "Fill her up, Devin."

Finn pulled the empty mug over to his side. When Crawford glared accusingly at him, Finn said, "I think you've had enough for one night, Crawford. Why don't I just call you a cab? You're in no shape to drive anywhere."

The other detective instantly took offense. "Who the hell died and made you boss of the world?"

"I did," Devin informed his inebriated customer as

he came up to Crawford's end of the bar. "From where I'm standing," he continued, "a cab sounds like a really good idea."

Crawford's scowl just grew deeper. "Don't like other people driving me home, putting their hands all over me getting me in and out of the back seat of some guy's cramped little car," the police detective grumbled.

Devin spoke up. "It's either that or sleeping it off on my sofa in the back office." The bartender looked Crawford over, as if sizing him up. "You look a little big for the sofa."

Resigned, Crawford sighed dramatically. "Okay, okay," he said, surrendering. "Cab it is."

"Smart. Hey, Dan, call this man a cab," Devin called out to the man he had clearing off the tables.

"Sure thing, boss," Dan McGuire answered. At six foot five, with a frame to match, it was easy to see that Devin had him doubling as a bouncer whenever the occasion arose. Luckily for Devin, it rarely did.

Exercising great care for a man his size, Dan slipped his arm around Crawford's tilting form.

As Dan took the swaying detective in hand, Devin looked at Nik and aimed his apology at her. "Look, I'm sorry about that. The people here are usually a lot better behaved."

"Nothing to apologize for," Nik assured the owner. "Trust me, I've been subjected to a great deal worse." For a split second, she saw a look of mild interest flash in Finn's dark green eyes, but then it receded as if it hadn't existed at all. He was going to be a hard nut to crack, Nik thought.

Devin nodded in response to what she had just said. "Still, these are on me," he told the woman and Finn, indicating the two tall foamy drinks before them on the bar.

With that, Devin moved away to give them the privacy he naturally assumed they were looking for.

Nik turned back toward Finn. "So?" she asked, waiting.

"So?" Finn questioned. Because of Crawford's interjecting himself into the scene, he had lost the thread of whatever it was that she was asking him—and he was content to let it remain that way.

Because of the previous misunderstanding, Nik decided to reword her question. "Have you thought about what I said regarding our working together?" Before he could answer, she added, "Two heads *are* better than one, you know."

Yeah, he'd thought about it, Finn thought. And he'd totally rejected the idea from the get-go. He knew she had to be bright enough to pick up on that. "You are annoyingly persistent, you know that?" he said to the woman.

Again, she smiled, as if they were sharing some sort of inside joke. "I think the word you mean is *stubborn*. Polish women are known to be very stubborn," she told Finn. Before he could say anything, she added, "And if you think that *I'm* stubborn, you really should meet my sister."

"I think I'll just pass on that," Finn told her in a flat tone. He hadn't wanted to meet her, much less any other stray family member, he thought. All he wanted right now was just to get rid of her.

"Stubbornness really is an asset in my line of work," Nik assured him. Hoping he might be weakening, she added, "You've got nothing to lose if we work together… and everything to gain."

Finn finished off his beer in one long draw. It was clear to him that he was not about to get that peace of mind he'd come in for so he might as well leave.

"I'm not in the market for a hundred-pound headache," he told her, putting his empty mug squarely down on the bar.

Nik considered his remark. He obviously was referring to her. "Flattering," she called out to his back. "But I'm actually a hundred and twenty pounds."

"Even worse," Finn said over his shoulder as he walked out of Malone's.

For a moment Nik thought about following him out and continuing to try to win him over, but although she was every bit as stubborn as she claimed, it wasn't in her to try to wear him down by making a pest of herself. She was fairly confident that Cavanaugh would come around eventually.

And if he didn't, she had other contacts to turn to. Contacts who would let her know if and when Finn Cavanaugh and his team made any headway in the search for Marilyn and why she'd been part of that carjacking.

She remained where she was, nursing her drink until she was certain that Cavanaugh had driven away, and then she left Malone's.

The phone rang at a little after two o'clock in the morning, jarring Finn out of an unusually sound sleep. Focusing on the light his cell phone emitted, he was almost tempted to ignore it, thinking that that pushy woman had somehow gotten his phone number.

But being a cop was too ingrained in him to let his phone ring without answering it.

He picked up the cell and swiped open the screen. "Finn Cavanaugh," he all but barked into the phone.

"Yeah, I know," the voice on the other end of the line said. "Sorry to interrupt your beauty sleep, Cavanaugh, but I think you're going to want to hear about this." Recognition sank in. The voice belonged to the man who was sometimes his partner, Joe Harley.

Sleep instantly evaporated from his brain. Instincts honed on the job, as well as at family gatherings, told him this had to be about his current case.

"Go on," he urged.

"It looks like that woman who carjacked the chief's father's car might have just added murder to her list of offenses," Harley told him.

Maybe he *was* sleepy, Finn thought. He wasn't processing what Harley had just told him. Taking a breath, he waited for the information to make sense. "Start from the beginning," he insisted.

"Okay." Harley paused, then said, "A homeless guy looking for food in a Dumpster behind a restaurant found more than he bargained for."

Impatience flared. "Harley, I'm not in the mood for games."

"You're even less fun after midnight than you are before," his occasional partner complained. Enunciating very slowly, Harley told him, "A homeless guy found the body of a woman. She's been dead for less than a day," he added.

The way Harley had worded it, the body didn't belong to their suspect. So why—? "And you're telling me this because—?"

"The dead woman was clutching a piece of paper in her hand," Harley said. "CSI managed to get a print off it." He paused dramatically. "Guess who that print matches?"

At this point, Finn was really having trouble holding on to his temper. "Surprise me," he said between gritted teeth.

"It belongs to that girl you're looking for in connection with your granddad's mugging."

Since this investigation had started, he had already corrected Harley three times, explaining that Seamus was his grandfather's *brother*, not his grandfather. He decided that there was no point in restating that fact to Harley again. Besides, that wasn't the important part.

"Where's the dead woman now?" Finn asked, throwing off his covers and getting out of bed. There was no way he was going to be getting back to sleep at this point.

"They just took her body to the medical examiner for an autopsy."

So far, that was standard procedure. "And where are you?" Finn asked.

"Still at the crime scene." There was a pause and Finn assumed that the man was checking with someone, or looking at a street sign. "McFadden and Adams," Harley added.

"Okay, I'll be there as soon as I can," Finn said, walking toward his closet to get his clothes.

"The CSI night-shift team is almost finished collecting all the data they found near and around the body," Harley told him.

"Still want to see the crime scene for myself," Finn said, juggling his phone against his ear as he pulled on his slacks. They might have overlooked something. It wouldn't be the first time that had happened, Finn thought.

Harley sighed. "Knew you'd feel that way. I'll stay here."

Almost dressed, Finn looked around for his shoes. "I'll be there in fifteen minutes," he promised.

"That's about the only good thing about coming out at

this time of night," Harley responded. "There's no traffic to hold you up."

That didn't mitigate the fact that he would have much rather slept through the night. "I'll try to remember that," Finn said just before he terminated Harley's phone call.

Jake Newman, the head of the night-shift team, was just about to finish packing up so he and his people could leave, when Finn arrived. Newman's perpetually pained look deepened as he looked up to see who had pulled up.

"Can I help you, Detective Cavanaugh?" the rather nondescript, slightly hunched man asked.

"Did you find out the victim's name yet?" Finn asked as he came toward Newman.

Instead of answering him, Newman had a question of his own. "Things rather slow in the robbery division, I take it?" he asked as he snapped shut his kit.

Finn didn't care for the man's attitude, but he wasn't about to get into an argument with him if he could help it. "I have reason to believe that this is tied into Seamus Cavanaugh's carjacking case."

Newman sighed. He knew when to back off. "I won't have any answers for you until I've had a chance to go over everything. I'll leave anything I find for your uncle on the day shift." Newman couldn't help himself and let off one zinger. "Or do you people just operate by using mental telepathy?"

"No telepathy," Finn replied in a voice that was completely devoid of any emotion. "Just the regular forms of communication."

Newman frowned, picking up his case. "I'll try to remember that," the night-shift CSI leader said coldly.

Finn bit his tongue to keep from uttering a retort. Mainly he did it because he realized that the somewhat belligerent night-shift leader was using some of the same chip-on-his-shoulder comments that he had used when he'd talked to that stubborn insurance investigator.

He didn't care for being on the receiving end, he thought.

And she probably didn't care for it, either, Finn admitted. He supposed that he owed her some sort of an apology.

Later.

It took him until five in the morning to finish going over the crime scene to his own satisfaction, and also to stop wrestling with his conscience. He found the business card that the insurance investigator had given him. At the time, to keep from littering, he had shoved the card into his pocket. And then promptly forgot about its existence.

Because he'd changed his clothes, it had taken him a little while to locate the card. When he finally did, he called the number printed on it, expecting to talk to a recorded announcement at best. He was prepared to leave a message.

He wasn't prepared to hear the phone on the other end ring only once before it was picked up. And he definitely wasn't prepared to hear her voice breathing huskily in his ear. Nor was he expecting to feel that warm shiver dancing down his spine in response.

"Hello?" He had woken her up, he thought. Why that threaded a warm, sexy feeling through him was completely beyond him—and definitely not welcome.

Recovering, he asked, "Is this the pushy pain in the neck?"

Any trace of sleep on Nik's end vanished instantly. "Detective Cavanaugh, how lovely to hear from you. What can I do for you?" she asked.

He heard rustling on the other end and assumed that she was getting out of bed. He instantly shut down that image and forced himself to focus on the reason he was calling. "You can wipe that smile off your face for openers."

Nik grinned. "I'm not smiling, Detective."

There was no way he was going to believe that. "Yeah, you are."

"And what makes you say that?" she asked, looking for her clothes. She wasn't the neatest person when it came to her own things.

"Because you know I'm calling you because I—" He paused as he forced himself to form the words. She deserved to know why he was calling.

"Because?" she prompted, waiting.

It took him another minute before he could get the words out without choking on them. "Because I might need your help."

Chapter 5

Finn's somewhat surly, tersely worded statement left her speechless.

Almost.

"Wait," Nik responded after a beat had passed by, "let me look outside my window and see if there are four horsemen riding up to my door."

Finn blew out an annoyed breath. "What the hell are you talking about? *What* four horsemen?" he demanded. Was the woman still asleep, or was she just given to babbling nonsense?

"You know," Nik answered him calmly, knowing that would probably irritate him even more. "Like the ones that are supposed to be approaching when the end of the world is coming."

The biblical reference caught him off guard. His mind hadn't been going in that direction. He'd been trying to make sense out of what she was saying.

"Very funny," Finn retorted darkly. "Are you interested or not?" he demanded.

It was obvious to Nik that the detective was one second away from hanging up. She kept her voice cheerful as she backtracked.

"Oh, you had me at 'because,'" she said. "I am definitely interested." But he had also piqued her curiosity for another reason. "Am I allowed to ask you what caused this sudden change of heart?"

Finn knew that the insurance investigator would find out what had motivated him to call her once she got here, but every word he volunteered was uttered grudgingly. "A woman was found in a Dumpster last night."

"Okay." That didn't really answer her question. Nik waited for more. When the detective didn't enlighten her any further, she tried prompting him as she held her cell phone close to her. "And?" she asked as she pulled clothes out of the closet and quickly began to get dressed.

He knew why this was hard for him. He didn't like asking for help, even if there was no way around it. Besides, he felt this somehow put her in the driver's seat. "And they found a note in her hand."

She felt as if she was pulling every word out of his throat. Calling her was his idea, not hers, but she refrained from pointing that out. She didn't want him being any more defensive than he already was.

"What was in the note?" she asked.

Belatedly he realized that *he* hadn't asked that question and thus had no answer for her. That was a grave oversight and one he wasn't about to admit to. "That's not the important part."

"All right, what is the important part?" Nik queried. There had to be some sort of a connection for Cavanaugh to have called her.

"There was a partial thumbprint on the paper," he said.

Nik finished pulling on her jeans and zipped them. "Let me guess. Marilyn's?"

"Give the lady a cigar," he said, imitating the voice of a game-show announcer. "You got it on the first try."

Pulling her hair out from inside her sweater, she shook her head to let her hair fan out down her back. "Where are you?"

"Still at the scene of the crime," Finn answered.

Getting information out of this man was definitely like pulling teeth—slowly. But at least she *was* getting it, she thought. That was something.

"And the scene of the crime is?" Nik asked, her voice going up at the end of the question.

"McFadden and Adams."

She knew where that was. One of her favorite Mexican restaurants was located there.

"Don't go anywhere," she told him. "I can be there in twenty minutes."

Twenty minutes. Finn did a quick calculation. If it took her twenty minutes to get here, that meant that she lived somewhere in his vicinity, he thought—unless she was coming from another direction, he amended. He supposed he could get Valri to find out where the annoying investigator lived—if he was really interested in finding out.

The next minute he decided that he would just be buying trouble if he went that route.

"All right, get a move on. I'll wait," he told the woman grudgingly.

Finn realized that he was saying the last part to a dead phone. The insurance investigator had terminated the call.

Saying a few choice words under his breath, Finn tucked away his cell phone.

Nik got to where the detective was waiting in just under seventeen minutes.

As she came to an abrupt stop, he stepped to the side and waited for her to get out of her car.

"How many lights did you go through?" Finn asked her the second Nik got out of her car.

"None." Nik saw the skeptical look on Cavanaugh's tanned, handsome face. "I learned how to time the lights," she said. She could tell that he didn't believe her, so she explained. "If you get the first one and keep going at a certain speed, you can catch a green light at all the intersections. I learned that from my dad."

"Your dad," Finn said.

He still sounded as if he thought she was making things up, she thought. "Yeah, my dad was part of the original work detail that put in the traffic lights back when Aurora was still in its planning stages."

Finn didn't really know how to respond to that. He certainly didn't want to travel down memory lane with this woman, so instead he focused on the reason he'd called her in the first place.

"Let's go. It's this way," he said.

Finn brought her to the location where the body had been discovered. They both looked over the area very carefully, although there really wasn't anything to be found.

"I'm not really sure if this has any sort of a connection to the woman we're looking for," the detective admitted.

"You said there was a note," she reminded him. That would mean a connection, Nik thought.

"Yes, and her thumbprint was on it, but for all we

know, the dead woman might have just picked the piece of paper up and had it on her person when she was killed. I don't know if it actually had anything to do with her murder."

And she got the impression that he really didn't know what was on the note, so there was no sense in asking him that again, Nik thought. She tried another tack. "How did the woman die?" Nik asked him.

That much he could tell her, even though the information was secondhand. "According to my partner, who called me, she was stabbed through the heart."

Nik filled in the blanks from the way the detective worded his answer. "Then you didn't see her?"

Finn looked at her sharply. "And what makes you say that?"

Nik answered automatically. "Elementary, my dear Watson," she teased. Then, seeing that the man appeared to be in no mood for a lighthearted answer—why didn't that surprise her?—she replied seriously. "It was the way you phrased your answer."

"Well, you're right." She was surprised he actually admitted that. "They had already taken the body to the medical examiner when I arrived," Finn told her, his voice sounding exceedingly serious.

Nik automatically glanced at her watch as she asked, "What time does the medical examiner's office open?" She began to walk back to her car.

This was a mistake, Finn thought. He had really managed to open up a can of worms by calling her. Whatever she could add to the investigation, it wasn't worth having to put up with this would-be insurance detective stomping through his investigation.

"Why do you want to know that?" he asked her.

She stopped and turned around. She would have thought

the answer to that would have been pretty self-evident. "So we can confirm her time of death and the manner in which she was killed. Why are you asking me 'why?'" she asked. "I know this isn't your first investigation—and, believe it or not, it's not mine, either. You called me so you obviously want me here. Why don't you stop pretending that you find me annoying and let's get on with this and be on the same page?" she told him.

"I'm not pretending about finding you annoying," he replied. "But let's just put that on hold for now." This wasn't just a mistake—this was a *huge* mistake. A huge mistake for a number of reasons. But he wasn't about to say as much to her out loud. She would undoubtedly go on and on about that if he did.

Finn sighed. "All right," he agreed like a man who was resigned to his fate, "but before we go anywhere, I want to make certain things perfectly clear."

Uh-oh, here it comes, Nik thought, bracing herself for another lecture. "Such as?"

"Such as that as long as you're with me on this investigation, you're going to play by my rules. If I tell you to do something, you won't argue with me, you'll just do it."

His wording left something to be desired. "First, I don't think there's going to be any time for 'playing,' Cavanaugh. And as for the second part of that 'commandment,' people have gotten into trouble adhering to that."

He frowned. "This isn't the time for cracking jokes, either," he informed her. "Now, if you're not going to take this seriously—"

"Oh, I take my job *very* seriously, Detective. I always have." She looked up into his eyes, a silent challenge in hers. "How about you?"

"I take *everything* seriously," he informed her somberly.

"I can believe that," she quipped. "You know," she continued, "that just might be your problem."

About to get into his vehicle, he looked at her sharply. "Are you actually analyzing me?" he demanded.

Her expression was innocence personified. "No, just trying to be helpful."

Yeah, right, he thought. "Well, *don't*," Finn ordered.

Nik cocked her head, looking at him. "Message received. To the medical examiner's?" she asked, waiting for him to confirm that that was their next destination.

But it was obvious that Finn had a different idea. "You said you were friends with Marilyn Palmer's mother—or was that an exaggeration?"

"No, that wasn't an exaggeration." She could feel herself getting annoyed and banked down the feeling. He probably didn't realize that he was accusing her of making things up.

Pressing her lips together, she studied him for a moment, trying to decide whether working with this man was going to be a mistake. Well, she was here, so she might as well see where this led. But she did want to get something out in the open. "You don't play well with others, do you?"

His expression darkened again. "What is that supposed to mean?"

"Well, you really don't know me, but you just accused me of making things up to further what you assume is my agenda." She waited for him to deny it—or to have an epiphany, if that was possible.

His darkened expression only lightened by a fraction. "Sorry if I insulted you," he said sarcastically.

Finn wasn't prepared for the smile that came over her face—it seemed to light up the whole immediate area, even though the sun had already risen.

"Okay," she said brightly. "Apology accepted," Nik told him.

He scowled at her. He didn't like having her think he was apologizing for anything. "I take it you're not acquainted with sarcasm."

"Oh, I'm acquainted with it," she assured him. "I was just hoping that your lack of social skills made what you meant as an apology sound as if you were being sarcastic." She grew serious. "I think that if you stop thinking of me as someone interfering in your investigation and start thinking of me as an asset to utilize, we stand a chance of getting along a whole lot better."

Finn chose not to reply to that. Instead, he told himself that the sooner he and the others working with him on this case could pull all the stray pieces together, the sooner he could be rid of this irritating woman.

At least he could hope.

"Do you think that Marilyn Palmer's mother will be up yet?" he asked Nik.

"Oh, I know that she is," Nik assured him. When he raised his eyebrow, appearing doubtful because of the hour, she explained. "She hasn't really slept since Marilyn didn't come home the other night."

That wasn't all that unusual, he thought. Nodding, he suggested, "Why don't you lead the way?" And then he added, "Slower, this time," he added.

"I didn't speed," she told him, throwing a grin over her shoulder. "I was just anxious to see you and, like I said, it turned out that all the lights were in my favor."

There was laughter in her eyes, most likely at his expense, Finn thought. Ordinarily, he would have taken offense that she was laughing at him, but for some reason, he didn't.

"Yeah, right," he muttered. "Let's get going," he ordered, waving a hand at her car.

"I'll go slow so you don't lose me," Nik said, remembering his instruction with a smile as she pulled open her driver's-side door.

"I should be so lucky," Finn murmured under his breath.

"I heard that, Detective," Nik responded with a laugh.

"Just go. Don't worry about losing me." Even if she did, he had the address to the Palmer house.

Finn got into his vehicle. Again, he told himself that he really needed to have his head examined for having called this woman. Still, he supposed that there was an outside chance that this woman that Nik Kowalski was initially looking for was involved in not just Seamus Cavanaugh's carjacking, but in the murder of the woman who had been found in the Dumpster as well.

In any event, he wanted to interview Marilyn Palmer's mother and he had a feeling that taking this annoying blonde chatterbox with him to run interference might make things a little easier. She was right about one thing, he grudgingly acknowledged. He wasn't as good as some of his cousins and siblings when it came to questioning people and getting them to trust him.

Finn started up his vehicle, pulled up directly behind her and they departed.

It didn't take him long to realize that if this woman was driving any slower, she could have been accused of actually going backward.

He trailed behind the woman ahead of him for approximately three city blocks. Then, having had enough of this charade, he sped up and passed her.

Which was when she did the same thing.

Finn suppressed the urge to speed up again. He wasn't

usually competitive, but there was something about this woman with the laughing eyes that certainly had a way of pressing all his buttons, he thought.

This, too, shall pass, he promised himself.

Maybe it would, he thought, but definitely not soon enough for him.

They wound up reaching Kim Palmer's house faster than he had intended. The modest one-story house had all the lights on despite the fact that it was now a little after seven in the morning. There was no need for so many lights to be on—unless they had been deliberately left on overnight to act as a beacon for her missing daughter.

"What was that all about?" Finn asked, getting out of his car at the same time that Nik emerged from hers.

She looked at him as if she didn't know what he was talking about, her eyes wide.

"You started out going slow, but you sped up," he told her.

"Oh, that," she responded.

"Yes, 'that,'" he repeated, waiting for her to explain.

"I was just helping you get the lead out," she answered him amicably.

"Maybe I didn't want to get any lead out," he pointed out.

Her grin told him she thought otherwise. "Sure you did," Nik said.

He was about to respond when, out of the corner of his eye, he saw the front door of the Palmer house opening before either one of them had a chance to reach it or ring the doorbell.

Nik saw the change in his expression and followed his gaze. Seeing what he was looking at, she instantly turned her attention to the ashen-faced woman framed in the doorway.

Kim Palmer, a once-attractive-looking woman, looked as if she had aged a decade in the last few days. She was holding on to the doorway on either side for support as she appeared to be struggling to keep her knees from buckling beneath her.

Her breathing became labored, as if she was trying to get her heart under control.

"Oh, lord, you found her, didn't you, Nik? You found my baby and she's dead, isn't she?" Covering her mouth, Kim Palmer instantly began weeping. And then her knees gave way.

Finn reached the woman just in time to catch her and keep her from hitting the front step a second after she fainted.

Chapter 6

"Bring her inside," Nik instructed, quickly taking charge of the situation. "The sofa's right over here." She pointed it out as she led the way over to a light gray, faded sectional.

As Finn followed her, Nik grabbed one of the two bright blue-and-white throw pillows. She placed it so that it would be just under the unconscious woman's head as he put her down.

Finn was careful not to jolt the older woman as he set her on the sofa. Focused on Marilyn's mother, he didn't realize that Nik was leaving the room until she was almost out.

"Where are you going?" he asked.

"To the kitchen—" she pointed where she was headed "—to get a wet towel for her forehead. Hopefully, that'll make her come around."

"Oh." He thought the insurance investigator was ducking out, leaving him to deal with the unconscious woman while she did who knew what. It hadn't occurred to him to get Mrs. Palmer a compress. Fainting women weren't exactly his forte. Nodding, he gave his consent. "Go ahead," he urged Nik.

He didn't hear what she said as she left the room. Maybe it was better that way, he thought.

Taking Mrs. Palmer's hand, he pressed his thumb against her pulse and found that it was strong. Well, at least she hadn't suffered a stroke or a heart attack. The worn-out, haggard-looking woman was under a lot of stress, and he was afraid that it could have generated the worst sort of disabling reaction.

"Got it," Nik declared, her voice coming from the kitchen.

The next moment, she returned carrying a totally wet, almost dripping towel. As she approached, Finn stepped back out of her way. Kneeling next to the unconscious woman, Nik ran the towel along Kim Palmer's throat and face, then folded it so that she could place the towel on her forehead.

"C'mon, Kim, you need to wake up. Open you eyes for me, Kim." When she repeated the entreaty a second time, the pale woman's lashes fluttered, then her eyes finally opened.

The next minute Kim Palmer suddenly gasped and bolted upright, looking wildly at Nik.

Kim grabbed her arms, as if anchoring Nik in place somehow helped.

"Is she—is she—?" Although Kim was obviously trying to ask a question, she couldn't get herself to do it. The words burned on her tongue and refused to come out.

Nik came to her rescue. "No," she told the frightened woman. "Marilyn's not dead."

"At least not that we know of," Finn qualified.

Stunned by the addition, Nik instantly shot him a dirty look.

"What?" he asked. He had no clue what he had said or done wrong.

Nik did her best to redirect Kim's attention to another part of the investigation. "Marilyn's partial fingerprint was found at the scene of a carjacking," she told her.

"A carjacking?" Kim repeated as if she didn't comprehend the word. And then her features clouded over. "I knew it! I knew he'd get her in trouble. I told her to stop sneaking off and seeing this mystery man of hers." Clutching Nik's hand again, the older woman looked at her, totally at a loss as she pleaded for help. "Why wouldn't she listen to me?"

That was easy enough to answer, although she knew it was painful for Kim to hear. "Because girls that age don't listen to their mothers. They think they know better and that their mothers are far too old to understand what it means to be in love with someone."

Kim Palmer looked like a woman who had been beaten down by life. Distressed, her eyes went from one person to another.

"So what do I do?" Kim asked, totally at a loss as to how to handle this news and, more importantly, how to get her daughter back. "How can I deal with this? How can I *fix* this?"

"You pray, and when she turns up, you hold her and tell her that you'll be there for her no matter what," Nik told the woman with such feeling, she had Finn believing her. Or at least believing that she believed what she was saying.

"No matter what?" Kim repeated numbly, almost wide-eyed.

"No matter what—but that doesn't mean that you condone whatever it is that Marilyn and this man might have done if what they've done is something wrong," she explained.

Out of the corner of her eye, Nik caught the detective watching her. She had to admit she was surprised that he hadn't tried to interject his own philosophy into what she was saying to Kim, or to at least correct her. Was he biding his time so he could come down hard on her when they left—if not before—or was there some sort of other motive going on here that she was missing?

Nik realized that she couldn't second-guess the detective, but right now there were more important things on her mind.

"Now, this is very important, Kim," she said to the woman, speaking slowly as she sat down on a corner of the sectional next to her. "I want you to think. Do you know the name of the guy Marilyn's been hanging around with?" Nik asked.

"It's Charles, or Chandler, or maybe Chad." Kim raised her wide shoulders and then dropped them again helplessly. "I don't know. She never brought him around to introduce to me. He was like this special little secret of hers. I only overheard her talking to him on her cell a couple of times, making plans to get together. Otherwise, I wouldn't have even known he existed."

"So, no last name?" Finn asked.

He had been silent up until now, so when he asked his question, the sound of his voice caught both women by surprise, startling them, although for totally different reasons.

"None that I heard, no," Marilyn's mother answered, shaking her head. "Do you think she's in danger?" She directed her question to Finn.

Nik turned her head and gave him a silent warning look not to say anything. She didn't want Marilyn's mother to become any more upset than she already was. But, to be honest, she had no idea if Finn even understood what she was attempting to get across to him—or if he would have even listened if she *had* gotten through to him.

Nik just mentally crossed her fingers.

"I think the faster we can find her, the better off she's going to be," Finn told the older woman. It was the best he could offer the woman.

"By any chance, you wouldn't have any photos of Marilyn and this guy, would you?" She knew the woman had said she barely knew of his existence, but it was worth a try. "When I was Marilyn's age, my father kept snapping pictures all the time, claimed it was his hobby, but I think he was just trying to capture pictures of my boyfriends and my sister's boyfriends in case one of them did something he didn't approve of." She smiled fondly, remembering how, at the time, she and her sister felt as if he was barging into their life. "I think he figured he could get his buddies to back him up if he ever decided one of those guys act was acting disrespectfully toward us."

If possible, Kim looked even sadder than she'd already appeared. "It would have been a lot easier for all of us if Marilyn's father had stuck around, but..." Her voice trailed off as she shrugged her shoulders helplessly. "He didn't."

"So, no pictures?" Nik asked.

"I told you, I never even saw what he looked like," Kim answered, frustrated by her own helplessness.

"Is there anything else that you can remember?" Finn asked. "Anything this guy might have done or said that your daughter might have repeated?" He thought of something. "Did your daughter mention a favorite hangout place that she liked to go to with him, or anything of that nature?"

To each question, the woman just shook her head. "My mind's a blank," she admitted, tears filling her brown eyes.

Finn merely nodded. "That's all right. Maybe it'll come back to you. If you do think of anything, give me a call," he said, handing the woman one of his cards.

She glanced at it, but it was obvious that she wasn't making out any of the letters at the moment. "I have Nik's number," she told him.

"You can call either one of us," Nik told her. "Detective Cavanaugh is with the Aurora Police Department, but I'm not."

The information clearly was news to Kim. "Oh, I just assumed he was a friend of yours and not…" For a second, the woman's voice trailed off. Kim paused to take in a breath, as if that could somehow help her focus. "She really is in trouble, isn't she?"

Finn was about to answer her, but Nik spoke up first, raising her voice to drown him out just in case he was going to talk over her and say something that would upset Kim all over again.

"Let's not assume anything just yet, not until we have more of the facts." Nik looked a little more closely at the haunted woman. She really was in a bad way, Nik thought. "Is there anyone we can call to come stay with you? A relative maybe, or a friend?" she asked. "You really shouldn't be alone right now."

Kim nodded. "I can call my sister," she said, as if the thought had suddenly occurred to her.

"Do you want us to stay until she gets here?" Nik asked. "Or at least one of us?" she amended. The detective was probably not in any mood to stick around and hold Kim's hand, Nik thought, and it might be better if he just left.

But Kim shook her head, turning down the offer. "No, that's all right. Claire doesn't live that far away from me. I'll be all right," she assured the two people in her living room. "Really," she added when they didn't immediately get to their feet.

Reluctantly, Nik rose. "Call her," she urged. "*Nobody* should be alone at a time like this. It doesn't take much for your mind to get carried away."

Kim nodded in response to the advice, then impulsively, she got up, threw her arms around Nik and hugged her. "Thank you."

When she turned around and hugged Finn, the woman caught him completely off guard. The detective stiffly endured the woman's hug, then slowly, after a beat, he put his arms lightly around her.

"Thank you both," Kim cried, her voice sounding as if her throat was filling up with tears again.

Nik murmured something appropriate, then reminded the woman again that if she needed to call, day or night, for any reason, she shouldn't hesitate. They made their way to the front door, and Nik pulled the door closed when she and Finn left.

"You look shell-shocked," Nik commented, glancing at Finn. "That was probably a totally new experience for you," she said, referring to being hugged by the suspect's mother.

"I usually deal with thieves," Finn told her as they walked back across the street to where their cars were parked. "Thieves don't usually hug me."

Reaching his vehicle, Finn stopped as he remembered something. He looked at Nik. "Why did you give me that dirty look back there?"

Her mind was already racing ahead, sorting out various details. His question managed to catch her up short for a minute.

"What dirty look?" she asked him.

"In the beginning, after Mrs. Palmer came to and asked about her daughter, you gave me a dirty look," he answered.

Now she remembered. The memory brought an impatient frown to her lips. The man really needed to work on his people skills. "Because you don't reassure a frightened mother who doesn't know where her daughter is by telling her that the girl 'might' be dead."

"I didn't say she was *dead*, I said that we didn't know that fact yet," he corrected. Finn was still in the dark about his supposed transgression. The way he saw it, he hadn't done anything wrong, other than not coddle the person he was questioning.

Nik sighed. The man just didn't get it. "Never mind. Maybe you'll get it later." She tried to salvage this session. "Right now, I guess you did better than I thought you would."

Talk about backhanded compliments. "What is *that* supposed to mean?"

"It means that you displayed more sensitivity than I would have given you credit for if I hadn't been there myself. It also means that there's hope for you yet," she added, punctuating her words with a broad smile.

"Are you insulting me?" Because at this point, he honestly didn't know if she was or not. From where he stood, her words and her tone were at odds with one another.

And then there was that smile that, no matter what he thought about her, somehow just seemed to light up the immediate world. He was going to have to be careful that he didn't allow it to get to him.

"On the contrary, I'm complimenting you," Nik informed him. And then she relented, seeing things his way. "I guess I do take a little getting used to."

"Oh, you take a lot of getting used to," he quipped. And then he added, "But luckily, I'm never going to find out."

She unlocked her car door, then paused to study him. "And why's that?" she asked, not bothering to hide her amusement.

"Because as soon as Seamus Cavanaugh is lucid enough to be able to answer a few of my questions, we'll have the answers we need and I can wrap this thing up."

She thought of the body in the Dumpster. "What about that murder scene you called me to?"

"Murder's not my department," he answered. He was ready to chalk that up to Harley making the wrong call. "Theft is, and as long as I can solve who stole his car, then we're done."

She didn't see it as being that easy. "Unless these two crimes wind up being linked in some way," she reminded him.

He recalled the blood that was found in the trunk. What if it belonged to the dead woman who'd just been found? For now, he preferred not to think about that. "Bite your tongue."

He didn't expect her to grin in response to his words. "If I do, I won't be able to talk."

For the first time since she had met the solemn, surly detective, Finn Cavanaugh smiled. "Exactly," he answered.

"Hey, wait," Nik suddenly cried as he started to get into his car. He stopped and looked at her, waiting. "Where are we going?"

We.

He was going to have to resign himself to that pronoun for the time being, Finn told himself, no matter how irritating it was. And, he had to admit, she had turned out to be helpful in her own way around the suspect's mother. He wasn't sure what he would have done if she hadn't been there to do and say the right things to calm Kim Palmer down enough so that he could ask her a few questions.

Granted, the questions hadn't been productive, but who knew? Maybe down the line the questions could still yield answers he could use in the investigation. He had been taught to leave no stone unturned and once those stones had been turned, he was taught to go back to the beginning and turn them all again.

Sometimes answers took their own sweet time to form and gel.

Finn saw that she was still looking at him, waiting for him to answer her. He knew what she was waiting to hear and there was no getting around it.

"*Now* we're going to go to the medical examiner. With any luck, the autopsy's been done, or at least the preliminary one," he explained, knowing that these things couldn't be rushed.

"I suppose we shouldn't stop for breakfast first," she said. Her stomach kept rumbling in protest because it was empty.

He looked at her in disbelief. "You want to eat *first*?" he asked.

Most people he knew had trouble facing an autopsy even if they were used to the concept. He'd just assumed that this was her first. That meant a queasy stomach at best. At worst, it could turn a whole lot messier.

"I am hungry," she confessed. She bit her bottom lip. "But maybe that wouldn't be such a good idea."

He shrugged. "Up to you," he said, leaving it entirely in her hands. If he told her it wasn't a good idea, she would undoubtedly go out of her way to prove him wrong.

"Well, as long as the ME isn't going to vividly re-create any scenes for us, or illustrate his findings with visual aids," she began, "I could go for some pancakes and sausages."

Now that she had mentioned it, breakfast did sound rather good. But he was certain she was going to regret it.

"Okay," he told her, "but just remember, this is your idea."

She looked at him, bemused. "Do people usually blame you for their having breakfast?"

"I mean if you have any side effects," he said.

"From breakfast?" she asked in feigned wonder.

"No, from having breakfast and then viewing the autopsy." She couldn't be as dense as she was pretending, he thought.

"No worries," she assured him cheerfully. "I was pre-med before I changed my mind. C'mon, I know this cute restaurant that serves breakfast around the clock."

"Of course you do," he said with a sigh.

Premed. Like he believed that.

He got into his car and started it up.

Chapter 7

"Good?" Nik asked, leaning forward over the small table for two.

She had kept quiet longer than was her habit, watching Finn eat his order of scrambled eggs and cheese—plus toast and Canadian bacon—but at this point, she felt she was entitled to some sort of feedback from the man. Not that she thought the food served in the small, all-but-hidden restaurant was bad. On the contrary, she knew for a fact that it was excellent. It was just that she had never brought anyone here who hadn't proclaimed it to be a wonderful revelation for their taste buds.

But this solemn, silent detective was just sitting there stone-faced as he continued to consume his meal.

Lost in thought, Finn looked up when he heard her asking about the meal. He was about to shrug and say that the breakfast she'd ordered for him was "okay," but even in his lost mental state, he knew that wouldn't be giving the meal its due. Even he knew it was better than just "okay."

So, taking a breath, Finn answered, "Good," and went on eating—and thinking.

Nik frowned, taking offense for the man who had prepared the meal. Roberto's son never did anything halfheartedly. "That sounded as if it was really hard for you to say. Don't worry, I'm not recording you if that's what you're worried about."

There was a lot more that she would have wanted to say to the detective, but she left it at that. She reminded herself that she needed to choose her arguments with this one, because something told her there would be more than a few arguments coming up before this matter was settled—*if* it wound up being settled.

Finn looked at her pointedly. "*That's* not what I'm worried about," he told the woman sitting opposite him at the small table.

At that point, rather than become defensive, Nik just laughed. "Good, then you *are* enjoying this. I'm glad."

Again, he looked at her, his glare turning razor-sharp. "The *food* is good," he said, deliberately emphasizing *food*. Under no circumstances did he want her to get the idea that he was enjoying himself sitting here like this with *her*. Heaven only knew where that would lead.

Nik nodded as if they were having a genial conversation and not one where she had to drag every word out of him.

"Well, that's all I can ask for. I've been coming to Roberto's ever since I started working and buying my own breakfasts. In all that time, I've never been disappointed. Roberto's got his whole family working here now."

That was a lot more information than he would have wanted. Every time she opened her mouth, there were things spilling from her lips, miscellaneous facts and information he had no use for.

"How do you *know* all these things?" Finn asked in exasperation.

"Things?" she repeated, not sure what he was referring to.

He rattled off just the three things he remembered off the top of his head. "The timing on traffic lights. Mrs. Palmer's concerns about her daughter. That all of this 'Roberto' person's family works here at his restaurant."

Nik didn't see how that was such a big mystery, or why it seemed to annoy him, but she could tell that it obviously did. She began to wonder if the stories she'd heard about the Cavanaughs' warmth and friendliness was just a fabrication. Maybe they weren't such outgoing, friendly people after all, she thought.

"I ask questions," she replied.

He knew what *that* was shorthand for. "In other words, you're nosy," Finn concluded.

"No, 'interested,'" Nik corrected him. "I'm *interested* in a lot of things," she said, emphasizing the word. "Aren't you?"

Her head must be crammed full, he thought—like a junkyard. "Just in things that have to do with my job and closing a case."

The man had tunnel vision, and she felt sorry for him. "That makes for a very one-dimensional life," she said.

He took that as a criticism. "It lets me focus."

She didn't quite see that as an advantage, not if he did that to the exclusion of all else. "You need someone to open up your world," she said. Finished eating, she wiped her lips. "I could help."

He realized that watching her do that was a distraction all on its own. Finn forced himself to look directly into her eyes—which didn't really help that much, either. But at least it was better than looking at her lips.

"You could help by focusing on this case and not letting your mind wander here, there and everywhere," he said sharply, annoyed with her *and* with himself for letting her lead him astray like that.

Rather than answer, Nik just smiled at him, like she knew something he didn't. Or maybe he was just reading into her expression, Finn thought.

Damn it, the woman was unnerving him and that was really getting to him, Finn thought, exasperated.

He quickly finished up his breakfast. His fork met the plate with a sharp sound that proclaimed he was finished eating. He raised his head to look at her. "You ready to go?"

"Anytime you say," she told him. "Although you probably should know that—"

He pushed his plate toward the center of the table and squared his shoulders, braced for a confrontation. "Now what?" he demanded.

"Eating your food so fast is bad for your digestion," she concluded. "It can give you heartburn."

It was really hard for him not to roll his eyes. It wasn't eating fast that was giving him indigestion. "Let me worry about my digestion," he told her, stopping short of being curt. He rose to his feet, then looked at her expectantly. "Ready?"

"Ready," she replied cheerfully.

Roberto Perez stood proudly by his cash register. He was barely five foot five and had a full head of hair that had been gradually turning salt-and-pepper in the last five years. In all the time that Nik had known him, she had never seen the man without his broad smile.

"Was something wrong with your breakfast?" Roberto asked, concerned as she handed him her bill.

"No, it was perfect as always, Roberto," Nik assured the man.

It was obvious that something wasn't making sense to the restaurant owner. "Then why are you leaving so quickly? I did not get a chance to refill your coffees," he said, looking from Nik to the man she had brought with her.

"I would love to stay, Roberto, but I'm afraid that work calls," she explained.

Roberto nodded his head, strands of unruly hair falling into his eyes. "I understand," he told her. "Come back when you have more time." His dark black eyes swept over both her and the guest she had invited along with her. And then the restaurant owner added with feeling, "Both of you."

"We will," she promised, although she really didn't know if she was speaking for Finn. She just didn't want to offend Roberto. As for Finn, she was starting to think the man was as friendly and outgoing as a pet rock. Pulling cash out of her purse, she paid her bill and then added a healthy tip to the sum. "For Manuel," she told Roberto, lowering her voice.

Finn stepped up the second she drew away and handed the man a twenty. Then he walked away before the owner could give him his change.

"Sir, you have change coming," Roberto called after him. He stepped out from behind the register, ready to hand the man his change, but Finn just kept walking.

"That's okay, keep it," Finn told the owner without turning around. Right now he just wanted to be out of there as quickly as possible.

As soon as they got out the door, Nik turned toward

him, wanting to say something about his being nice and giving a tip to Roberto, but she never got the chance. Finn started talking immediately.

"Do you *always* try to make friends with everyone you meet?" he asked. Given the line of work she was in, he found that rather an unusual trait.

"I don't try," Nik answered him. "It just happens. Why does that seem to annoy you so much?"

He didn't like being second-guessed—or having her act as if she could see right through him. "It doesn't annoy me," he snapped.

She didn't believe that for a second, not given his tone of voice. "Yes, it does," she said, contradicting him. "You know, I think you'd get along a lot better if you just loosened up a little."

"Stop and smell the roses, is that it?" he asked. Was she for real?

Nik mulled over the question in her head, as if she was actually thinking about it.

"Might not be a bad idea," she answered. "This is California. We have lots of roses, as well as a whole bunch of other flowers for you to choose from," she said, her eyes dancing.

It really annoyed him that he noticed things like that about her. He didn't trust himself to comment on what she had just said.

Instead, he asked, "You still want to follow me?"

He was curtailing the conversation, she thought. If she was being honest, she was surprised he had put up with it as long as he had. Maybe she was wearing him down a little.

"Absolutely," she answered with a broad smile.

"Then get in your car and let's go," he ordered.

Having a change of heart, Finn decided that he was

going to enjoy bringing this woman to the medical examiner's. In his opinion, she could use a little sobering up. The woman was just too damn cheerful and chirpy for her own good.

The medical examiner on duty, Dr. Jonah Grady, looked none-too-happy to see Finn approaching him, although his expression changed when he saw that the detective wasn't alone.

"I've only had a chance to do a preliminary autopsy on that body you found in the Dumpster," the doctor said. "I only have two hands," he protested, holding them up to illustrate his point. And then he flashed a welcoming smile at the woman next to Finn. "I'm sorry, where are my manners?" the medical examiner apologized. "I don't believe I've had the pleasure." He put his hand out to Nik. "I'm Dr. Jonah Grady. And you are…?"

"Just passing through, Doc," Finn informed him. "No need for you to make any lengthy introductions. She's just interested in the cause and time of death for the woman who is currently occupying your table."

She saw the annoyed look flash over the medical examiner's face and quickly stepped in to smooth down any possible ruffled feathers. Didn't the detective realize that he got more things done using honey than rubbing in salt?

Stepping forward, Nik slipped her hand into the medical examiner's extended one and introduced herself. "Nikola Kowalski."

"And why are you here in my exam room, Ms. Kowalski?" And then a look of horror passed over Grady's face as an answer occurred to him. "The deceased wasn't a loved one, was she? Because if she was, I am so sorry that I—"

"She wasn't," Nik quickly assured him, stopping any

apology that might have been on the tip of the man's tongue. "The victim is part of a case that Finn and I are working on together."

She heard Finn clear his throat, most likely registering his displeasure at her choice of words, she thought, but she didn't look his way. Her attention was focused on Grady.

Interest was very evident in the medical examiner's craggy features as he looked at her.

"'Finn,' is it now?" he asked with amusement as he turned toward the detective.

"Can we get on with this, Doc?" Finn requested tersely. "You said you did a preliminary autopsy on the victim. What did you find?"

It was obvious that the medical examiner would have rather focused on the detective's companion, but he nodded. "Okay, we'll do it your way." He crossed over to the table that still had the body on it. "Cause of death was a stab wound to the heart. She bled out, although there were a few other stabs wounds to her chest that were shallower than the one that actually killed her. Time of death was between midnight and two. From what I can tell, she put up a struggle—all her nails are broken but, as you can see, she was obviously overpowered." He looked up at them, glancing from Finn to Nik. "Anything else?"

"Are there any signs that she was sexually assaulted?" Nik asked. She wanted a clearer picture of the type of person they were dealing with. If the person who had killed the victim had also violated her, then they would turn their attention to the sex offenders who were currently at large.

"No, if that's any consolation. This appeared to be a thrill kill," Grady told them. And then the medical examiner said, "I've got a question."

"Go ahead," Finn told him.

Grady turned toward Nik. "Did you intentionally leave your ring at home," he said, apparently very interested, "or are you single?"

Nik gave no indication that the question had caught her off guard. Instead, she smiled at the man. "I'm spoken for. But thank you for the compliment."

He didn't appear quite ready to back off just yet. "Sure I can't change your mind?" the medical examiner asked hopefully.

Nik let him down gently as she shook her head. "No, sorry."

Grady shrugged his wide shoulders, taking the disappointment in stride. "Ah, well, can't blame a guy for trying. Oh, there's one more thing," he said, suddenly remembering something as he looked at Finn. "Her blood is a match for the blood that was found in the trunk of the chief's father's car."

That stopped both Finn and Nik in their tracks. "That explains the carjacking," Nik cried.

"How do you figure that?" Finn asked.

"The killer needed a car to transport the body to the Dumpster. That obviously wasn't where he had killed her," she reminded Finn.

He didn't want to admit it, but that impressed him. "Good guess," he told her.

"I like to think of it as a deduction," she replied. Turning toward the ME, she said, "Thanks for all your help, Doctor. We'll get out of your hair and leave you to your work."

She walked out of the morgue leaving the medical examiner beaming, with Finn following.

"You're married?" Finn asked, making no effort to hide the fact that he was surprised by that piece of information. They were in the elevator, on their way up to the first floor, before he decided to ask her about what she had said to Grady. The conversation with the medical examiner had been enlightening on so many levels, he thought.

"No," Nik answered.

Okay, now he was confused. "But you just told the ME—"

"Something to spare the man's feelings," she explained. "The ME looked like the persistent type and I thought it would be easier if I just let him believe I was 'taken' instead of 'not taken' with him."

"But you're not. Taken," he ventured, wanting to be perfectly clear on the subject.

"No," she replied. Then her own curiosity got the better of her. This was probably the most personal the detective had gotten with her. "Does that make a difference?"

"Not to me," Finn said, perhaps too quickly even in his own opinion. The elevator came to a stop on the first floor and they both got out. "Just trying to clear some things up, that's all," he added, avoiding her eyes.

The elevator doors closed behind them and the elevator car left.

"So now what?" she asked, turning toward Finn.

He looked at her, surprised. For a second, he thought the insurance investigator was asking him what was next for the two of them and then realized that she was talking about what was next with the case.

"Well, now that there appears to be a reason for the carjacking, I'm going to see if Uncle Andrew brought his father home from the hospital to let them know that Seamus's car was taken to transport a body. I haven't had a chance to talk to Seamus to get his version of what happened. He was drifting in and out of consciousness when I saw him.

Maybe he did see who took his truck, and if he did, then I'll get a sketch artist in with him to see if he can re-create a likeness. It'll give me something to go on."

Nik nodded. "That sounds good to me," she agreed. She gestured toward the outer door. "Let's go."

Finn realized that she intended to go along with him. He tried to discourage her. "Look, if I find out anything, I'll let you know."

Nope, not going to happen, she thought. He'd called her out on this and now he was stuck with her. "You won't have to because I'll be right there with you."

"There's no need to drag you around—" he began only to be cut off.

"You don't need to drag me," she assured him. "I can pull my own weight." She tried to appeal to his kinder side. It had to be there somewhere, right? "Look, Detective, you saw Kim Palmer. The poor woman is teetering on the edge of a breakdown. I've got to be able to give her something to hold on to. Ideally, I'd like to give her her daughter to hold on to."

Wasn't she forgetting an important point? "A daughter who might have mugged Seamus Cavanaugh and stabbed a woman to death," he reminded her.

"We don't know that for sure yet," Nik responded. "And besides, if she *was* involved in these horrible acts, she couldn't have acted alone."

He folded his arms in front of his chest, waiting to be convinced. "What makes you say that?"

Nik had met the girl briefly a few years ago. "Because she's five foot three and maybe a hundred pounds. There is no way she could have lifted that dead woman up and tossed her into the Dumpster. That takes far more upper-body strength than Marilyn Palmer is capable of," she explained.

"You have a point."

Nik smiled, pleased that she'd finally convinced him. "I know."

He scowled at her as he headed to his unmarked vehicle. "Anyone ever tell you that you're really irritating?"

"You mean other than you?" she asked innocently.

"I didn't say that to you," Finn told her.

"No, not in so many words," she agreed. "But your eyes did. Several times," she added.

The woman had an answer for everything. "My eyes, huh? I had no idea I was so expressive."

That was when she grinned again. "You are, but that's okay. I won't hold it against you."

"Lucky me," he retorted sarcastically.

"Well, now that you mentioned it," she said, touching his face, "maybe you are."

She'd had caught him off guard again, touching him like that. For just a single moment, he allowed himself to react to the feel of her fingertips on his skin.

But a moment later, for the sake of sanity, not to mention getting this case solved, he tamped down his reaction and silently insisted that he hadn't reacted to this outspoken woman.

He found that denial was a hell of a lot safer.

Chapter 8

"Nice house," Nik said as she caught up to Finn. He had pulled up into the chief's driveway, but in the interest of leaving the man's garage access clear, she had parked her car across the street.

Her comment had Finn looking at the house as if he hadn't really taken notice it for a long time. "Yeah, I guess it is," he agreed. He rang the bell.

The front door opened within less than a couple of minutes.

"I've been expecting you," Andrew said as he opened the door wider. "Come on in," he urged.

"Is your father up to talking?" Finn asked. He smiled at his aunt as Rose came into the foyer and joined them. "Because I'd really like to get his statement about what happened that night if I could. I haven't been able to speak to him so far."

The look on the former chief of police's face was skeptical. "Well, Dad's lucid but I'm not sure if you're going to be able to get anything useful from him at the moment," Andrew warned him.

"No recollection of the mugging?" Finn asked. "Temporary amnesia isn't unheard of in these kinds of cases. I know I'm not telling you anything new," he added, not wanting his uncle to think that he was talking down to him.

"It's not amnesia so much as, well, withdrawal," Rose said.

"Head injuries can cause that," Finn said, doing his best to comfort the couple. "A lot of times it's just temporary. There's every chance that it'll go away in time."

"I'm afraid that it's not so much of a head injury as it is a spirit injury," Andrew explained.

Finn's brow furrowed. "I don't think I understand," he confessed.

Nik knew exactly what the man was talking about. Sadly, she had seen this sort of thing before. "It was because he was caught by surprise and wasn't able to defend himself, wasn't it?"

Both Andrew and his wife turned in unison toward the young woman who had managed to hit the nail on the head as far as assessing what was wrong with Seamus.

"I'm sorry, who are you again?" Andrew asked politely. He had met a lot of people in the last few days and although he recalled this woman's face, he wasn't sure what her name was.

"Chief, this is Nikola Kowalski. She's an insurance investigator," Finn explained.

"An insurance investigator," Andrew repeated as if each word represented a mystery to him. His father's auto-insurance company had been notified, but he'd already spoken to someone while Seamus was still in the hospital. "I'm afraid I don't see—"

"It's a long story, sir," Finn admitted, hoping that at least for now, he could skip having to go into an explanation.

Nik stepped in with a quick summation, hoping that would be enough to explain her presence. "A friend of mine is afraid her daughter is somehow involved in this. The Aurora crime-scene investigators found a partial print on the back of your father's rearview mirror. The print appears to belong to my friend's daughter." She moved in a little closer as she continued explaining. "I thought if I could just ask your father to look at her picture, he might be able to identify her—or better yet, exonerate her," she added. That was the result that she was secretly hoping for.

Andrew exchanged looks with his wife. The latter nodded, giving her consent and adding it to his.

"Well, I have my doubts, but it's worth a try," Andrew told the two people in his living room. "Follow me. For the time being, my father's staying in the downstairs guest room."

The room was just down the hall.

Andrew knocked on the door. At first there was no response, but after a couple of minutes and another knock, a barely audible voice said, "Come in."

Andrew opened the guest-room door slowly. Looking in, Nik saw an older man sitting on the bed. The man had his back toward the door and he appeared to be staring out the window, which faced the backyard and extensive patio.

"Dad, Finn's here," Andrew announced. "He'd like to talk to you if you're up to it."

"I could come back if you're tired, sir," Finn offered.

The note of kindness evident in his voice surprised Nik. She found it encouraging. There *was* a heart inside that chest somewhere, she told herself.

Meanwhile Seamus shrugged indifferently at Finn's offer. "Doesn't matter," he responded in a disinterested voice. "Come in."

The older man sounded listless, as if all the energy had been leeched out of him, Nik thought.

Andrew looked at the two people he'd brought in. "He's been like that ever since he regained consciousness in the hospital," he told them. Andrew clearly looked distressed, as did his wife. "I'm afraid that he's just not himself," the chief confided.

The Seamus Cavanaugh everyone knew carried himself with confidence and verve, but this was a subdued, demoralized version of the man and it really distressed Andrew to see his father like this.

Seamus looked over his shoulder, a flash of hostility in his green eyes. But it disappeared almost as quickly as it appeared, almost as if it hadn't existed at all. And when it went, it seemed to take the very light out of him along with it.

"So what do you want to ask me?" Seamus asked.

Nik stepped forward, holding up Marilyn Palmer's photograph. "Have you ever seen this woman before?" she asked.

After a beat, Seamus took the photograph from her and looked at it. An image flashed through his mind, but he couldn't catch hold of it and then it was gone. He continued to stare blankly at the photograph.

"Maybe," Seamus murmured. He handed the picture back to Nik and shrugged. "I don't know."

She tried to pin him down. "You didn't see her the

night you were mugged?" Nik persisted, searching the lined face.

"I didn't see anything," Seamus snapped. And then he seemed to physically withdraw. "I'm an old man. I need to rest now."

He had all but told them to leave, Nik thought.

"Of course," she replied, backing away from the man's bed. "We'll come back later," she promised. Leaning in, she squeezed his hand.

Seamus looked as if he was a million miles away when he turned his head to look at her.

"Don't," he told her. "The answer won't be any different then."

Closing his eyes, he stretched out on the bedspread and seemed to quietly withdraw into himself.

The foursome walked out of the room. Andrew shut the door.

"He's been like that since before we brought him home." Andrew reached for the photograph and looked at it closely. "Is this the woman who mugged my father and stole his car?" he asked Nik.

"We're not sure if she was part of the carjacking, or if she wound up being taken herself and was collateral damage in the carjacking." Putting the photograph away, she told the former chief, "Her mother thinks she might have been abducted."

"Did you check all the surveillance camera footage taken in the area that night?" Andrew asked.

Nik answered before Finn had a chance. "It was a dark night and although we made out what looked like a couple of images of your father's car, it was too dark to see anything clearly. All we know is that there were two people in the car and that a woman was driving, whether willingly or under duress is still up for debate," she admitted.

"Marilyn?" Rose repeated quizzically.

"Marilyn Palmer, my friend's daughter," Nik explained.

"What else do you know about that night?" Andrew asked.

"Marilyn's—the suspect's—prints were discovered on a piece of paper that a dead woman was clutching when she was found," Finn told them.

"Dead woman?" Rose repeated. "What dead woman?"

Nik told the chief everything that she knew. "The one who was found early this morning in a Dumpster."

Andrew was still unclear about the details. "How is she involved in my father's mugging?" he asked, looking from Finn to the woman he had brought with him.

"She might have been the reason for the mugging. There was blood found in the trunk—the blood belonged to the woman found in the Dumpster," Finn explained.

"The theory is that your father's vehicle was taken so the killer or killers could transport the body without attracting attention," Nik added.

"Have you put out an APB on this Marilyn woman?" Andrew asked, looking at Finn.

"Not yet, sir," Finn answered. "If she's responsible for any of this, it might spook her and cause her to go into hiding."

"And if she's not responsible, but knows who is, the APB might help you find her," Andrew countered. "One way or another, it'll answer some questions for you."

Nik raised her hand. Finn looked at her quizzically. "If we're voting on this, I'd say go with the APB," she said.

Finn frowned. "It doesn't work that way," he informed her coldly. "It's not up for a vote—and even if it were, you don't get to vote."

"But the APB *is* a good idea," Andrew told the younger detective with authority.

This was the chief of police. Retired or not, Finn was not about to argue with the man. After all, this was the man's home territory *and* his father.

"Maybe you can talk to someone to get that moving, then, sir," Finn said.

Rose smiled at what she found to be the young man's naivete.

"Oh, I think he might know somebody, don't you, dear?" she said, looking at her husband.

"Well, I don't like throwing my influence around," Andrew told them evasively.

Rose laughed, totally amused by the image her husband was attempting to project for the benefit of the two people who had come to speak to her father-in-law.

"Uh-huh. Nobody believes you, dear. Not even Nik." As she said the name, Rose became aware of something. She looked around the immediate area. The younger woman was nowhere to be seen. "Where *is* Nik?" she asked.

"She's...not here," Finn said, realizing that he couldn't just point to her the way he had intended to. He scanned the area. There was no sign of Nik and he hadn't seen her leave. "Where did she go?" he muttered under his breath.

While the others were debating on the course of action to take regarding the APB, Nik had impulsively taken the opportunity to double back and return to the guest room. She wanted to take another stab at talking to the chief's father.

She knocked lightly on the door, then opened it and peered inside. The chief's father was exactly where they had left him, lying on the bedspread.

"Mr. Cavanaugh?" she asked. When the man didn't stir, giving no indication that he had heard her, she repeated his name, then asked, "May I come in?"

Seamus's eyelids fluttered ever so slightly, and then he slanted a look in her direction. The old man sighed. "What do you want?"

Her father had always told her she was far too brazen for her own good, but she was certain that he had meant it as a compliment. In any event, she used his assessment to bolster her courage.

Slipping into the bedroom, she closed the door behind her.

And then she started talking. Because she could always relate to people, words had always been her best tool.

"When I was growing up, my great-uncle Walter was this great big, burly guy. You know, one of those guys who just seem like they are larger than life. He was a construction foreman. One day when I was about thirteen, Uncle Walter was in this really bad construction accident. I don't know exactly what happened, but he fell two whole stories." As she talked, she drew a little closer to the chief's father. "We honestly didn't think he was going to make it," she continued solemnly as she relived the incident. "But somehow, he did. He hung on. It took his body a long time to heal."

"What does this have to do with me?" Seamus asked.

"Well, I'm getting to that," she told the man. "It took Uncle Walter's mind even longer to heal than his body. You see, because he had had the accident and fell—something he felt with all his experience he should have been able to see coming and prevented—he felt he had become a useless old man. A useless old man with absolutely nothing to offer."

Seamus nodded to himself. "Yeah," he said bitterly, "it happens."

She came around to the foot of the bed to face Seamus. "But it doesn't have to. And it wasn't true," she insisted. "Uncle Walter *wasn't* useless, he still had a great deal to offer," she told the man lying on the bed. "But he had to stop feeling sorry for himself in order to realize that."

"A lot to offer," Seamus scoffed. "Like what?"

"Like experience and knowledge," she told him without any hesitation. "Uncle Walter had a great deal of experience stored up in his head—experience he could pass on to younger men." She drew even closer to Seamus, trying to get her point across. "It took my great-uncle a long while to realize one very crucial thing."

"What's that?" Seamus asked.

"That we all do have to get older, but none of us, not a one," she said with emphasis, "has to get old. Because 'old' is a state of mind that happens when you give up." Finished, Nik looked at Seamus hopefully, searching for a sign that she had gotten through to the man.

But he just closed his eyes. "I'm tired, little girl. Let me rest."

Her heart sank.

"Yes, sir." There was no point in arguing with the man right now.

Even so, she made a mental note to come back and see Seamus Cavanaugh again. It wasn't in her nature to give up. She refused to allow him to be a casualty of the person or persons who'd mugged him.

But for now, she knew she needed to go.

Nik slipped out of the guest room. After closing the door behind her, she walked smack into Finn.

"What were you doing in there?" he demanded.

She struggled to stifle her surprise. "I was just talking to the chief's father."

His eyes darkened as he looked toward the door she had just closed.

"Yeah, I figured that part out," he told her. He had to struggle to keep his temper from flaring. "Did you think that if you batted your eyelashes at him, he'd wind up telling you something he wasn't sharing with the rest of us?" Finn demanded hotly. "Damn it, that's an old man who's lucky to be alive, Ko-val-ski. Maybe you could try to keep that in mind the next time—when and *if* you get to talk to him again," he snapped.

"I wasn't 'batting my eyelashes' at him," she retorted. "I was just telling him about my great-uncle Walter."

"About who?" he asked, completely bewildered.

"Uncle Walter, my dad's uncle," she told him. "He was this big bull of a construction worker who fell two stories—"

"Let me guess," Finn interrupted sarcastically. "He flew, right?"

Nik stopped abruptly. "Never mind, the story's wasted on you," she told him, turning her back on Finn and going toward Andrew and his wife. She followed the sound of voices. They were coming from the rear of the house.

She kept going until she found Andrew and his wife in the kitchen.

Andrew half rose in his chair when she entered. He saw the angry look on her face. "Everything all right?"

She assumed he was asking about things between Finn and her. She had never been the type to turn to other people to defend her or fight her battles.

Nik smiled politely at the former chief and told him in the cheeriest voice she could summon, "They just couldn't be better."

Andrew knew when he was being lied to. He also knew when to leave things alone. So he asked, "Would you like something to eat before you go?"

"My husband has a great reputation for making sure everyone who crosses his path is filled to the gills," Rose told them, smiling lovingly at Andrew.

"Maybe next time," Nik said, declining the offer.

"What she's trying to say is that we've got to get back to the case," Finn explained.

"You'll keep me posted?" Andrew asked.

"Us," Rose corrected. "Keep *us* posted. My husband sometimes forgets that we're a unit and that I love that old man just as much as he does," she said, nodding toward where the guest room was.

Nik nodded. "If you love him," she advised the pair just as she began to leave, "don't call him old."

"Sorry." Finn threw the apology over his shoulder as he hurried out. Nik was sticking her nose into things that weren't any of her business, and Finn felt obliged to apologize for her.

Chapter 9

"So now you're giving my uncle advice on how to treat his father?" Finn asked as soon as he caught up to her outside of the chief's house.

Nik turned to face him. He obviously appeared to be annoyed at what he apparently viewed as her newest transgression. She had begun to think that they were past his finding fault with her.

Looked like she was wrong.

"I was just trying to be helpful," she told Finn.

He scowled at her, dismissing her excuse. "Well, don't be," he told her.

She was doing her best to be understanding, but the man was really wearing her patience thin. "What is your problem, Cavanaugh?" Nik asked.

"Maybe my problem is I don't like people horning their way in where they don't belong." The words came out before he had a chance to think them through. If he had, he might have had second thoughts about saying them. Then again, he might not have.

She looked at him sharply. He *had* to be kidding. Nik refused to back off. "That would make more sense if you hadn't asked *me* to join *you*. I didn't call you at five this morning, you called me." She raised herself up on her toes. "Remember?"

Damn it, she was right, he thought belligerently. Annoyed with himself for the oversight, Finn backed off. "My mistake."

He did an about-face so fast, her head was spinning. Was this a trap? she wondered. "Is that what you really think?"

Whatever he was going to say was going to have to wait because at that moment, his cell phone rang. It was the beginning notes from "The Pink Panther Theme." Surprised, Nik stared at the phone as Finn pulled it out and answered the call.

"You're kidding," he said after listening to the caller for a minute. "Valri, you're a genius. I owe you one… Okay, I owe you more than one," he amended. "Be right there." He terminated the call only to see Nik looking at him. "What?"

"'The Pink Panther Theme'?" Nik asked incredulously. "Really?"

He shrugged. "It just seemed appropriate when I input her number."

Since he wasn't volunteering anything, she decided to ask. "So what did she find?"

"The name of the woman in the Dumpster," Finn said as he got into his car.

Nik immediately ran to her own vehicle across the street and got in. She wasn't about to be left behind. She gunned her engine and took off after Finn, who had already pulled away from the curb and had hit the road. She had a pretty good idea where he was going, but just in case she was wrong, she wasn't about to lose sight of him if she could possibly help it.

Nik managed to stick to him like glue.

When he pulled up in the rear parking lot behind the police station, Nik was right there with him. She found a space one row over and parked there.

"Where did you learn how to drive?" Finn asked, slamming his car door shut. He'd watched her the entire time in his rearview mirror. "By playing a video game?"

Instead of answering his question, Nik told him, "I didn't go any faster than you did."

He didn't know what to say to that because she was right. It was just that he had deliberately squeezed through yellow lights, thinking he could temporarily lose her or at least impede her. But she had managed to fly through all the lights, making it through by a hair-breadth before the lights turned red.

He decided that it was safer just to drop the subject altogether. "Well, you're here now so you might as well come along," he told her.

Nik smiled broadly up at him and said, "Thank you."

Finn didn't detect a note of sarcasm, but he would have bet his soul that it was there, anyway, woven in just underneath.

"So who is the dead woman?" Nik asked as he hurried up the steps into the police station.

"Valri wants to show me when I get there," he told her, walking toward the elevator. The grin on his lips wasn't for Nik, it was there because of something that Valri had said to him. "She said if she had to work to find a match, I can get my butt down to her office so she could show me." He shook his head. "She's definitely getting feistier. When she first started working in the computer lab," he told Nik, "Valri was the meekest, mildest person you ever wanted to meet."

She could definitely see that happening. "I guess she realized how important she was to getting the crimes solved."

Finn thought over her response. "I suppose it could be something like that."

Nik decided to get on slightly more even footing with the detective. She knew that she was only here because he was tolerating her presence. She didn't want to sacrifice that.

"By the way, thanks for having a change of heart," she told him. When he raised one quizzical eyebrow, she elaborated. "You're letting me come with you. When we left the chief's house you sounded as if you wanted to have me banned not just from the police investigation, but just possibly from the planet as well," she added. Her smile widened.

"Maybe I did let my temper get away from me," Finn admitted, although his tone stopped short of being apologetic.

"Everyone has a right to be protective when it comes to their family," she said. She actually believed what she was saying, so she wasn't fabricating an excuse for his benefit.

They had reached the computer lab. Finn held the door for her, then followed in right behind Nik as she entered the large room.

As always, Valri was at her computer. Preoccupied, she didn't even seem to hear them approaching until they were practically on top of her. It wasn't until Finn said her name that she realized she wasn't alone.

Swallowing a gasp, Valri's hand flew up to her chest,

presumably where her heart was. Taking a large breath to steady her nerves, she looked at Finn accusingly.

"Don't you know any better than to sneak up on someone like that?" she demanded. "You could have given me a heart attack."

"I didn't 'sneak,'" Finn replied. "I came in the way I always do. I could break something next time if you'd prefer to be alerted that I was here."

"Heaven willing, there won't be a next time," Valri answered. "I've got enough people leaving their puzzles on my desk to keep busy until Christmas. Maybe even next Christmas," she added. Valri raised her eyes to look at the woman beside her cousin. "Someone new on the force?" she asked, nodding at Nik.

Nik smiled broadly at the lab tech. "I'm Nik Kowalski," she told her, extending her hand to Valri. "Just think of me as an adjunct investigator."

Valri looked at her, slightly bemused. "O-o-okay," she replied, stretching the word out. She looked toward Finn for a further explanation.

He, on the other hand, wanted the answer he had come for. "The dead woman's identity?" he prompted Valri, waiting.

"Right." She nodded her head, returning to the information on her monitor. "That would be Julie Everett. According to what I found, she was working at Hanover and Wallace." Valri scrolled down to the next screen. "It says here that she was a temp at the firm. She was there a little more than three weeks."

"Wait," Nik suddenly blurted as the name of the firm rang a bell. "I think that's the name of the place that Marilyn works."

"Marilyn," Valri repeated. "Are you talking about the woman who left a rearview-mirror partial print?"

Nik smiled, surprised that the other woman had made the connection. Valri's mind had to be filled to overflowing with the various pieces of information she gleaned thanks to the numerous searches she wound up conducting day in, day out.

"You really *are* good," Nik said, complimenting the other woman with enthusiasm.

Valri in turn beamed at her, grateful for the recognition. She laughed. "That's what I've been trying to tell all these people who keep trooping through my office, making requests. They take the information I come up with and are off and running without so much as even a single word of acknowledgment for all my efforts."

Nik saw Finn opening his mouth, about to protest the generalization. She jumped in instead.

"Oh, I'm sure they appreciate you. Some people just have trouble being vocal—unless they're yelling," Nik qualified.

"Are you through yet?" Finn asked, looking at her. The edge she'd previously heard in his voice had made a return appearance.

Rather than retreat, or become defensive, Nik merely exchanged looks with Valri. "See what I mean?"

Finn ignored Nik and just focused on Valri. She was the one with the answers, in his opinion. "You have anything else of significance to tell me?"

"I've got an address for the dead woman," she said, writing it down on a piece of paper. She held it out to Finn. "And some advice."

"Advice?" Finn asked, slightly confused. He had no idea what this could be about.

"Yes. Keep this one," she told him with a wink, nodding at Nik.

"I think you've got the wrong idea," he said. One that

he intended to clear up quickly. "Kowalski is not part of the department. She's an insurance investigator—" he slanted a glance at the woman who had followed him into the computer lab "—or so she claims."

"Trust me, nobody claims to be an insurance investigator if they're not," Nik assured both of them. "It's not the attention getter in a crowded room that you might think." She looked at her watch. "It's still early enough to go to Hanover and Wallace to find out who the last person was who saw Julie alive. Although…"

"Although what?" Finn asked, curious where Nik was going with this.

"If this Julie Everett was just a temp, nobody might have even noticed her."

He hated to admit it, but she was right. It was a definite possibility. They'd find out soon enough.

"Thanks, Val," he said as they turned to leave the computer lab.

Valri glanced up for a split second and murmured, "Right," then went back to her current project. There never seemed to be any downtime in her line of work, she thought.

"What's Valri's favorite drink?" Nik asked Finn as they went to the elevator.

The detective looked at the diminutive woman beside him, thinking that was rather an odd question to ask, especially out of the blue like that.

"I really don't know," Finn admitted. And then he allowed his curiosity to take over. "Why?"

"You might want to find out and bring her a bottle of it the next time you 'drop' by with another riddle for her to solve. That would definitely show her that you appreciate her efforts on your behalf. Just a thought," she added with a shrug.

As he got out of the elevator when it stopped on the ground floor, all Finn could do was study his temporary companion for a long moment.

Nik endured the scrutiny, convinced that he was going to tell her what was on his mind eventually.

And he did.

"You missed your calling, you know," he told her as they walked to the outer doors. "You should have been a social director."

Nik took it all in stride. "I know you meant that sarcastically but I'll take that as a compliment regarding my people skills."

He had a feeling she would. Finn lifted one muscular shoulder in a dismissive half shrug. "Whatever floats your boat," he said. "You want to come with me to Hanover and Wallace?" The suggestion surprised her. Nik thought she was going to have to talk him into letting her come with him. "I'll drive," he added.

She sensed he expected her to make a counteroffer. "We could go together and I could drive," Nik said as they went down the back steps to the parking lot.

Finn looked at her, surprised that she had made the offer in all seriousness. He laughed dryly. "Not unless you want to learn a whole bunch of new words—and not even then," he added with finality.

If he thought that would embroil them in an argument, he was wrong, she thought. She was totally amenable to his suggestion. She was just glad to be going along.

"Since you put it so nicely, how could I refuse?" she asked with a broad smile.

Just when he felt he had her all figured out…he didn't, Finn thought. The woman definitely kept him up on his toes.

Preoccupied with the newest information that Valri

had given him, Finn didn't fully realize that the latter fact didn't really bother him.

Hanover and Wallace was a prestigious accounting firm located on the southern edge of Aurora. There were no run-down sections in the city, but the southern section was known to be particularly upscale. The area was right next to Quail Hill, which was currently the last word in expensive homes and upscale buildings.

"Wonder what the rents run here," Nik mused as she got out of the passenger side of Finn's unmarked vehicle.

This ritzy area was way out of his league, Finn thought. Out loud, he said, "You know what they say, if you have to ask…"

"You can't afford it," Nik concluded, nodding. "That's okay," she said. "I'm not looking to move. I like where I am."

Which stirred his curiosity. "Where is that, by the way?"

"In Aurora," she answered vaguely.

She was playing games, Finn thought. Why? Did she think he was going to stalk her if he knew where she lived? If he really wanted to do that, he could find out where she lived from Valri.

But the fact that she was deliberately withholding the information had him pressing her. "Just where in Aurora?"

Nik smiled. "In a nice section," she answered evasively.

"They're *all* nice sections in Aurora," he pointed out.

"I know," she replied brightly. "That's what I like about the city. It's incredibly neat and clean—and safe," she added. She'd lived here ever since she was a teenager. "At least for the most part."

It irked him that she refused to tell him where she lived. It irked him even more that that fact bothered him. It shouldn't matter to him *where* she lived. All that should matter was whether or not she was an asset to his case.

He had far more important things on his mind than this woman's little evasive games.

That fact didn't really seem to help.

The offices of Hanover and Wallace were located on the twelfth floor of the newly renovated Atwater Building. Nik and Finn took the express elevator up.

"I think I left my stomach on the ground floor," Nik told the detective when the elevator doors opened on the twelfth floor in a matter of seconds. She was definitely queasy, she thought.

"You can pick it up when we go back down," Nik told her dryly.

Instead of getting annoyed at him, as he expected, he heard Nik laugh at his comment.

"Humor." She nodded her head in pleased approval. "You know, I guess there is hope for you yet, Detective Cavanaugh."

His eyebrows drew together. He did his best to look at her darkly, although he didn't quite succeed. "I'm glad you think so," he told her. "That means a lot."

Nik would have had to be deaf to miss his intonation. "But sarcasm is still your go-to move, isn't it?" she said.

The expression on his face grew just a tiny bit darker. "I really don't suggest analyzing me, Kowalski. Not if you know what's good for you."

"Too late," she replied brightly. "I'm afraid that you're just too fascinating a personality to ignore, Cavanaugh."

He blew out an irritated breath. "Now who's being sarcastic?" he asked.

She turned her head to him just as he was about to open the firm's door. "I guess you're rubbing off on me."

He sighed, shaking his head. He was allowing himself to get sidetracked. "Look, if you can't get yourself to focus on the reason we're here—"

"I'm focused," she told him, then repeated for emphasis, "I'm focused." And then, just before he opened the door leading into the firm, she said, "I'm sorry. I get carried away sometimes."

He only wished that she would get carried away—literally.

Tamping down his growing irritation, he gave her a scrutinizing look. "Are you ready?" he asked.

In all seriousness, she answered, "I'm ready."

And then, right before his eyes, the woman he'd regarded as annoying seemed to transform back into the serious investigator he had first decided to join forces with.

Finn nodded his head. "Then let's do this."

Chapter 10

Hanover and Wallace's receptionist, Miriam Harris, according to the nameplate in the middle of the oversize desk she was standing behind, was more of a moving target than a stationary figure. She appeared to be so busy that she didn't even realize they had entered the large outer office until Finn had cleared his throat to get her attention.

"I'm sorry, I didn't see you standing there." She tapped her monitor, pulling up a screen. "Who do you have an appointment with?"

"Actually," Finn began, "we don't have an appointment."

The woman sighed as she shook her head. Wisps of auburn hair were coming undone around her face and neck. She looked as if she was weathering a windy day right here in the office, Nik thought. The woman appeared to be on the verge of unraveling.

"I'm sorry," the receptionist said with what seemed like genuine distress. "We're not taking any walk-ins right now. The assistant who's supposed to be here sched-uling the appointments hasn't been in in two days and everything is just falling to pieces…appointment-wise," she added as an afterthought. "If you'd like to call back in a couple of days, we can see about fitting you in with one of our accountants. I'm sure everything will be back to normal by then."

The woman seemed to be doing her best to be conge-nial, but it was obvious to Nik that the receptionist was caving in under the pressure.

"Is this the assistant who hasn't been in the office the last couple of days?" Finn held up his phone, showing the receptionist a photograph of Julie Everett that had been taken in the morgue after the dead woman had been put back together following her autopsy.

Despite the fact that she had been cleaned up, there were bruises evident on Julie's neck and on the side of her face. It was obvious that she had been the victim of some sort of an assault—and that she had not emerged the victor.

Miriam Harris's brown eyes widened. "That's her!" she cried. "That's Julie!" Her eyes darted from Finn's phone to his face. "She looks awful. What—what hap-pened to her?"

Not trusting Finn to break the news to the already fragile-looking woman, Nik took over. "I'm afraid she's dead, Ms. Harris."

"Dead?" the receptionist repeated in a shaky voice fraught with disbelief. When she could finally form words, she asked, "When? How…? Who?" The third question came after a beat.

"That's what we're trying to find out," Finn told her,

his voice a little less abrupt than it had been a moment ago. He took out his wallet and held up his ID and his badge. "Detective Cavanaugh with the Aurora PD," he told the woman. Then, because he felt it might cut down on any unwanted questions, he added, "This is Investigator Kowalski. We'd like to ask you a couple of questions about Ms. Everett."

The receptionist looked as if she was suddenly folding up right in front of them. Not because she had something to hide, but because of the idea that someone she had interacted with so recently was abruptly no longer among the living.

"Ma'am?" Finn persisted.

"I don't think there's much I can tell you," she told him nervously. "I mean, we weren't friends or anything. I just knew her from work," the receptionist explained, her eyes going from the detective to the woman beside him. "From here," she clarified. "Julie was sent here by a temp agency. Our regular scheduling assistant is out on maternity leave," she added. "Are you sure that Julie's, you know, dead?"

"Very sure," Finn replied. He got back to questioning the woman. "So you never saw her talking to anyone outside of the office?"

Miriam shook her head, her hair becoming more and more undone. "I'm way too busy to keep track of the comings and goings of the other people in the office," the receptionist said, her voice quaking. And then she lowered it, her eyes furtively looking on either side of her. "I just notice if they don't do their job."

"And did Julie do her job?" Nik asked in a friendly, conversational manner.

It was obvious that the receptionist was torn between

telling the truth and speaking well of the dead. After a beat, Miriam compromised.

"She did as much as could be expected, but you could see that she wasn't all that interested in it, not that you could really blame her." The woman became a little more animated in her answer. "Although why take on a job if you don't intend on doing it right?"

Sensing the woman was looking for someone to agree with her, Nik answered, "Absolutely." She knew that Finn wanted to establish a timeline if that was possible, so she asked the receptionist, "When was the last time you saw Julie? Do you remember?"

"Oh, yes," the receptionist said without hesitation. "She came to tell me that she had to leave for a doctor's appointment. Right in the middle of the day," the woman said with disapproval, "and she never came back." A look of horror suddenly took over her features, washing away the annoyed one that had begun to take hold. "You don't suppose that was when she was killed, do you?" Her distress instantly doubled. "I've been complaining about her not coming back and all along, she was lying dead somewhere. Oh, I'm a terrible person," Miriam cried, clearly distressed by her own behavior.

"Her body was discovered early this morning," Finn told the receptionist. "All indications were that she was killed either late last night or early this morning, not two days ago."

Miriam exhaled, apparently finding some sort of solace in the information. "Oh, all right then, I feel better." She looked stricken again as her words played back to her. "I mean, I don't feel better, but...you understand?" she asked, as she looked from one of them to the other.

"We do," Nik assured her. She saw Finn taking a card out of his pocket.

"If you think of anything else, please call," he told the receptionist. "My number's on the back," he said, pointing to it. Then he added, "The department's number is on the front."

Nik noticed that the receptionist only seemed to be interested in the number on the back of the card. She wondered how long the woman would wait before calling him on the pretense of giving him some miscellaneous piece of information.

"You know she's going to call you, right?" Nik asked him as soon as they walked out of the accountants' suite of offices.

"As long as she has some more information..." Finn responded, his voice trailing off.

He was missing the point, Nik thought. "I had no idea that you were an optimist," she said with a laugh. "You know, the more I think about it, the more interesting you become."

He stopped at the elevator and pressed the down button. He wasn't following her. "So what are you saying? You don't think that she's going to call?"

"No," Nik answered, stepping into the elevator and bracing herself for its swift descent. "She's not going to have any information. Once the shock of actually knowing someone who was murdered started to wear off, she started looking at you like she was a hungry lioness and you were a very large cut of T-bone steak." She smiled up at him despite the queasy feeling in the pit of her stomach as they went down. "Rare."

He laughed, but there was no humor in the sound. "Very imaginative."

"Very accurate," Nik corrected.

She mentally blessed the elevator when it arrived at the ground floor.

They walked out of the elevator, and the doors closed immediately, even before they reached the outer exit. "Well, I don't know about you," Finn said, "but I think that I'm going to call it a day." He held open the exit door for her.

"Don't forget that you have to drive back to the station first." When he looked at her with confusion, she reminded him, "My car's there, remember?" She was fairly certain that he probably wasn't happy about having to chauffeur her back. Taking pity on him, she gave Finn an alternative. "Or I could just call a cab and have the driver take me over there."

But he shook his head as they walked over to where his car was parked. "It was my idea to use just one car—*my* car," he said. "So I'll take you back."

Right now, a cab still sounded like the way to go in her opinion. She didn't like putting someone out—especially when they made her feel that they were being put out.

"You make me feel like your own personal penance," she told him.

He nodded, approving her choice of words. "That's a very good description."

"I'll find my own way back," she informed Finn.

But he caught hold of her arm as she began to take out her cell phone, ready to call for a ride. "I said I'd take you, so I'll take you. End of story."

"End of story," she echoed, putting her phone back in her pocket. She offered him a smile, which he ignored.

"So, same time, same place tomorrow?" Nik asked him cheerfully once Finn pulled his car up next to her vehicle.

His eyes gave nothing away, not even a hint of whether or not she had guessed right. "I'll let you know," he told her solemnly.

Nodding, she assured him, "I'll be here."

"I meant I'll call," he told her.

That didn't change her answer. "Funny, I meant I'll be here. In the flesh," she added. When she saw the impatient look on his face, she reminded him of one crucial fact. "We still haven't found Marilyn," she reminded him. "And I promised Kim that I wouldn't stop looking until I found her daughter."

The frown on his face was not one of censure, but was one of mild surprise. "Are you always this diligent about keeping your promises?" he asked.

Nik didn't waver or hesitate even for a second. "Always," she answered.

He nodded as she got out of his car. "Okay then."

She realized that he hadn't said anything one way or the other about meeting her tomorrow.

"That's not an answer," she pointed out as he began to drive away.

"It is in my book," he said, then he was gone.

This man took a *lot* of getting used to, she thought grudgingly.

Wanting to check on Kim, she swung by the woman's house and saw another car parked in her driveway.

Had Marilyn come back, or did the car belong to Kim's sister? Knowing she couldn't take anything for granted, Nik sat in her car across the street from Kim's house and dialed the woman on her cell phone.

Kim's voice sounded thick, as if she was crying, when she answered after several rings. Nik refrained from asking her about it.

"Hi, Kim, it's Nik—"

Instantly the other woman seemed to come to life, and asked, "Have you heard anything? Is Marilyn all right? Is she—?"

"We're still looking," Nik told the woman. "I just thought I'd check with you to see if she had tried to call you."

"No." Nik could almost see the woman's chest deflating. "Nothing," Kim answered in a voice that throbbed with fear.

"Did your sister come to stay with you?" Nik asked, staring at the car in the driveway.

"Yes, she's here now." Kim's voice took on a note of complaint. "But all she does is lecture me that I was too soft on Marilyn."

"Your sister means well—and she's worried," Nik added, hoping that would make a little of what was happening tolerable. "I'll check in on you tomorrow," she promised.

"And you'll call me if you hear anything about Marilyn?" Kim pleaded.

"You'll be my first call," Nik assured her. "Kim, I've got to go," she said, sensing the other woman's reluctance in letting her hang up.

"She *is* all right, isn't she?" Kim asked, her voice begging for reassurance.

Nik honestly didn't know the answer to that and she didn't want to lie to the woman, but at the same time, she didn't want to crush her, either. So she said, "Just remember to keep positive thoughts."

And with that, Nik took the opportunity to terminate the call.

Nik stayed up, making a list of all the different possible scenarios, but she had to admit to herself that it was just an exercise in futility. The scenarios all led nowhere. There just wasn't enough available information to go on, despite the fact that both Marilyn and Julie were connected to the accounting firm, one permanently and one just as a temp. It might mean something, but most likely, it was just a coincidence.

"Think, Nik. *Think!*"

She had to be missing *something*. But what?

The thought throbbed in Nik's head until she finally fell asleep on her sofa minutes shy of midnight, surrounded by notes and scribblings that had gotten less and less coherent the later it got.

When her phone rang at five the next morning, the first thought that occurred to Nik's semiconscious, exhausted brain was that she had somehow gotten caught up in a broadcast of the movie *Groundhog Day*.

But as she forced her brain back into a conscious state, that notion disappeared…only to make a reappearance when she heard the voice on the other end of the call.

It was Finn.

He was calling her, just as he had the previous morning.

His voice was almost weary. "It happened again!" he declared.

She blinked, trying to focus and shake off the last remnants of sleep. He just couldn't be saying what she thought he was saying…could he?

"What happened again?" she asked, fairly confident that the next words out of his mouth were going to totally dispel this lingering nightmare buzzing in her head.

"A patrolman found another dead woman. She was stabbed through the heart, just like the first victim."

Nik caught her breath. Her heart was pounding wildly. "Was she in a Dumpster?"

"No, but the body was dumped in the alley behind another restaurant. She was stabbed like the last one," he said. "I just got the call. I'm heading to the crime scene," he told her.

She could hear the rustling of his clothing. He was getting dressed even as he was talking to her. She kicked off her own covers and headed toward her closet. "Where's the restaurant?"

"Rafferty's. Over on Main and Jeffery," he told her.

She blinked again, trying to focus on the clock back on her nightstand in an attempt to kick-start her brain. "I can be there in thirty minutes."

"That's all right," he said, negating what she'd said. "I can swing by and pick you up."

The offer to come and get her was unexpected and she hesitated for a moment. If he came to pick her up, then he'd know where she lived.

He probably already did, she thought. Which meant that there was no point in telling him no. Besides, the man was obviously trying to extend an olive branch for the way he'd behaved toward her.

"Sure, why not?" she finally said.

"I need an address," he told her.

Then he *didn't* know where she lived. Oh, well, that ship had sailed, Nik told herself. The next minute she rattled off her address to him.

"You don't live all that far from me," he revealed.

"I know," she replied. "Let me go get ready," she said just before she ended the call.

For a split second, she thought about calling Kim with this latest bit of news, then decided to let the woman sleep—providing she had been able to, Nik amended.

In any event, this latest murder could have nothing to do with Marilyn's being missing. In addition, she wouldn't be doing Kim any service by frightening her with the possible scenarios that might have taken place involving her daughter. For one thing, they might not have happened in Marilyn's case.

It was best for the woman to hang on to hope for as long as she could. If Marilyn did turn up alive, all the better.

And if the opposite turned out to be true, well, she wanted her friend to be able to hang on to the slim shreds of hope while they were still available to her.

"That does it," she told herself as she rushed into her clothing so that she'd be ready by the time Finn knocked on her door. "I am definitely not having any kids. My nerves wouldn't be able to stand this kind of tension."

But even as she discounted the hypothetical scenario that might or might not be in her future, she knew she didn't really mean it. She liked kids too much to reject the idea of having them someday.

It was finding a father for those kids—or kid—that was going to be the problem, Nik decided.

The doorbell rang just then.

Chapter 11

After checking through the peephole to make sure it was Finn standing on the other side of the door, Nik unlocked it and slipped out of her apartment. "You came."

He heard the surprise in her voice and couldn't help wondering why it was there. "I said I would."

That still didn't change the fact that part of her doubted that he would show up. Yet here he was, she thought.

"You know," she told him as she locked her door, re-setting her alarm system, then began walking ahead of him, "we really should stop meeting like this."

Finn stared at her as she turned around, confused by her comment. "I called to tell you I'd be here."

She smiled, shaking her head. "You really don't have any sense of humor, do you?"

"I don't see anything humorous about my line of work," he told her flatly. The woman said the strangest things, he thought. "My car's over there," he said, nodding toward one of the general parking areas.

"You have to find humor in everything," Nik told him, trying to explain why she felt the way she did as she followed him to his car. "Otherwise, you'll lose your sense of humanity."

He stopped in front of his vehicle and pressed a button on his key fob. All four car door locks popped up at attention, signaling that the doors were open. He spared her another glance as he prepared to get in. Thinking of what she'd just said, he told her, "My family would really love you."

"I take it you mean that as a compliment," she said a little uncertainly. "Anyway, I'm going to take it that way."

"Do whatever you want with it," he muttered. He waited for her to get in on her side, then got in and started the engine. Pulling out of the spot, he asked, "Do you want to hear about the latest victim or not?"

She didn't usually get sidetracked like this. "Please," she answered. "Give me the details."

He went around a car that was traveling much too slowly in his opinion. He could feel his impatience building. Was it because he was handling a murder case, something outside his usual purview, or because he hadn't solved the case yet? He really wasn't sure. "The patrolman who was the first one on the scene and found the body noticed the similarities to the first victim. He called it into Dispatch, and they called to alert me."

"Similarities," Nik repeated, trying to keep things straight. "You're talking about the fact that she was stabbed through the heart, right?"

"That's just the first similarity," he told her. "The victim was around the same age as the first woman, and she was dressed up just the way victim number one was."

He certainly liked to use a minimum of words, Nik thought. "You mean she was wearing the same clothes?"

"The same *kind* of clothes," he explained. Pressing down on the accelerator, he made it through a yellow light before it turned red. "You know, like what a woman would wear on a night out. Sexy dress, heels, that kind of thing." He glanced at Nik to see if she understood what he was saying.

Nik was considering the significance of what he'd just told her. "So you think this might have been a date that went bad?" she asked.

He felt it was more diabolical than that. "I think our perp is a serial killer who picks up his victim at a fancy restaurant or bar, gets them drunk and then satisfies his bloodlust."

"That sounds plausible enough. Gruesome, but plausible," she said. She had one question, though. "How does Marilyn figure into this?"

"That part I haven't figured out yet," Finn admitted. The restaurant was still two long blocks away. He started to look for it. "Maybe she was actually his first victim and we just haven't found her yet."

Something didn't add up for her, Nik thought. "But the killer didn't try to hide the other."

Technically, that wasn't true. "He put Julie into a Dumpster," Finn reminded her.

"That's not really hiding," Nik said. "He would have known that she'd be discovered sooner or later—most likely sooner," she told Finn.

She was reasoning this out on the fly, he thought, and he grudgingly told her, "You know, you're not half-bad at this."

Nik pretended to clutch her heart and throw back her head in shock. "Two compliments in one day and the sun's barely risen," she cried. "I don't know if I can stand this."

Finn scowled at her. "Okay, I take it back."

"Sorry, too late," she responded with a laugh.

He turned the corner and then pulled up in front of the restaurant. Despite the early hour, the area was already busy, but not because of customers. There were three patrol cars as well as the crime-scene van and the coroner's wagon.

Nik leaned forward, taking it all in. "Looks like the party's already in full swing," she noted grimly. She was out of Finn's vehicle the second he brought it to a full stop.

"Remember, don't contaminate the crime scene," he warned, calling after her. He felt like a parent with an eager child in tow.

The fact didn't annoy him as much as he would have thought it would.

"Not my first rodeo, remember?" Nik said over her shoulder as she approached what she assumed was the scene of the crime.

Why did he keep doing this to himself? Finn silently demanded. He didn't *have* to let this woman know about these crimes when they happened. There was no law, written or unwritten, that said he needed to notify her. He'd done it simply as a courtesy, nothing else.

Maybe, he told himself following behind her, it was time to stop being so damn polite and just focus on the crime he had accidentally managed to get pulled into. It was robbery, not homicide, that was his regular line of work.

Hearing the sound of people approaching, Sean Cavanaugh looked up. "Ah, Ms. Kowalski, I didn't realize you'd be gracing us with your presence," he said, smiling at her. "I thought you were looking for your friend's daughter, the young woman who was involved in my father's carjacking."

Nik smiled back at the genial investigator. "We think

this might be connected somehow. At least that's what we're trying to figure out."

"We?" Sean repeated, both curious and intrigued. Then he saw Finn coming up behind the woman he had greeted. "Finn, are you part of the 'we'?" the head of the CSI's day shift asked the younger man. By the amusement on his face, it was obvious that he felt he already knew the answer to that.

Finn bristled, not because of what the man said, but of the implied assumption. He and this woman were *not* a pair in the usual sense.

Rather than attempt to argue that point, he ignored it altogether and asked Sean, "What do you have for me?"

For the sake of family harmony, Sean diplomatically refrained from making any further mention about the elephant in the room. Instead, he turned his attention to the details he had already uncovered.

"I can tell you that whoever did this was really angry. The stab wounds in the victim went in really deep."

"Could a woman have done the stabbing?" Nik asked.

Sean considered the question. "If she was enraged enough, I'd say it was possible. But as far as what your average woman is capable of, the answer is most likely not. The stab wounds looked as if they were delivered using a great deal of force." In his mind's eye, Sean re-created the scenario. "Most women would have difficulty overpowering another woman and at the same time stabbing her to this extent. Of course, there are always exceptions," he added.

Finn knew what Nik was trying to do. She wanted to rule out Marilyn without actually saying the words. It was obvious that she wanted Sean to do it.

"Would a one-hundred-and-ten-pound woman of average strength be such an exception?" he asked Sean. He could see that he had surprised Nik with his question.

"I'm going to go out on a limb here and say no," Sean told him. The man paused for a moment, looking over at the latest victim as she was being zipped up into a body bag. "Did the last victim have a full tox screen run on her?" he asked Finn.

Tox screens were standard. However, full ones weren't. "Not that I know of," Finn answered.

"Have them run one," Sean told him. "There were no defensive wounds on this one. She might not have seen the guy switch gears just before he killed her, but my guess is that she was too out of it to really see anything at all or realize that she was in trouble until after the fact."

Finn agreed. "I'll ask the medical examiner to run a full panel."

Sean nodded. About to get back to work, he suddenly remembered something just before the duo left him. "Oh, by the way, I'm supposed to tell you that Andrew's throwing a party next Saturday for Seamus."

The information surprised Finn. "I was under the impression that Seamus didn't want a party, or any fuss made over him, either," he said to Sean.

Sean shrugged. "You know Andrew. When he gets his mind fixated on something, nobody's going to talk him out of it no matter what. I think that he just wants to express his gratitude that his dad came out of all this safe and sound."

"Well, safe and sound," Finn said, "but I wouldn't say that he's exactly his old self." He looked at Sean to see if the other man agreed, or if there was something new that he didn't know about.

But it was Nik who spoke up, bringing up what she felt was an important point.

"Maybe this party is just what he needs," she said more to Finn than to the other man. She realized that Finn might not appreciate her putting in her two cents, but on the other hand, she felt she had nothing to lose here and it was her opinion that the presence of his family and friends might just help the older man heal and realize how lucky he really was. "If Mr. Cavanaugh is around his family and friends on a large scale, maybe he'll appreciate being alive instead of the alternative," she said.

"I'd say that the lady is on to something," Sean said with a chuckle.

"Oh, please don't encourage her," Finn complained.

Sean did a quick assessment of his own. "You want my opinion, that one doesn't need any encouragement from anyone," he told his nephew. "She knows exactly what she has to contribute to the game at any one given time," he said with a wink.

"I like your uncle," Nik said as she and Finn began to walk toward the medical examiner's vehicle.

"Oh, Finn," Sean called after him, raising his voice. When Finn paused to turn around in his direction, the older Cavanaugh said, "Andrew also said to tell you to be sure to invite the insurance investigator you brought with you to the party."

Nik looked at Finn, surprised and delighted. "Does he mean me?"

"Looks that way," he told her flatly. "We currently don't have any other insurance investigators hanging around."

Nik's eyes crinkled as she looked back toward Sean. She called out, "I'd love to come."

Sean gave her a thumbs-up.

"I'm sure he never doubted it for a minute," Finn told her.

Something in Finn's voice caught her attention. "Would it bother you if I went?" she asked him.

"Could that stop you?" he countered, although he was certain he knew the answer to that.

Or thought he did, because the one Nik gave in response to his question didn't jibe with the one he had assumed she would say.

"Actually, yes," she told him.

Finn abruptly stopped as they headed toward the medical examiner's vehicle. He turned so that his words were more private.

"How's that again?"

"I said yes, it would stop me," she answered in all seriousness. "If you didn't want me to attend the party, I wouldn't go."

Like he believed her. Finn took a guess at the altruistic reason she would give. "You're going to tell me that you don't want anything to damage this 'wonderful working relationship' we've developed, right?"

That was the general thought, but those were *not* the words she was planning to use, Nik thought. She put it into plainer language.

"Well, very honestly, you're not exactly Mr. Sunshine right now and I'm afraid that if I did anything to tick you off any further, you'd ban me from the case and then I won't be able to keep my promise to Kim about finding her daughter. Or at least," she continued in the spirit of honesty, "it would be a great deal more difficult if I had to try to work this without your resources."

He looked at her for a long moment and she found she couldn't make an educated guess as to what was going on in his mind.

And then he told her.

"I'm impressed. You've really thought this all out, haven't you?"

She couldn't tell if he was mocking her, or if he was being

serious. All she could do was level with him. "Whether you believe it or not, loyalty's very important to me. I gave my word to Kim that I was going to find Marilyn and I intend to move heaven and earth to do just that." The smile on her lips was tinged with sadness. That sadness bothered him, and that, in turn, surprised him. "If that means passing up on an invitation to one of Andrew Cavanaugh's famous get-togethers, then I guess I'll just have to pass it up."

Either she was serious, or she was one hell of an actress. He decided to go with the former. "Well, good news. If the chief wants you there, I'm not going to be the one to stand in your way. My having to spend the entire time explaining to the chief, his wife and heaven only knows who else why I was the one responsible for you not taking him up on the invitation is not something I would relish—so you get to come," he told her.

Nik held her breath until he finally finished. And then she allowed herself to react.

Finn had to honestly admit that he wasn't prepared for the amount of wattage that suddenly seemed to burst out all over the woman's already more-than-attractive face as she smiled.

"Thank you!" she cried.

He wasn't expecting that, either. Or the quick embrace that went with the words.

Releasing him, Nik asked, "What time do these things usually begin?"

"Anytime after dawn," he said. "And before you ask, they last for as long as anyone wants to remain at the old homestead. People have been known, on occasion, to stay until the following morning. The parties are without any bounds—not unlike this investigation," he said with a sigh, bringing the discussion full circle.

Right now Nik was feeling much too happy about the

invitation to be brought down by his last statement. She had heard a great deal about the people who comprised the inner framework of the Aurora Police Department. This would be an opportunity to watch them when they *weren't* working a case, which to her was as important as gaining access to them when they were working one.

Seeing the medical examiner, Finn strode over, wanting to catch the man before he loaded the victim into his van.

"Hey, Doc, do you have an approximate time of death for the victim?" he asked Grady.

"Best guess now is sometime around two this morning," he told Finn. "I can be more precise once I get her on my table."

But Finn was mulling over the medical examiner's first assessment. "Just like the last one," he mused. "Hey, Doc," he said, stopping him again just as the man and his assistant were about to load the gurney into the back of the vehicle. "Can you do me a favor?"

"That depends," the ME said. "What's the favor?" he asked.

"Can you do a tox screen on the victim?"

"I always do one," the ME answered. "It's standard procedure."

"I know," Finn said, not wanting to get into a discussion. "I mean a full one."

The medical examiner frowned slightly, thinking over the request. "Okay, but that's expensive. You looking for anything in particular?"

"How about evidence of a date-rape drug?" Nik asked, speaking up.

"All right, but from what I could tell, the victim wasn't raped," the ME said. "So looking for a date-rape drug would be a waste of time."

She thought otherwise. "Not if the killer used the drug to ensure that the victim wouldn't fight back when he went to kill her." Nik glanced over at Finn to see if he agreed.

The look on Finn's face was inconclusive, but the medical examiner sounded as if what she had just proposed made sense to him.

"Okay, you've got it," he said. "Looks like your new assistant scored a few points," he said to Finn. "I'd keep an eye on her if I were you." And then he chuckled. "But then, you're probably doing that already," he said, eyeing Finn.

Finn shut down any further speculation when he asked the medical examiner, "How long before you have the results of the report?"

"It'll be ready when it's ready," the ME answered, sounding somewhat annoyed. "This isn't some TV show where I can get the answers to you magically by the time the first bunch of commercials roll across your screen. Cavanaugh or not, this is still real life, you know. And there are tests that are waiting to be done ahead of yours." The man looked at Finn sharply. "Remember that," he said as he climbed into the van and slammed the door shut.

"I guess someone forgot to give him his morning coffee," Nik told Finn.

Finn shook his head. "I guess so."

Chapter 12

"Well, the medical examiner certainly doesn't sound like he's in any sort of a hurry to get us any answers," Nik commented as she and Finn rode the elevator from the morgue back up to the first floor. "Most likely, the reverse is probably true. He's going to deliberately drag his feet, isn't he?" she asked.

She saw a glimmer of a smile curving Finn's mouth. She was getting to him, Nik thought, feeling a little shiver of triumph despite the situation.

"I think it's a safe bet that he's going to take his time with this," Finn answered. "In his defense, I hear he's swamped."

From what she'd heard, that wasn't exactly anything new. "Aren't they all?" she countered.

Finn inclined his head. "You have a point," he agreed.

She was surprised that he was taking this so calmly. When she'd met him, he'd seemed as if he was eager to put this whole case to bed…fast. "Isn't there someone you could turn to, you know, someone who could lean on the ME to at least run the tox screen if not do the actual autopsy?" she asked Finn.

"That's not the kind of thing we do," he told her.

By "we" she knew he was referring to being part of the Cavanaugh family. They had a higher standard than most. Nik had to admit that she was surprised by his attitude. If anyone would have asked her, she would have said that Finn was the kind of detective who pulled rank whenever he needed to in order to solve a case, not refrain from that sort of behavior.

That Finn didn't pull rank actually raised his stock in her eyes—but since she was trying to find answers for her friend, not to mention find that friend's daughter and bring the girl home, Finn's attitude also frustrated her.

"Do you know what time that last restaurant opens today?" she asked suddenly as they reached the first floor.

He thought for a moment. "The sign on the door said that the doors opened at eleven, so I'm going to take a wild guess here and say…eleven," he answered.

Now *that* sounded more like Finn, she thought. Sarcastic and flippant. She could deal with that since she knew what to expect.

"So we've got some time to kill before we can talk to anyone inside the place," she concluded, thinking out loud. She turned toward him as ideas began forming in her head. "Why don't we talk to various people around that vicinity, see if any of them have surveillance cameras facing the restaurant, or the restaurant's alley. Maybe we'll get lucky and one of them caught our dead woman with a companion."

"You mean with the guy who murdered her?" Finn asked bluntly.

She nodded. "It's worth a try. For that matter, we could also go do the same thing around the first restaurant, see if anyone stands out there." She could feel Finn's resistance and she couldn't tell if he was resisting because he didn't think it was a good idea—or because it was *her* idea. "Besides," she added in a lighter tone, "what else do you have to do?"

Finn gave her a dark, quizzical look. "You're kidding, right?"

"I've been known to do that," Nik admitted. "But not this time. We scan all the available footage to see if anyone stands out." Maybe she wasn't explaining herself correctly. "You know, if the same face pops up in both places."

But Finn shook his head. "We can't arrest anyone because of a coincidence," he pointed out.

"No," she agreed. "But we can use that as a basis to allow us to ask that person more in-depth questions that might lead us somewhere."

He shrugged. He supposed she had a point. And, she was right. As far as this case went, they were at a standstill for the time being. "All right," he agreed, "let's go."

She looked at him, stunned. That was way easier than she thought it was going to be. "I convinced you?" she asked incredulously.

"Let's just say you had a point when you said we've got nothing else to do right now," Finn conceded.

"But—"

"Kowalski, take the win and quit while you're ahead," he told her.

Grinning, she did as he said.

* * *

The people who ran the shops that littered the immediate area around the restaurant were of little help. The surveillance cameras they had mounted either didn't work, or the footage was shot from a vantage point that didn't give Finn and Nik a view of the people who came and went from the site where the second body had been found.

The restaurant, when it opened, wasn't really any better.

Max Baldwin, the assistant manager who opened the restaurant's doors and let them in, looked rather doubtful when they explained what they were looking for.

"We've got a camera out front and one facing the back alley, but we don't have one inside the actual restaurant. Our customers don't like to have their privacy invaded," Baldwin explained.

"As a private citizen, I can sympathize," Finn agreed. "But as a cop, this definitely interferes with being able to solve a crime," he said.

Nik held up her phone for the man to view. She slowly swiped through three of the photographs. "Can you tell us if you've seen any of these women in here?"

"You mean last night?" the assistant manager asked.

"Anytime," Nik told him. "Say, did they come in here anytime in the last few weeks?"

Finn looked at her, puzzled. "What are you doing, Kowalski?"

"Trying to establish whether or not these women knew each other, or even talked to one another in passing." She paused, trying to be clearer. "I guess I'm trying to find some kind of connection between them."

Finn looked at the assistant manager. "Well?" he asked, waiting for Baldwin to respond.

The assistant manager shook his head. "I didn't see them together—or apart," he admitted. "But Henri has the evening shift and he closes up. Maybe *he* saw them," Baldwin said, stepping back from Nik's phone.

"All right, where can we reach Henri?" Finn asked the man.

The assistant manager didn't hesitate in his answer. "Henri's off today."

"Of course he is," Finn said, struggling to hold on to his patience. "Where does he live?" he asked. Now that they had decided to go down this road, he was determined to track down this Henri and talk to the man.

"I've got an address for him," Baldwin said. "But he won't be there," he added, preventing Finn from asking the next logical question—what that address was.

"And why is that?" Finn asked, already fairly certain that he wasn't going to like the answer he was going to get.

The assistant manager looked intimidated. He answered the question in a less-than-confident voice. "Because he said he was going to go hang gliding in the desert with his friends."

Nik couldn't tell if the assistant manager was on the level, or if the man was covering for one of his own. Anything was possible.

"Now all we have to do," she said to Finn as they left the restaurant, "is pray he doesn't break his neck before we get a chance to ask this 'flying squirrel' a few questions."

Finn allowed himself a lopsided grin, which he aimed in her direction.

"Ah, always the optimist," he said with a touch of sarcasm.

"I like to think so," she replied. "There is something else we could do."

He was open to any suggestions that could be doable. "Go ahead."

"We could canvass the area around the first crime scene, see if there is anyone that pops up on *those* surveillance camera videos that might vaguely resemble Marilyn."

She was being more specific than she had been. He considered her suggestion with interest. "So are you thinking that your friend's daughter is a victim, or a perpetrator?"

"Honestly, I don't know," she responded. "I'd like to think she's a victim, but in reality, I really can't say for sure. Other than those partial fingerprints that were found on the back of the rearview mirror and the note, there's nothing to suggest that she is part of all this. For Kim's sake, I'm trying really hard to keep an open mind," she confessed. "Right now, I would just like to collect any evidence that is available to help make up my—our," she corrected, glancing at Finn, "minds."

"So let's go," he told her, unlocking his vehicle and getting in.

Canvassing the first crime scene led nowhere. The available surveillance videos they gathered were, at best, unclear. As for the people they spoke to who worked within the restaurants, they had conflicting opinions. One waiter was positive that he saw the first victim come in with someone, but the hostess who greeted patrons as they came in and brought them to their tables said that the victim had come in alone.

A busboy swore that the woman was not only *not*

alone, but when she left, she'd also been seen with a man *and* a woman.

"In other words, they had a threesome," Nik concluded after the busboy left.

Finn laughed dryly under his breath. "Put your money down and take your pick," he commented.

As they exited the restaurant, he noticed the thoughtful look on Nik's face. "What are you thinking?" he asked her.

"I'm thinking that the busboy might have gotten it right," she ventured. "Let's face it, he's low man on the totem pole and he doesn't have much to focus on." She could see that Finn didn't quite understand what she was getting at. "He doesn't have the responsibility of properly seating patrons and he doesn't have to make sure that the food he's bringing is still hot when it reaches the table because he doesn't bring them their food. He's also not trying to do anything that would get him any kind of a big tip. All a busboy has to focus on is cleaning up. That gives him time to study the patrons and form a quick opinion of them."

"Or," Finn said, going a different route, "he can just let his mind drift and make things up to entertain himself as he clears the table."

Nik sighed. Finn did have a point. She really couldn't argue with what he was saying.

"You could be right," she replied. She caught her lower lip between her teeth, chewing on it. "So where does that put us?"

"The way I see it, I'd say that we're stuck in first gear," Finn told her as they reached his car.

At that moment, his cell phone dinged, announcing an incoming text message. When he looked at the screen, the corners of his mouth curved downward in what amounted to a half frown.

"What?" Nik asked, sensing that what had just come in had to be about the case.

He looked at his message again. "Valri just identified our victim."

That was good, wasn't it? she thought. So why was he frowning?

"We have a name?" she asked.

He nodded, then said grimly, "And a family to notify." He put away his cell phone. "Theresa Allen was twenty-two and lived with her parents, Joannie and Bill."

Something didn't sit right for her. "Didn't they notice she was missing?"

He shrugged. If this had happened in his family, even if the victim *hadn't* lived at home, there would be members combing the streets, searching for her. But not all families were like his.

Out loud he said, "Apparently this wasn't unusual behavior for Theresa. She stayed out often, sometimes crashing with friends instead of coming home."

She knew that old dodge, Nik thought. "Or so she told her parents."

Finn conceded that point. "Undoubtedly to avoid being lectured to," he mused.

"Or to spare their feelings," Nik said, speculating. "Or maybe she actually did crash with friends," she said. "We don't know."

Finn had a skeptical look on his face as he got into his vehicle and then waited for Nik to buckle up.

"Nobody dresses the way the victim did just for friends," he pointed out.

"Oh, I don't know. Women can be pretty competitive.

A 'night out with the girls' might really mean getting all dressed up just to bolster her own ego."

"I still have my doubts," Finn told her as he turned the vehicle in the direction of the address that Valri had texted him.

"This is the part I really hate," Finn said less than half an hour later as he and Nik pulled up in front of a quaint-looking two-story house. "Telling people someone they cared about won't be coming home again." He took a breath. "Ever."

She wouldn't have thought that he would have had to deal with that sort of thing. "I thought you said you worked in Robbery."

"I do, but I deal with that sort of thing when things go sideways during a robbery, or a home invasion," he told her grimly as he got out of his car.

Nik quickly got out on her side, matching his pace in an effort to catch up to him.

Surprised, Finn glanced at her over his shoulder. "You don't have to come in with me," he said, his voice distant.

"I'm coming in for support," Nik explained.

That didn't make any sense to him. He stopped short of the front door.

"You don't know these people—do you?" he suddenly asked. It occurred to him that he hadn't found that out, he'd just taken it for granted that she didn't.

"It's you I'm supporting," she clarified. His eyes widened as he stared at her. Nik suppressed a sigh. The man needed a road map drawn for him. "You said you hated this. I thought having someone with you might make it a little less unbearable."

She was serious, he thought. The woman kept surprising him. Ordinarily he would have said something flippant in response, or at the very least something to show his disinterest, such as "suit yourself."

But this display of selflessness on her part earned something more than that in his view. He wasn't comfortable with that, but he couldn't very well ignore it, either. So he murmured, "Thanks," and left the word just hanging there between them as he walked up to the front door.

He had to ring the doorbell twice before anyone came to answer it.

When the front door finally opened, a white-haired woman of average height who was wearing what looked like a full-length colorful caftan stood in the doorway. The wide smile on her round, affable face drooped a little as she looked at the pair on her doorstep.

"May I help you?" she asked in a slightly uneasy voice.

"Mrs. Allen?" Finn asked her.

Powder blue eyes turned toward him. "Yes?"

There was no point in delivering the news twice. "Um, is your husband around?" Nik asked.

"He's in the backyard, pruning one of our trees." She nodded toward the rear of the house. "It's a hobby," she confided. "I told him to hire someone, but oh, no, he has to do it himself. Says he needs to save money because Theresa—that's our daughter—spends it like it's going out of style." She smiled tolerantly. "I told him it was just typical for someone her age."

She was rattling on, Finn thought. The woman was nervous, as if she sensed what was coming. "Mrs. Allen," Finn said, interrupting her, "maybe you should ask him to come join you."

The last of the woman's smile vanished. Her expressive eyes moved from Finn to Nik and then back again. "Why?" she asked in a hushed, frightened tone. "What's this about?"

Instinctively Nik moved in closer to her. "We have some bad news, Mrs. Allen."

"What kind of bad news?" she asked, spacing each word apart as if she was trying to find the courage to say the next one.

"It's about your daughter, Theresa," Finn began.

He got no further. Tears instantly sprang to the woman's eyes and she shook her head violently. "No," she cried. "No!"

"Mrs. Allen—" Finn moved toward her, attempting to place a hand on her shoulder, but the woman pulled away. "No!" she yelled, covering her ears with her hands. "I'm not listening!"

A man raced toward her from the rear of the house. "Joannie, what's wrong?" He looked accusingly at the duo on his front step. "What did you say to her?"

"I'm sorry to have to be the one to tell you this, sir, but we're here to notify you and your wife that your daughter, Theresa, was found in an alley this morning." He could see the horror building in the man's face. "She was stabbed to death."

Instantly, the big, barrel-chested man looked as if the very life had been drained out of him, even as he put one bracing arm around his wife to keep her from collapsing.

Chapter 13

"You're right, that had to be one of the worst experiences I've ever had," Nik told Finn as they left the Allen house. It was close to an hour later and she felt emotionally wrung out and almost totally drained. "I felt so awful, so helpless," she confessed. It was even worse than what she had felt when she had gone to talk to Marilyn's mother. At least with Marilyn, there was still hope that things might turn out for the better. "I just didn't know what to say to those poor people."

"There's nothing *to* say," Finn told her. He glanced over his shoulder back toward the house, although he honestly tried not to envision the couple he had left there. "The only thing you can do at this point is offer them closure by catching the person or persons responsible for killing their daughter."

Nik looked at him as they reached the car. Something suddenly occurred to her. "So you are letting me hang around?"

He raised an eyebrow, scrutinizing her. Like he had a choice, he thought—outside of threatening to arrest her in order to make her leave. "If I told you to back off, would you?"

She paused for a moment, then admitted what he already knew. "Not really."

"Then I won't waste my breath," Finn said. "Besides, it seems that for some reason, Uncle Andrew and Uncle Sean are rather impressed with you, so I really *can't* get rid of you."

About to get into his vehicle, Nik stopped short. "All right," she said, "now I know you're just pulling my leg."

His mouth curved ever so slightly. "I wouldn't dream of pulling anything on you."

She stared at him, genuinely surprised. That was a joke, wasn't it? "Then they really are impressed with me?" she asked Finn. "Why?" she asked. "What did I do?"

He sighed. At times he asked himself that same question. But there was no denying that the two men—not to mention several others on the task force—were taken with this open, friendly insurance investigator. "I'll let them explain it at the party."

"Party?" she repeated as she got into the car.

"The one you're coming to next Saturday," he reminded her, closing the driver's side door. He started up his car.

Nik had gotten so caught up in investigating the second murder that she had forgotten all about the invitation. She noticed that Nik referred to it as the one she *was* coming to. Apparently, her attendance was not up for debate.

Despite the weight of the situation she had just been through, Nik smiled. "I forgot," she confessed.

"Well, now you've been reminded," he said. "I've got to get back to the squad room," he told her, laying out his immediate agenda once he got back to the police station. "There are reports that are waiting to be written up and if I don't get to them, left on their own they have this nasty habit of just multiplying. I can drop you off at your place," he volunteered.

She had a different idea. "I can come with you to the station. Maybe I can help you remember some details that might have slipped your mind. In any event, I can help you tackle the reports."

Paperwork and writing up reports in general were the most tedious parts of his job. Finn usually avoided having to face them until he ran out of options. This time around, though, because the case involved Seamus, he felt that tackling the chore sooner than later was a better way to go.

"Not that I don't appreciate the offer," he told her, as he continued driving to the police station, "but don't you have a job to go to?"

The insurance investigator had been with him for a couple days now and he would have thought that she'd be getting back to her day job. Apparently, Finn surmised, he'd thought wrong.

"I took a sabbatical," Nik explained. "I didn't feel I could do what I had to if I had to divide myself between my job and looking for Marilyn—so I made a choice. Besides, I have a great deal of vacation time accrued."

"Very conscientious of you," he quipped.

Her eyes met his. "I don't like to do things halfway," she told him simply.

Finn nodded. Dark brown hair fell into his eyes and he pushed it back. "Good to know," he murmured.

At least, he thought, forewarned was forearmed.

Leaving his vehicle in his designated spot, Finn rode up to his floor and brought Nik into the robbery squad room. Looking around, he found her a desk.

"Take that one," he said, gesturing toward it.

The desktop was neat, but was far from empty. Nik looked at it uncertainly.

"Won't whoever sits here want their desk back?" she asked. She didn't want to settle in only to be told that she had to move again before the day was out.

"Monroe might want it back," Finn answered, "but right now, he's home, recovering from a broken leg. He probably won't be back for a few weeks at least." A bemused expression crossed his face. "He likes to make the most of situations like this."

"What happened to him?" Nik asked.

He heard the sympathy in her voice and wondered how she could possibly feel sympathy for someone she'd never met and didn't know. "He was trying to chase down a robber driving away from the scene of the crime when the guy suddenly turned his car around and drove straight at him."

She could visualize that in her mind's eye and shivered. "Oh, wow! Did the robber hit him?" she asked.

"Almost. Monroe jumped out of the way and avoided getting hit by the car, but he didn't avoid tripping over a pile of rubbish that was right there. He came down hard and wound up breaking his thighbone."

Nik winced. Her sense of empathy made her feel the shock of the blow. "Ouch!"

Finn laughed dryly. "That wasn't exactly the word that Monroe used, but I guess the sentiment was similar." He realized that she'd managed to pull him into a vortex. Given half a chance, he had a feeling that Nik would have him giving her background stories on all the people who worked in the squad room. "Okay," he declared, "let's get you settled in so you can provide that backup you promised."

"Absolutely," she responded.

* * *

Nik's presence in the squad room did not go unnoticed right from the start. Whenever she looked up, she found herself on the receiving end of interested looks as well as an occasional nod and/or smile. She had a natural tendency to engage in conversations and found that she had to block that tendency in order to help Finn fill out the reports she'd told him that she'd help with. But it wasn't easy. Especially since there seemed to be an endless parade of people who were either milling around the area or coming into it from another floor.

She immersed herself in working on the reports, getting involved in writing them up to the total exclusion of everything else.

She didn't even hear Finn at first when he tried to talk to her.

When his voice finally penetrated her brain, she blinked, looking up. "Did you say something?" she asked him.

Finn raised his voice, deliberately speaking more forcefully. "I said you don't have to finish them all in one day."

"I don't like leaving something to be finished at a later time," she told him. When he looked at her quizzically, she elaborated. "You never know what might crop up down the line, interrupting your work. It's better to get it all done while it's still fresh in your mind."

Finn regarded her thoughtfully. "Maybe you *are* a long-lost Cavanaugh after all."

That, she thought, might raise a whole different set of problems. "Lord, I hope not," she said, more to herself than to him.

Even so, it almost felt as if her voice rippled right

through him, creating a mini-tidal wave. "Me, neither," he agreed quietly.

Neither one of them said anything further on the subject, but it was obvious to each of them that, at least when it came to this, they were on the same page.

The next victim wasn't found until almost two days later. Another attractive young woman in her twenties, dressed for a fun night out that obviously ended all too abruptly. Technically, Finn thought, Homicide should have taken the lead on the case. But because of its similarity to the other two cases, Brian Cavanaugh, the chief of detectives, made an exception and assigned Finn and his team members...including Nik.

He called Finn into his office to tell him about this newest twist. "Because you and your people have been working on this, I'd say that you're the most familiar with the details here. I take it that that insurance investigator is still helping out."

Finn answered Brian's questions without allowing himself to make any comments on the situation. "Yes, sir. We have reason to believe that the young woman Ms. Kowalski was initially looking for—Marilyn Palmer— is somehow involved in all this, either as one of the victims, or possibly as something more."

Brian looked interested. Very little happened in his precinct that he didn't know about and this definitely wasn't a exception. "And by something more?" he asked, waiting for Finn to fill in the blanks more succinctly.

"One theory is that she might be working with the killer." He paused, then added, "It wouldn't be the first time a woman tried to cull the favor of a killer by helping him."

Brian nodded. "You have a point," he agreed. "Keep

me posted, Finn. This one's personal—for all of us," he added.

Finn was keenly aware of that. "Yes, sir, I know. It is for me, too," he said as he walked out of the man's office.

While Finn talked to the chief of detectives about this newest development in the case, Nik was left to cool her heels in the squad room until he returned. By now, even though she was focused on the reports, she still managed to have conversations with the various members of Finn's team as well as some of the other members in the Robbery squad room.

But even so, she wasn't so distracted that she didn't instantly know when Finn came back into the room. She raised herself in her seat the moment he crossed the doorway.

"Well?" she asked. The question referred to the reason that Finn had been called into Brian's office in the first place.

"Looks like our serial killer struck again," Finn told her. "Or rather, he struck before."

Grabbing her shoulder bag, Nik crossed the room and was at his side in a matter of seconds. Her brow furrowed. Had she missed something?

"Mind saying that again?"

Finn obliged. "He struck before," he repeated.

Nik shook her head as she looked up at the detective walking beside her. That they were going somewhere was obvious, but she didn't ask about that. She wanted him to clarify his statement.

"That still doesn't make any sense," she confessed.

"Our killer killed this one before he killed what we thought were victims one and two. According to the chief of detectives, the medical examiner said that this one was killed around the same time frame that Seamus was mugged."

"Are you saying that the person who mugged Seamus didn't have anything to do with the other killings?" she asked, trying to get the information straight.

"No, that's not what I'm saying. He could have killed this woman just before he killed the other two. We just missed this body somehow." It was obvious that he didn't like things that didn't seem to make sense to him. The one thing that seemed certain was that they were dealing with someone whose bloodlust was growing stronger.

"Does that mean he was better at hiding the body previously?" she asked, struggling to put the pieces into some sort of order.

"I'm not sure what that means," he confessed.

She reexamined what Finn *had* said. He thought this was the same killer. That had to mean that there were similarities between the three victims.

"Was she stabbed?" Nik asked as she walked quickly beside the detective.

He nodded. "She was stabbed, she was attractive and she was dressed to kill…so to speak," Finn said, adding the last phrase when he realized the way his words sounded.

Nik went to the next important detail. "What does her tox screen say?"

Finn shook his head as he pressed for the elevator. The car arrived almost immediately, its doors yawning open. "It's too soon to tell. And this didn't happen in a restaurant, either," he told her as they went down to the ground floor. "The body was found behind a nightclub."

"Surveillance cameras?" she asked hopefully.

"There's some video available," he answered, but before she could ask, he told her, "But from what I hear, the quality's rather poor and the video looks pretty grainy."

"I think they're probably still worth a look," Nik told him as they got out of the elevator.

Finn headed for the rear doors. "Are you volunteering for the job?"

Sitting still and going through numerous videos wasn't something she relished, but it needed to be done, she thought. "If it helps bring this case to a close, then absolutely."

"You realize that you just volunteered to go cross-eyed, Kowalski," he told her. "I'm serious when I said the videos all looked rather poor."

She was undaunted. Nik was focused on the bigger picture: finding a killer. He had to be in there somewhere, she told herself. "Then it's a good thing I have twenty-twenty vision," she answered.

Finn laughed.

"What?" she asked. She hadn't said anything particularly funny in her opinion.

"Valri's going to love you," he told Nik. "This is usually her job."

"Then I'm glad I could make her happy," she replied.

Nik didn't see this as a chore to slog through; she saw it as an opportunity to bring this case one step closer to being resolved.

And hopefully, she thought, one step closer to finding Marilyn.

"Here," Finn said several hours later as he stopped by the computer lab. He placed a bottle of water on the desk in front of Nik and a bottle of extra-strength headache tablets directly beside it. "I thought you might need these."

Nik blinked her eyes twice as she looked up and then focused on what Finn had brought her. Her sigh resounded with appreciation.

"My hero," she said in what sounded like sincerity to him. She opened the container, then shook out three pills into her palm and was about to pop them into her mouth.

"Hold it," Finn said. "I don't think you're supposed to eat them like candy."

She had a different opinion. "It's either that, or ask you to hit me over the head with a hammer and put me out of my misery."

He looked at her sympathetically. "That bad?"

"I'll let you know how bad it is when I can focus on your face," she told him.

"I'm making an executive decision," he told her, turning her chair away from the computer screen. "I think you've had enough for the day."

"But I haven't found anyone," she protested. "Not even that woman you showed me in the photograph, the one who is our new first victim…maybe," she said, hesitating. At this point, she wasn't convinced that there weren't other, older victims who might qualify for the first space in this tragic lineup.

Nik succeeded in getting his attention. "What do you mean 'maybe'?" Finn asked.

"Well," she began, "we have reason to believe that this victim was killed before the other two women who were found—"

When she paused, he persisted, "Yes?"

He wasn't going to like this, she thought. But she couldn't believe he hadn't thought of this, too. "Who's to say that there weren't others before her? Others who *weren't* found earlier and connected to this killer, but now that we know what we're looking for—"

"We can connect them," Finn concluded.

"You know," Valri said, overhearing the last exchange when she walked in to check up on Nik's progress, "for a nonprofessional, you're pretty good, Nik."

Nik smiled, albeit weakly, at the woman. "I'll thank you as soon as the drums in my head stop pounding," she told the head of the computer crime lab.

"I'll look at it as an IOU," Valri said with a laugh. "Is there anything I can do to help?" She looked from Nik to Finn, waiting for an answer.

"I thought you said you were swamped." Finn reminded his cousin about the excuse she had given him before he had taken Nik up on her offer to help.

"I was—and still am," Valri insisted, then nodded toward Nik. "But she looks like she's in pain and I know what that feels like, so I thought I'd offer to lend a hand."

"Well, as it turns out," Finn told his cousin, "Kowalski here is calling it a day."

But Nik wasn't quite ready to walk away yet. "It's early," she protested, then stopped, uncertain. "Isn't it?"

"Not really," Finn answered. "Valri just likes to stay late—"

"I don't *like* to," Valri interrupted. "It just somehow happens."

"That's called denial, little cousin," Finn told her with a grin. "But whatever it is, I'm taking Kowalski here away from the computer screen before she goes totally blind on me. C'mon," he said to Nik. "I'll buy you a drink at Malone's. You've definitely earned it."

"But I didn't find anything," she protested again.

"No, but you tried," he reminded her. "And by not finding anything, you did rule a few things out," he told her.

She looked at the detective. "That'll make more sense to me when the headache finally goes away, right?"

Finn wasn't about to lie to her. "Maybe" was all he would commit to.

Nik took a deep breath, trying to focus her thoughts. She made her way toward the elevator. "Just let me go and get my car."

This was worse than he thought. "You left your car at your apartment, remember?"

It took her a moment to put the pieces together. "Oh, right." She turned toward him. "Then I guess you're driving."

He laughed despite himself. "I guess so," Finn agreed.

Chapter 14

Devin Wilson's face broke into a wide, welcoming smile as Nik and Finn came into Malone's and walked up to the bar.

"Nice to see you back again," the bartender said. His words were directed toward Nik since Finn was considered to be a semiregular in the establishment. "What can I get you?"

"I'd like a screwdriver, please," Nik requested.

"A screwdriver, huh?" Amused, the bartender exchanged looks with Finn. "I haven't heard that one in a while. I guess there's nothing like the classics," he told Nik as he reached for a bottle of vodka.

"Go heavy on the orange juice," Nik instructed.

The retired police officer inclined his head. "Yes, ma'am. And you?" he asked, turning toward Finn. "The usual?"

Finn nodded. "Just a beer. Whatever you have on tap."

"In other words, the usual," Devin repeated. "Why don't you two find yourselves a table and I'll bring your drinks over to it."

Finn looked skeptically at the bartender's instructions. "We weren't planning on staying here too long."

"The length of time doesn't matter. It's a known fact that drinks go down better at a table," he told them with a wink. "So does the conversation. Go on," he urged. "The place isn't so big that I won't be able to find you," he promised.

"What was that all about?" Finn said as they walked away from the bar. "That one okay with you?" he asked Nik, pointing to a table for two that was off to the side.

"That one's fine," she told him. "And I think Devin thinks we want to be alone."

He stared at her as she led the way to the table he'd pointed out. "Why would he think that?" Finn asked, puzzled.

She would have thought it would be obvious to the detective. "Because the last time we were here together, you gave the impression that you were restraining yourself from trying to strangle me."

He remembered. Finn's mouth curved. "And now?" he asked.

"And now you're buying me a drink," she pointed out. "To his bartender mind, things seemed to have definitely improved. So he's thinking maybe we want some privacy," she told him, looking around, "if that sort of thing can be found here."

Finn laughed at the idea. "It's amazing what finding three bodies can do."

Devin was almost right behind them. As soon as they sat down, he was putting their drinks in front of them. "A screwdriver for the lady, domestic beer for Cavanaugh," he said with a flourish, tucking his tray under his arm. "You two need anything else? Hamburgers? More privacy?" He was about to indicate the small back room, where occasional private parties were held.

"A bartender who doesn't ask questions comes to mind," Finn answered.

Devin looked thoughtful for a minute, then shook his head. "Not sure if they make that model. I'll ask around, though," he said with a semiserious expression.

"Are you hungry?" Finn suddenly asked her. To the best of his recollection, she hadn't had anything to eat since before she had started reviewing the surveillance footage earlier today.

"My headache has completely wiped out my appetite," she told him. "I'll just finish this drink that you sprang for, then call a cab to take me home."

Overhearing, Devin turned around to look at Nik. "I wouldn't trust him to drive me home, either," he agreed, giving her a pronounced wink.

Finn frowned at the older man. "Don't you have a bar to tend to?"

"Maybe you didn't notice, but it's slow tonight," Devin pointed out.

"Yeah, I noticed," Finn answered. "That could have something to do with the bartender," he said, giving Devin a long, penetrating look.

"Drink up, darlin'," Devin said, turning toward Nik. "When you're done, I'll call you that cab myself."

Taking a sip of her drink, she watched the bartender make his way back to the bar, then take a customer's card to ring up a sale.

Nik blinked. It hit her like a ton of bricks. Why hadn't she thought of that before?

"Credit card!" she cried suddenly, looking up at Finn.

He had no idea where that had come from or what she was trying to say. Taking a guess, he told her, "No, I paid for our drinks with cash."

Nik shook her head. He didn't understand, she thought, and who could blame him? She hadn't exactly made herself clear. She'd started talking when she was right in the middle of her thought.

"No," she said, doing her best to talk slower. "I mean we should go back to those two restaurants and that night-club to ask if we could see their receipts from each night that a victim was found behind their premises." She was growing excited now. This could have very real possibilities. "Don't you see? That might give us a handle on who was there at the time. And if we find a credit card that was used in all three places, then we've got ourselves someone to actually question!"

Finn frowned. She was overlooking one small problem, he thought, thinking of the way he had paid. "Unless the killer paid for his tab with cash."

Nik sighed. Finn did make things difficult. "Please don't rain on my parade yet. Let me bask in the sunshine of my idea for at least a couple of minutes."

"Hey, it might work," he allowed. "And it's a pretty good idea. Our killer might have slipped up."

"Not bad for someone using only half their brain," she said.

"Half?" he asked.

"Yes. The other half is out of commission because there are these fierce little elves pounding on it with their little pointy hammers," she reminded him.

Finn grinned. She did have a unique way of saying things, he thought. "At least they're not using sledge-hammers."

"They did, but that was before you came with the aspirin," she told him.

He looked at the glass she was holding in her hands. "You know, if it hurts that much, maybe you shouldn't drink," he advised.

She feigned surprise. "And give up the chance of having you buy me a drink? Not on your life." She took another sip, finishing the drink that was, after all, mostly orange juice. "Besides, the aspirin you gave me did take the punch out of it."

"Good." Finn drained his mug and put it down. "Okay, Kowalski, let's get you home," he said.

He hadn't had a lot to drink, but he had disposed of it quickly, she thought, hesitating. "Would I be offending you if I asked if you needed a minute to let your drink metabolize?"

His grin was lopsided. "More than you could possibly know. Devin waters his beer down," he told her, lowering his voice. "And even if he didn't, it would take more than a mug—or two—to affect me. You ready?"

Nik pushed back her chair and slowly rose to her feet. "I'm ready," she answered.

"Then let's go," he told her, leading the way out of Malone's.

The parking lot looked as if it was filling up when they walked outside. Finn crossed to his vehicle. There were no available spaces anymore.

"Well, this'll make Devin happy," Nik commented.

But Finn laughed, shaking his head. "No, it won't," he told her.

"Why? He was just complaining about it being a slow night," she reminded him, getting into the passenger side. She buckled up and waited for him to do the same.

"And now he'll complain about it being too busy for

him to catch his breath. I've known him for a long time. Devin isn't happy unless he's got something to complain about," Finn told her. "The man is a world-class complainer."

She tried to wrap her mind around what Finn was telling her. After a moment, she came to her own conclusion.

"So, ultimately," she said to Finn, "this'll make him happy because he can complain about it."

Finn laughed. Putting his key into the ignition, he turned it on. "You know, in a lopsided way, I think you're catching on, Kowalski."

"Could you call me Nik?" she asked him. Then, before he could make some sort of a comment or ask her why she was making things so personal, she told him, "Every time you say my last name, you make me wince."

He shrugged, looking back on the road. "Sure. So, for the duration—which shouldn't be all that long—you're 'Nik.'"

She'd gotten what she wanted, but now he'd raised another point and she wanted that clarified. "Why shouldn't the duration of our association be too long?" she asked.

"Because I've decided that maybe you *did* have a decent idea with the credit-card receipts. If there's even one repeater in the batch, it could be our man, or at the very least, he—or she—could lead us to our man," he said.

He caught her satisfied smile out of the corner of his eye.

Because the car ahead of him was going at a snail's pace, Finn switched lanes. After passing the driver, he switched back.

"Hopefully before another body turns up," Nik added solemnly.

"That goes without saying," Finn responded with feeling.

* * *

The drive back to Nik's garden apartment complex took only a little over twelve minutes. It surprised Finn how fast the trip went.

"We're here, Cinderella. Safe and sound," he announced as he drove the winding path leading into the complex.

He noticed that she sat up just a little straighter.

"You can just let me out here," she told him.

Finn glanced at her. Was she serious? Apparently, judging by her expression, she was.

"I'm not having you jump out of the car," he told her. "I'm going to park my car and then bring you to your door."

Why would he want to go through all that trouble? "This is Aurora, one of the safest cities of its size in the country," she reminded him. Something, she thought, he should already know.

He pulled up in an empty space that was marked Guest Parking.

"Tell that to the three women in the morgue," he told her grimly. "Besides, this is my Cavanaugh training, take it or leave it."

"Cavanaugh training?" she queried.

He nodded. "You drive a woman home, you have to bring her up to her door."

He was missing one crucial point. "But I'm not a date," she reminded him.

"Nobody said anything about 'dates,'" he said. "The operative words here are *woman* and *home*."

This wasn't a debate she was going to win. And the truth of it was, she kind of liked the idea of his walking her to her door. Maybe it was old-fashioned, but it was also rather chivalrous in her opinion.

"All right," she said, relenting. "I won't argue."

He laughed shortly just as he opened the door on his side. "And here I was, just about ready to give up on miracles."

Nik eyed him before she unbuckled her seat belt. "Don't make me regret not taking a cab," she told the detective.

"I'll try hard not to," he countered.

Getting out of the car, he rounded the hood and came to her side just as she began to get out. He held the door open.

"Okay, you've impressed me," she said, swinging her legs out. She wasn't oblivious to the fact that he didn't take his eyes off them, or to the fact that there was an appreciative look in those eyes. "You can go home now," she said, waving him away.

"We're not at the door yet," Finn dutifully reminded her.

"You're really serious about this, aren't you? You know that you don't have to do this. You can just sit in this space with the engine idling and watch me walk to my door." Her apartment was located across the courtyard, but it wasn't *that* far away and he could easily see it from where he was.

"Sorry," he said, shaking his head, "but that's not the deal." He locked his door. "Habit," he explained when she raised an eyebrow.

"We didn't make a deal," Nik told him.

"I know." Before she could ask what deal he was referring to then, he said, "It's a deal I made with my mother. She insisted that all her sons make sure the women they were with were brought to their doors. *Safely*," he said, emphasizing the last word.

A word he'd used caught her attention. "All?" she repeated. "Just how many sons did your poor mother have?" Any number larger than two sounded like total chaos in her opinion.

"Five, counting me," he told her.

"Five sons?" she said, marveling. She was right, that had to be absolute chaos.

"And a daughter," Finn added.

"That poor girl," Nik said, sympathy all but throbbing in her voice.

"Why poor?" he asked. "She had five brothers ready and willing to defend her honor," he said, only half kidding.

"I think you answered your own question. Your sister probably never had any dates as a teenager. If you're any indication, nobody could get through that solid wall of protective brotherhood around her."

"Oh, she could hold her own, trust me." He looked thoughtfully at her. "I think you and Skylar would get along great," he said.

"Well, at any rate tell her she has my full sympathy," Nik told him.

She took a deep breath. "Well, here it is," she said unnecessarily as she came to a stop before the door with 164 on it. "My door. Consider me brought to it. I'm sure you'll be happy to know that you've made your mother very proud."

She wasn't prepared for the rather solemn look on his face. "I'm afraid that's not possible."

"Your mother's a rather demanding woman?" Nik asked.

"Not anymore." Then, because he could see the question coming into her eyes, Finn said, "Mom's been gone now for five years."

Well, she'd certainly put both feet into her mouth, Nik thought, keenly embarrassed.

"I'm sorry," she apologized with sincerity. "I didn't mean to be so flippant. I didn't know." The words sounded rather empty to her.

"No reason you should," Finn replied.

His absolving her only made things worse in her opinion. She should have known, she upbraided herself. She had found out things about other members of his family. Why had she overlooked looking into his background, of all of the Cavanaughs?

It didn't make any sense to her—unless, she thought, she had done it deliberately out of some sense of self-preservation. That could be it. There was something about this particular Cavanaugh that seemed to just really get to her.

No, she argued, that wasn't it. This was just the headache and the exhaustion talking, nothing more. Nothing else made sense, right?

"Well, thanks for the drink," she said. "And for seeing me to my door, safe and sound," she added with a smile.

"Don't mention it," Finn told her. But he continued to remain where he was.

Was there something else? Something she had overlooked?

"You're still here," Nik told her, expecting that to rouse him and finally make him go. But he didn't move a muscle. "Why?"

He nodded at her door. "You haven't unlocked your door."

"You mean that's part of the process?" she asked him in disbelief.

"Sure. What did you think I meant when I said I needed to see you home?"

Talk about the old-fashioned type, this man actually belonged in a museum.

"Obviously I wasn't thinking of what you meant. Does this include you clearing each room in the apartment, or is my unlocking the front door enough?"

His mouth curved into the smallest semblance of a smile. "You're not the only one who doesn't like to do things in half measures," he said, reminding her of what she had told him earlier.

Nik sighed. "I suppose I had that coming," she commented.

His grin grew just a little wider. "Yes," he agreed. "That and so much more," he said. "But I'll settle for this for now."

"Very decent of you," she quipped.

When she turned from her unlocked door, holding her key tightly in her hand, Nik realized that she was standing much closer to Finn than she had thought.

Chapter 15

Time seemed to stand still. Nik could have sworn the electricity between them was all but crackling audibly.

And then she felt a wave of heat flash through her, making her very skin tingle.

For one long, heart-pounding moment, she thought Finn was going to kiss her.

Or maybe she was even going to kiss him. She was certainly tempted. All her thoughts were all jumbled up in her head.

Nik's breath caught in her throat as she waited to see if either of them would make the first move—or if their senses would make a sudden return, preventing them from making a mistake.

Because it would be a mistake, right? Nik silently argued. After all, she couldn't allow herself to get carried away like this. There was absolutely no future for her with Finn and she wasn't the type who gravitated toward relationships that were, by definition, just casual. That just wasn't her, she insisted.

But despite this mental debate she was conducting, Nik couldn't shake the overwhelming desire that was gripping her, making demands and causing the guard that she usually kept up to just splinter apart into a thousand little pieces.

But what would it hurt? the little voice in her head whispered. *One kiss, one small contact. Would it really be so bad?*

Would it—?

And then, just like that, the time for inner reflection, for wondering and wavering, had passed.

Because Finn was kissing her.

Nik felt his arms encircling her, felt his breath on her skin as he brought his face down to hers. Her heart slammed against her rib cage as his lips covered hers.

When it happened, it was hard to say who was more surprised, Finn or Nik.

Or which of them was more pleased.

She tasted of everything sweet, just exactly as he thought she would. He could feel his pulse racing as he tightened his arms tightened around Nik, bringing her slender, supple body closer to him. The scent of her hair filled his head, intoxicating him.

Nik felt her head swimming. And then she could feel Finn smile against her lips, his lips warming her.

Seducing her.

"Why are you smiling?" she asked hoarsely as she tried to drag air back into her lungs.

"Because that was exactly the way I imagined it would be," he confessed.

And then the reality of what he had just done hit him. Finn sobered, realizing that she might misunderstand what had just happened. "Sorry, that wasn't the reason I wanted to see you to your door." And then he decided that confession—in this case—was good for the soul. "But I would be lying if I said that it wasn't to have a few more minutes with you."

Reviewing their relatively short association, she looked at him skeptically. "I thought you couldn't wait to get rid of me."

"In the beginning," he conceded. "But I have to admit that you do have a way of getting to a guy." He was saying too much and making this way too personal. He dialed it back a little. "And I have to say that you are pulling your own weight."

"You sure do know how to turn a girl's head with sweet talk," she told him wryly.

Okay, maybe he was being a little too cautious. "You know what I mean."

And then she smiled, taking pity on him. The man would never be accused of having a silver tongue. But at least he was trying. And he *was* honest, which meant a great deal to her.

"Fortunately, I do," she told him. "See you tomorrow?" She assumed that she would, but she knew she couldn't appear to take that for granted, just in case that would cause him to change his mind.

Finn nodded in response. "Sure. Monroe's desk is still free and we're still looking for a lead, so I expect you to be in the squad room."

"Tomorrow, then," she replied, trying not to sound as pleased as she felt. Nik turned away and started to go inside her apartment.

She heard Finn's cell phone ringing just as he began to walk away. Something—instinct, a sixth sense maybe—

made her turn around again and listen to Finn's end of the conversation.

"When?" he asked the person on the other end of his call.

The second he said that to whoever had called him, she could feel goose bumps popping up all along her arms and upper torso.

This had to be about the case, she thought.

Another body? So soon?

"Yeah, I'll be there as soon as I can. It's not like I was going to go home and sleep or anything," he said with a touch of sarcasm. "'Bye."

Ending the call, Finn tucked away his cell. After a beat, he turned around to face Nik. He knew she'd been listening.

"It happened again?" she asked, fairly certain she knew the answer to that.

"It did, but they're not sure about the time of death yet. The victim has started decomposing," he told her. "That means she's been dead for a while."

Instantly her heart went out to the poor woman who would never see another sunrise. "Same MO as the others?" she asked.

"It sounded that way," Finn admitted, although Harley had been short on details. "I'll know more when I get there."

She didn't like the way he said that. "You're not going solo on me now, are you?" she asked.

"Actually," he told her, "I thought I'd let you get some rest…"

Nik frowned. Was the man serious? "Right, like I could sleep now," she scoffed. "Just give me a couple of minutes to put on a fresh shirt and change my shoes. These are killing me," she confided.

Finn looked down at her footwear. The woman had been wearing heels all day. "I was wondering how you managed to walk around in those shoes," he quipped.

"They don't usually bother me, but eighteen hours is my limit," she confessed. "C'mon in," she told him, opening her door all the way. "You can wait for me on the sofa."

Finn followed her inside, but he didn't take her up on her suggestion. "If it's all the same to you, I'll stand," he told her. "If I get comfortable on the sofa, I might wind up falling asleep waiting for you."

"I'm not going to take that long," she said, laughing softly.

Finn found himself reacting to her laugh. Something in his gut tightened and quivered just for a second. What was that about? She must have laughed before, he told himself. Why was the sound affecting him this way now?

Maybe he *was* getting punchy, he thought. He'd been able to go around-the-clock before, he argued, but he had to admit that was back when he was a rookie.

Face it, Cavanaugh, he told himself. *You're getting old.*

It wasn't something he accepted easily. Nor was it actually true, but at the moment, he felt older than his years.

The noise coming from behind him caught his attention. When he turned around, he saw that Nik had changed her whole outfit, and instead of high heels, she was wearing a pair of shoes that had heels only half as high.

To each his own, he mused. "That was fast," he told her.

"Well, to be honest, I thought if I took too long, you'd use that as an excuse to leave without me," she confessed.

His mouth curved as he glanced at his watch. "You still had five minutes left," he teased.

Apparently, that kiss had not only broken the ice between them, but it had also been instrumental in having him gain a sense of humor.

"Well, luckily, I don't need the extra time. I'm ready now," she told him. "So, what do we know about this victim?" she asked as she locked up her apartment and followed him into the courtyard.

"Not much except that it does look like the work of the same guy." When she suddenly stopped walking, Finn looked at her, confused. "Something wrong?" he asked.

"I was just wondering if we should take separate cars," Nik told him.

"Why?" he asked. Then he said, "Don't like me bringing you home?"

"I don't like imposing," Nik said, correcting him.

"You're not. Don't worry, I'll let you know when you're imposing," he promised her. And then his voice became serious as he instructed her, "Just get in the car."

Nik suppressed her smile as she opened the passenger door and did as he directed.

"Is it just me, or are there more police cars out than there normally would be?" Nik asked, taking in the area as Finn pulled up to what appeared to be the crime scene.

"No, it's not just you," he assured her, scanning the entire block. "There have to be at least twice as many cops, detectives and crime-scene investigators than usually come out for a homicide, even one involving a serial killer."

Finn turned off the engine, then got out of his car and approached the head of the crime-scene investigators. He was surprised to see that Sean was still at work.

"Chief?" he said, raising his voice as he tried to get Sean's attention.

It took two attempts before Sean heard him. "I thought I'd see you here," Sean commented. "And I see you brought your lovelier sidekick with you." Sean smiled wearily at Nik. "Sorry to have to see you so soon again under these circumstances," he told her.

"Speaking of circumstances," Finn said, taking the opportunity to bring the conversation back around to the reason they were all here, "I take it that the MO is the same for this victim as it was for the others."

"No question about that," Sean confirmed.

"Harley told me that you said this one might have been killed before some of the others we've found," Finn said.

Sean nodded. "As near as I can tell at the moment, this one was killed six days ago. You'd think that by this time, there'd be fewer young women out there, risking their lives by dancing the night away. I don't understand why our possible victim pool hasn't been thinned out, at least a little," Sean confessed, shaking his head.

"It probably has been," Finn ventured. "Imagine how many more dead women there would be by this time if it hadn't been."

"Shh," Nik warned. "Don't say that. You'll jinx it and they still might turn up."

"I didn't know you were superstitious," Finn said, looking at her.

"I'm not. Usually," Nik qualified, looking at the woman who was still lying near a Dumpster. Just like the first victim they'd found, she thought. This serial killer was treating his victims like trash. He hated women even more than most killers, Nik couldn't help thinking.

Finn squatted down beside the victim's body, taking a closer look at the woman.

She appeared younger than the other victims, he thought. "Do we have an identity for this one yet?" he asked Sean.

"No wallet, same as the others," Sean told him. And then he said the same thing that Finn had been thinking. "She looks younger than his usual prey."

That was when Nik leaned over Finn and took a closer look at the girl.

He heard Nik suddenly draw in her breath. Both he and Sean turned to look at her.

"What?" Finn asked. It was obvious that something had struck her about the dead woman and he asked what.

Nik let out a long, shaky breath. "I think I know her," she told the two men. "In fact, I'm sure of it." Her eyes swept over both of them. It was obvious to her that they didn't recognize the woman on the ground. "I think that this case just got hotter."

"I don't—" Finn began, shaking his head.

He got no further before Nik interjected, "That's Senator Clark Heaton's daughter, Gretchen."

"Are you sure?" Finn asked.

"I'm positive. They did a story on her in the Sunday supplement of the paper last month. You know, what it means to be the daughter of an up-and-coming senator, the so-called responsibility that position holds, that sort of thing."

Finn still looked rather dubious. "And you're sure it's her?"

"It's an easy enough thing to check out," Sean told them. "If you're right," he said to Nik, "then you know that you're going to have the senator breathing down your necks, demanding you find the killer, the second he finds out about this."

Finn frowned. "Demanding," he repeated. "Like these

other women don't deserve that sort of concentrated investigation on our part." Rising to his feet, he said, "I'm going to need a bigger task force on this before the higher powers decide to take this investigation totally out of my hands."

"All you need to do is tell me what you want," Nik said. The smile that came to Finn's lips when she said that told Nik that she had chosen the wrong words in this case.

Rousing himself, Finn turned toward Sean. "As soon as you can pinpoint the approximate date and time of death, we can get started requisitioning and reviewing any and all surveillance videos in the area. I can't let go of the feeling that someone must have seen *something*, and the second we can find some sort of a match to someone else popping up on those other videos, then we'll be in business."

Nik took in a deep breath. "You realize that we need to talk to the senator, see if there's anything he can tell us about his daughter that might help us find her killer," she said. "Her habits, people she hung out with, places she might have frequented where she could have come in contact with the killer. These women have to have something in common besides being fancy dressers and in their twenties. Or, in the senator's daughter's case," she said, glancing down at the body, "*almost* twenty."

Finn looked down at the face of the young woman whose life had been so abruptly cut short. "Wonder what made him change his 'type.'"

"I don't think he changed his type so much as he might have broadened his scope," Nik answered. "Look at her. Her makeup is practically wiped off, but I'm guessing that when she had her war paint on, Gretchen was able to pass for someone older, maybe more glamorous and sophisticated. And *that* seems to sum up his type.

"Or the type he's trying to eliminate," she suddenly suggested. "This might be someone he's trying to get back at, over and over again. Maybe his mother, or some woman who rejected him."

"Hey, hey, let's not get ahead of ourselves," Finn cautioned. "Let's operate one step at a time, okay? Sometimes hoofbeats just means a horse, not a zebra," he counseled.

"Okay," she agreed, although it was obvious that the wheels in her head were still going at top speed.

Suddenly, the area lit up as bright as day. Headlights were bearing down on the scene at what seemed like top speed. The next second, a white, high-end Mercedes came to a screeching halt barely two feet away. Within moments, an ashen-faced, well-dressed older man all but exploded out of the vehicle. He was followed by another, far more solemn-looking man, most likely his bodyguard, Nik thought.

"Is it true?" the first man, Senator Heaton, demanded. Not waiting for an answer, he fired out another question. "Where is she? Where's my daughter?" The cry came out almost hoarsely as he scanned the area, his eyes all but wild.

"Senator, I don't think you want to see her this way," Finn said, attempting to place himself between the man and the sprawled-out body on the ground.

Suddenly seeing the form, the senator pushed aside Finn, displaying an extraordinary amount of strength for a man of his age and build. Finn chalked it up to adrenaline.

The second the man realized that he was looking at what was left of his daughter, an almost inhuman sound emerged from his lips. In less than a second, the senator transformed from a raging bull to a man who had his very life drained from him.

The man with the senator did his best to stabilize the senator's slumping figure.

Coming around and collecting himself, Senator Heaton looked around the crowd, frantic, angry and wild-eyed.

"Who did this?" he cried. "Who did this to my little girl?"

"That's what we're trying to find out, sir," Finn told the grieving father.

The senator suddenly turned on him, incensed, and shouted, "Try harder, damn it! Try harder," he repeated just before he completely broke down, sobbing uncontrollably.

"Senator, Detective Cavanaugh has been doing everything he can to find whoever has been killing these young women," Nik began, "and he and his task force won't stop until these women—all these women—have justice, and the person who did this horrible thing to them is brought to trial."

The senator blinked, looking at her. "Who are you?"

"Just someone who wants justice, too," Nik answered simply.

Chapter 16

Finn quickly stepped in, trying to redirect the senator's attention away from the scene, as well as from Nik. The older man gave the impression that he was liable to explode at any second. He didn't want Nik to be in his line of fire.

"Senator, when you're feeling up to it, I'd like to ask you some questions about your daughter," Finn said, carefully easing the man away, with Nik and the bodyguard following.

Fire suddenly spiked in the man's hazel eyes. "What kind of questions?" the senator demanded hotly.

It was obvious that he was growing defensive and he was not about to stand for anything that he considered the slightest bit defamatory being said about his slain daughter.

Trying not to provoke the senator, Finn kept his tone polite. "Just a few general questions to give us some kind of perspective as to the type of people your daughter might have hung out with—"

That only seemed to anger the senator even more. He looked as if he was going to take a swing at Finn at any second. "Are you saying that my daughter brought this on herself?" he shouted.

"No one is saying that, Senator," Nik assured him, attempting to calm down the man. "We're just trying to retrace her steps."

"Senator," the man's bodyguard said, "why don't you let me take you home, sir? You can talk to him in the morning—right, Detective?" Alexander Waverly, the senator's aide, asked, looking at Finn.

Finn stepped back, clearing an exit path for the two men. He wasn't insensitive to what the senator was going through. If anything, he felt sympathetic.

"Sure thing," he answered. "Take him home. We'll talk tomorrow."

"Home?" the senator shouted, stunned. "What do I have to go home to? There's nothing there anymore," he cried, his voice breaking.

Having been a silent witness, Sean stepped forward. "Do you need any help getting him home?" he asked the bodyguard.

"I can handle this, thanks," Waverly told Sean. Placing a hand on his employer's shoulder, the bodyguard steered the broken man toward his vehicle.

"That poor man," Nik murmured, watching as Waverly guided the senator into his car.

"Which one?" Finn asked, watching with her. "The senator or the bodyguard?"

"Both," she replied without hesitation. "For different reasons."

Finn turned away and looked at Sean. The medical

examiner had just placed the senator's daughter into a body bag and was zipping it up. The sound seemed to reverberate through the evening air.

"Anything different about this one that I should know about, Sean?" Finn asked.

Sean shook his head. "Other than the fact that she's younger than the others, nothing jumps out at me at the moment. I think it's just a coincidence that she's the senator's daughter."

The answer wasn't what Finn was looking for. "There's got to be some kind of a connection between these women that we're missing," Finn said. He looked at Nik, and Harley and Ramirez, two members of his task force who had arrived on the scene. "We need to do a deep dive into these women's social-media pages. Maybe we're missing something that's out in plain sight."

"That would make things a lot easier, wouldn't it?" Harley said. "Well, all we can do is hope."

But Finn's attention was back to the leader of the CSI team. "Let me know the moment the ME pins down an approximate time of death."

Sean nodded, giving Finn an encouraging smile. "You got it."

"Okay, Kowalski. Let's see if we can round up some surveillance videos from the last six days," Finn told her.

"I can hardly wait," Nik responded.

"You know, I am really starting to hate Thomas Edison," Nik said to Finn several hours later.

The moment she and Finn had gotten back to the station with copies of surveillance videos from the area where this latest murder had occurred, she and one of the other people on the task force settled in to review each one slowly.

Finn had come, as promised, to spell her.

"The inventor?" he asked, perplexed as he looked in her direction. "Why? What have you got against him?"

"Because if he hadn't invented film, we wouldn't be sitting here, going cross-eyed like this," she retorted in a less-than-genial tone.

"He didn't invent it. Someone else did. Edison invented the first film camera so to speak," Jerry Collins, sitting at the table next to Nik, said wearily.

"Why would you even know that? Never mind," Finn said, waving away the other man's words. He looked at Nik. "Want me to take over for you?" he offered.

She surprised him by rising from the desk. "Sure, why not?" Then, not wanting to seem as if she was shirking the responsibility he'd given her, she added, "Just until I stretch my legs—and get my eyes refocused and back in my head."

Finn sat down in her place and began to review the videos, picking up where she had left off.

Rotating her shoulders, Nik did her best to attempt to ease the ache she felt taking hold there. But even as she tried to distance herself from the videos, she couldn't help glancing in Finn's direction. More specifically, looking at the screen as he fast-forwarded through the videos.

And then she froze. "Wait!"

Finn gave her a quizzical look. "The idea is to try to get through this footage fast," he reminded her. "And I thought you were taking a break."

She hardly heard him. "Stop!" she cried. When he did, she leaned forward to get a better look at the people caught in mid-movement. Nik blinked, focusing on the frozen frame. She was right! "That's Marilyn," she cried. Stunned, she looked from the monitor to Finn and then back again. "It's her!" she declared more loudly this time.

"I'm sure of it." And then she looked at Finn, mystified. "What's she doing there?"

"Beats me," he admitted. "Maybe we've found our connection," he said.

"But what does it mean?" she persisted, trying to make sense out of the whole scenario.

"That I don't know. Yet," he replied. In his opinion, this *all* needed clarification. "We definitely need to mount all these victims on a board, see if we can find any more connections between them," he told Nik. Maybe if it was all spread out in front of him, it might start making some kind of sense. "I'm going to see if we can get some space set aside for the task force, maybe a room in the back."

Constructing the bulletin board with the various victims and what they had discovered about them took the better part of that day as well as part of the following one.

When it was done, Nik stood back, looking over what they had managed to piece together. There were still so many pieces that seemed to be missing.

Nik turned to Finn. "I'm going to go back to Marilyn's mother, see if she knows whether or not Marilyn actually knew Senator Heaton's daughter."

He nodded. That sounded like a good idea to him. "I'll come with you," he announced. And then he waved a hand at the board with its columns of dead women. "I'm not that good when it comes to social media," he confessed.

"You don't have a social-media page?" Nik asked him as they left the squad room together.

"No," he answered. "If someone wants to know something about me, I'd rather they asked me about it face-to-face."

"So you can shut them down in person?" she asked, trying to suppress the smile that rose to her lips.

He surprised her by laughing. "You're getting to know me," he said.

Yes, I think I am, Nik thought.

When Kim Palmer opened the door after Nik had knocked, there was instant fear in the woman's eyes. "Did you…?" she began breathlessly.

"No, we didn't find her," Nik answered, anticipating the woman's question. "There's been another murder, but it wasn't Marilyn," she said quickly.

"Then I don't understand," Kim said. "Why are you here?" There was still apprehension in the woman's brown eyes.

Finn stepped in to answer Kim Palmer's question. "While we were looking through the surveillance videos corresponding to the latest crime scene, we saw Marilyn in the background."

Kim gasped and clutched at his arm. "Marilyn? You're sure it was her?" Before he could say anything, she cried, "Then she's alive?"

Finn didn't answer the woman because he didn't want to get her hopes up in case this was no longer true. The video was from several days ago. Instead, he asked Kim about what they were trying to ascertain.

"Mrs. Palmer, does your daughter know Senator Clark Heaton's daughter, Gretchen?"

Kim appeared puzzled, as if she was having trouble absorbing the full meaning of the question. And then she finally shook her head.

"No, Marilyn never mentioned anything about a… Gretchen did you say?" she asked, struggling to make sense out of all this.

Nik nodded. "That's right. Her name was Gretchen Heaton."

"Was," Kim repeated. "Then she's…?"

"Yes," Nik answered as gently as she could. "The senator's daughter is another victim."

Kim swallowed. It took her a second to find her voice. "No, I never heard Marilyn say that name." She flushed, embarrassed. "I told you, Marilyn stopped telling me things a few months ago. She transformed into this extremely secretive creature these last few weeks." She blew out a breath, remembering an incident that showcased just how distant her daughter had become. "When I accidentally found out that she was going to see this doctor rather a lot and asked her about it, she suddenly started yelling at me, screaming that I needed to mind my own business." Kim raised her head, tears shimmering in her eyes. "Like she wasn't my business," the woman sobbed.

"What kind of a doctor was she seeing?" Finn asked her.

Kim shrugged self-consciously. "You know, one who concerned himself with female problems."

"A male?" Nik asked. Kim nodded her head. "Do you happen to remember his name?" Nik asked her. This might just be nothing, but then again…

"Garrett, Gallagher, something like that." Kim shrugged, unable to pinpoint the doctor's name at the moment because her mind was so weighed down. "Why? Is that important?"

"I don't know yet. I was just wondering why this set off your 'mom' radar," Nik told her.

Kim thought for a moment, trying to remember. "To be honest, I thought maybe he was trying to bilk her. You know, there are unscrupulous doctors around, taking advantage of naive patients—and Marilyn isn't exactly worldly," Kim confessed.

Though it cost the woman to admit this, she told Nik, "She's a very young twenty. That's why I asked you to look for her," she explained. "I even called the doctor's office," Kim suddenly remembered, "to see if Marilyn had had a recent appointment to see him, but the receptionist said she couldn't disclose that kind of information. Something about doctor-patient confidentiality," Kim scoffed. "But I'm her *mother*," she protested, looking from Nik to the detective with her. "I should be able to *know* these things, shouldn't I?"

Nik felt it best not to encourage the woman along this path. Instead, she said, "We'll get to the bottom of this, I promise."

"You said you found out about these visits accidentally. What did you mean by that?" Finn asked. "Was a bill sent to the house?"

Kim nodded. "I was emptying out Marilyn's wastebasket—it was garbage day," the woman explained. "And this bill fell out. I wasn't going to look at it, but…" Her voice trailed off and she shrugged again. "It wasn't as if I was going through her things," she cried. "It was in the trash for heaven sakes," she said as if that was her defense and she intended to stand by it.

"Would you still happen to have that billing statement?" Finn asked.

"No, Marilyn tore it out of my hands when she saw I was looking at it and she ripped it up into little pieces. She accused me of snooping!" Kim released a shaky breath and closed her eyes. And then her eyes flew open. "It was Garrett. His name was Dr. James Garrett," she announced triumphantly. Her eyes seemed to bounce back and forth, silently pleading with the two people in her living room for support. "Does that help your investigation?"

"Honestly, probably not," Finn told her, again not wanting to raise the woman's hopes. "But we'll check it out."

"What do you think?" Nik asked Finn the moment they had left Kim's house and were far enough away not to be overheard.

"Well," he said, rolling the last few minutes over in his head, "I'm beginning to see why Marilyn withdrew into herself. If you ask me, she probably felt she was being smothered."

"In Kim's defense," Nik said, "it's probably not that easy being a single mother and Kim has been one for the last decade."

They reached his car. "I understand your loyalty—and I think it's a very admirable quality," he told her. "But in my house, my parents set a good example and trusted us to do the right thing. Innocent until proven guilty, that sort of thing."

Nik got into his car. "Not everyone is fortunate enough to grow up a Cavanaugh," she told him as she fastened her seat belt.

"It has nothing to do with being a Cavanaugh," he protested. "It just has to do with trusting your kids." Finn looked at her. This case had raised questions in his head, questions that had nothing to do with the case and everything to do with the woman with him. "How about you?" he asked. "Your parents trust you?"

"Parent," Nik corrected. "It was just my dad, really," she told him. "My mom decided early on that she really wanted something else out of life than being a mother, so one night she just handed my sister and me over to my dad and come morning, she was gone. She left a letter, he told us, but that was the last contact he ever had with my mother."

She sounded almost detached when she spoke. Had she distanced herself from the incident that much? "That must have been hard," he said sympathetically.

Nik shrugged as he finally started up his car. "Actually, it wasn't. My dad and I always liked each other, so it was okay. He took over being both mother and father, like that was the way it had always been." She smiled. "He loved us enough to fill both slots, so I never felt as if I had been abandoned. And I've got some great memories."

"Is your dad still around?" he asked suddenly. "I'd like to meet him."

Nik looked at him, pretending to be "shocked."

"Are you getting personal, Cavanaugh?" she asked, recalling what he'd been like at the start of their association. It hadn't exactly been that long ago.

He shrugged. "Working together like this, it's hard not to," he admitted.

"Okay," she said, thinking over his request. "Maybe when this is all over, I'll introduce you to him."

"I'll take that as a rain check," he told her. "Right now, let's go talk to this Dr. Garrett, see if he can shed some light on the situation."

"Sounds like a plan," she told him as he picked up speed.

There was a sign on Dr. James Garrett's office door that read Closed for Renovations. There was also a date below that stated when the office was going to reopen again. There was also a phone number below *that*, referring patients to another doctor until the office officially reopened.

"Looks like the good doctor is playing hooky," Nik said, taking out her cell.

"What are you doing?" he asked, curious.

"I'm calling the number of the doctor listed here. It says he's standing in for Dr. Garrett so maybe he can shed some light on this," she said as she completed inputting the phone number.

"Well, I—" Finn stopped talking because Nik was holding up her finger, indicating that she had gotten someone on the line.

"Yes, I'm calling because I need to see the doctor," she told the woman on the other end of the line. "My own doctor, Dr. Garrett, seems to be away for the next couple of weeks. I was wondering if you know if there's been some mistake. Dr. Day is listed on the door as subbing for Dr. Garrett."

The woman on the other end of the call confirmed the bare essentials. "That's right. Dr. Garrett's office is being renovated and Dr. Day is taking on his patients. But I'm afraid that Dr. Day won't be able to see you until next week. We're booked solid."

"Do you know when Dr. Garrett will be back?" Nik asked.

"I was told he'll be back in two weeks, the way it says on the door," the woman said coldly. "But apparently that's not a date that's written in stone."

"Really?" Nik asked. "Why's that?"

"I have no idea." At this point, there were icicles dripping from the woman's voice. "Now I'm going to need your name, your contact number and the name of your insurance carrier," the woman told her.

Which was when Nik hung up.

Chapter 17

Listening to Nik's end of the conversation, Finn did his best to fill in the gaps.

"Maybe Marilyn ran off with her doctor and now the two of them are away somewhere, living the high life." He watched Nik's face to see if he'd guessed right.

"At this point, I'd believe anything," she said, trying to harness her frustration. "But there's still the matter of Marilyn's partial fingerprint on your grandfather's rearview mirror—and on the note that was found near what at the time was the first victim." She looked at him, stymied. "Just how does that figure into all this?"

"Good question," he agreed. "By the way, Seamus isn't my grandfather. He's my grand-uncle," Finn reminded Nik. "But that doesn't change the question you raised."

A tall, stately-looking woman wearing a conservative gray suit walked past them as she went to reopen the office located just across from Dr. Garrett's. As she unlocked her door, her eyes swept appreciatively over Finn and lingered for a moment.

"Can I help you with something?" the woman asked. Her question sounded as if it was intended for both of them, but she was still only looking at Finn.

Nik took the lead. "We were looking to talk to Dr. Garrett."

The woman laughed, obviously amused. "Good luck with that."

"Would you know where he is or when he'll be back?" Nik asked the woman.

"According to gossip," the woman told Finn, taking a step closer in his direction, "he's probably out tomcatting around. As to when he'll be back, well, that's anyone's guess. Don't get me wrong," she said a bit quickly. "James is a very good doctor—when he's doctoring," she qualified. "But he gets these…let's call them restless periods, and he just takes off. When he gets it all out of his system," she went on, "he comes back and picks up the reins of his practice as if nothing's happened."

Finn and Nik exchanged looks. "Does he do this sort of thing often?" Finn asked the woman.

"Actually, there was just that one time that I know of—until now," she added with just a touch of drama. In Nik's opinion, she was milking the situation for Finn's benefit.

"Hasn't anyone thought of disciplining him for this?" Nik asked.

The woman tossed her a look, then told Finn, "James is a charmer. He can talk his way out of anything, doesn't matter if it's a male or a female on the receiving end of his monologue." She shrugged, turning back to her own door. "I suppose it's harmless. He does have someone covering for him in case an emergency comes up. And I'm told that his patients were all rerouted until he returns."

"The doctor who's covering for Dr. Garrett, that would be Dr. Day, right?" Finn asked, glancing back at the sign on the door to make sure he had gotten the name right.

The woman nodded. "Yes, that's right. I heard that James and Dr. Day went to medical school together." The woman's look lingered on Finn again. "Anything else I can do for you?" she asked.

It sounded more like an offer than an actual question to Nik.

"No, thank you," Finn replied. "You've been a great help, Ms.—" He waited for the woman to fill in her name.

"Doctor," she informed him proudly. "Dr. Julia Bishop," she said, extending her hand to him.

Finn had no choice but to shake it. "Detective Finn Cavanaugh," he told her. "And this is—" He got no further because Dr. Bishop interrupted him.

"Yes, yes," she said, totally ignoring Nik. "You know where to find me if you have any more questions, Detective."

And with that the woman went into her office and closed the door.

"Well, looks to me like you just made a friend, 'Detective,'" Nik commented.

"If I did, it's all due to you." He saw the puzzled look on Nik's face and explained. "Don't look now but I think you're rubbing off on me."

"It's not me that Dr. Bishop would like to be rubbing against," Nik murmured under her breath as they went to the elevator.

"So, what are you thinking?" she asked Finn as they stepped back into the elevator and took it down to the first floor.

He wasn't sure if she was referring to the overly

friendly doctor in the hallway, or if she was talking about something else, so he asked, "What do you mean?"

She looked up at him as she stepped off the elevator. "You've got this look in your eyes, like you're working through something. Did something Dr. Sexy say get to you—I mean other than the obvious?"

He ignored the latter part of her sentence. "Bishop made it sound like Garrett is a ladies' man."

"And?" she asked. But before he could actually answer her, Nik had another question for him. One that had begun to buzz around in her own head. "You think he's involved in these murders?"

"I don't know," Finn answered honestly. "But my gut says that there's something off here."

"Your gut," she repeated. They walked out of the building and headed to where he had parked his car. "Wait, I think I've heard of this. The famous Cavanaugh gut, right? It's what you and your family call feelings that have absolutely no logical basis for existing, but you still fixate on them. Right?"

He had to laugh at her description. "You know, for an optimistic, cheerful person, you have a really downer way of putting things."

"Sorry," she apologized, flashing a smile at him. "I didn't mean to throw mud on a sacred institution." They had reached his vehicle and she paused at the passenger side. "So, what do you want to do next?"

"Off the top of my head, I'd say talk to Dr. Day and see if he can give us some insight into his old friend so we know whether or not we should continue on this path," Finn answered.

She nodded. It sounded like a good idea to her. "Provided we can get past his bulldog of a receptionist," she pointed out.

Finn patted his pocket where he had his badge pinned. "We will," he assured her.

"You could always try charming her," she told him.

He scowled, knowing she was referring to his exchange with Dr. Bishop. "Get in the car, Kowalski," he instructed.

She saluted. "Yes, sir."

He knew she was just kidding, but he still smiled and said, "You're learning, Kowalski."

She said something else under her breath, but he thought it wise to leave it alone.

"Wait, you can't go in there!" the receptionist declared indignantly. "Doctor's in with a patient!"

"Fine," Finn replied, stopping. "Then tell him to come out. I...we need to speak to him," he told the rather stern-looking woman.

The thin woman drew herself up to her full height of five foot three. "And what is this about?" she asked.

Nik smiled at the woman, answering for Finn. "You don't have a need to know that, ma'am," she informed the receptionist "politely."

Daggers shot from the woman's eyes at Nik as the receptionist turned on her heel and went to one of the rear examination rooms.

"Nicely done," Finn told Nik.

Pleased, she flashed a wide smile at him. "I have been waiting for a long time to say that to someone," she confided. "It always irritated the hell out of me to be on the receiving end of that line."

Finn laughed softly under his breath. "Remind me to keep you in the loop."

"I will," she promised.

A couple of minutes later, a small, aristocratic-looking

man with a pencil-thin moustache hovering on his upper lip came over to them.

"I'm Dr. Day," he said. "Stella tells me that you're looking for me."

"I'm Detective Cavanaugh, this is investigator Kowalski," Finn said, introducing himself and Nik. "Is there somewhere we can talk?" he asked, looking around.

"My office," the doctor responded. He led the way to another room in the back. "Will this take long? You might have noticed that I've got a waiting room teeming with patients."

"Yes, we know," Nik acknowledged. "You're doing double duty at the moment, taking on Dr. Garrett's patients as well."

"Yes." And then Dr. Day looked at her over his shoulder, perplexed. "How would you know that?"

They were in the doctor's office now and Finn took the liberty of shutting the door. "Dr. Garrett has a sign on his door, referring his patients to you. Tell me, does Dr. Garrett take off like this often?" Finn asked, wanting to hear Day's response to see if it jibed with what Dr. Bishop had told them.

"No, hardly ever," Dr. Day answered rather quickly. "As a matter of fact, I can't remember the last time he did this. Jimmy works really hard. He puts in longer hours than most. He's exceptionally dedicated," the doctor told them. "I guess he just needed to recharge his batteries, so to speak."

Finn played along. "Do you know where he goes to do this 'recharging'?"

To Finn's disappointment—although not to his surprise—Dr. Day shook his head. "I really don't know. But he'll be back soon enough if you need to talk to him for some reason." He looked from Finn to the woman beside him. "What's this all about, anyway?"

Finn remained deliberately vague. "Sorry, we have some questions to ask him that only Dr. Garrett can answer."

"Questions about one of his patients?" Day asked, hoping to get a reaction.

"Something like that," Finn answered. "Well, if you hear from Dr. Garrett, ask him to give me a call," he told the man, then handed the doctor his card.

Dr. Day glanced down at the card and then he put it away. "I will."

"Thank you. We won't take up any more of your time, Doctor," Finn said. He glanced at Nik. "Let's go."

"You know," Nik said, thinking out loud as they drove back to the police station, "you could ping Garrett's phone, get a location on him."

"I'd need probable cause before I could do that," he reminded her.

"Probable cause." She shifted in her seat to squarely face him. "That's so you can get a warrant to ping his phone, right?"

He glanced at her. She knew that as well as he did, he thought. But, for the sake of argument, he answered her. "Yes."

"From a judge, right?" Nik said, continuing her thought.

Okay, no more games, Finn thought. "What are you getting at?"

"Don't you people have judges you know, or in the family?" she asked. "I mean, if you wanted to go strictly the legal route."

"That would be the best way to go," he said sarcastically.

She smiled, making him think of pure mischief personified. "But not the only way."

It struck him that for all her irritating ways, she was

still rather adorable. "You know, you're as devious as my sister and some of my cousins," he told her.

Her eyes crinkled. "I'll take that as another compliment."

Finn laughed, shaking his head. "You keep this up and you'll become an honorary Cavanaugh," he told her. They were on their way to the squad room, but he could easily delay that for thirty, forty minutes. He'd been feeling his stomach pinching him for the last hour or so. "How about some lunch?" he suggested.

"We're past lunch," she told him. "This would be an early dinner."

"Whatever you want to call it," he said, turning his car down a street and heading toward a fast-food restaurant he favored, already assuming that she was going to take him up on his suggestion. "Do you want to grab some?"

Now that he mentioned it, the idea of getting something to eat sounded really good. "I never say no to food," she answered.

"Good to know," he told her.

"That was some good work back there," Finn told her as they sat at a small table in a fast-food restaurant.

The restaurant they'd gone to wound up being one that Nik favored—and it was closer than the one he had planned to go to. There was a logo of an adorable rabbit with huge eyes looking down at each customer as he or she walked through the door.

"Of course, I would have picked a different restaurant, but then, you can't be dead-on each and every time," he said philosophically, looking around.

"I like this place," she said defensively. "It meets my two basic requirements. The food is good and it's not expensive," she told him. "As for the first thing you said— thank you."

He nodded, taking a healthy bite of his cheeseburger.

"By the way, I was told to remind you that Uncle Andrew's party is tomorrow. Do you want me to come by and pick you up, or do you remember the way there?" he asked.

"I remember the way there," Nik answered. She paused for a moment, then ate a few fries and said, "But you can come by and pick me up."

He looked at her, surprised by her answer. "I would have thought you'd opt for being independent."

His reaction amused her. "You're not taking me into bondage," she told him. "You're just bringing me to a party. The way I see it, I'm saving on gas and the immediate world is being spared having a little extra pollution if we carpool."

"Carpool," he repeated, his smile growing. "Is that what we're calling it now?"

"What did you want to call it?" she asked, then took a guess at the label he would have used. "A date?"

"Definitely not a date," he answered. And then he raised his eyes to hers. "Unless that's what you think it is."

They were in the middle of a homicide investigation, but she realized that she was enjoying this. "I find that it's best to avoid labels in some cases," she told Finn.

"Yeah, me, too," he agreed.

They were both lying, and they knew it. From Finn's point of view, it was just a matter of time before they admitted it.

He glanced at Nik's tray. For a little thing, she could really pack it away quickly. The tray had had a healthy amount of food on it and it was now empty. "Ready?" he asked her.

She looked at him, a touch of suspicion entering her eyes. "For what?"

"I need to go back to the squad room and make a note of this latest bit of information about the doctor," he told her.

"You *do* think he has something to do with this, don't you?" she asked.

"Like I said, it's a gut feeling."

"Maybe we can question the other victims' families, find out if any of them were acquainted with the good doctor."

"That's a long shot," he told her.

"Why?" she asked. Was he changing his mind? "I thought you said you had a gut feeling about the doctor."

"I do," Finn confirmed. "But you're missing the point."

"Which is?" she asked.

"Does your father know the name of the doctor you go to?" he asked.

"He would," she answered, "if I had a doctor."

"You don't have a doctor," he said incredulously, looking at her.

"Nope," she freely admitted. "I am as healthy as the proverbial horse."

"Maybe," he said skeptically.

"No maybe about it," she assured him firmly.

"That still doesn't mean that you shouldn't establish a baseline, you know, have a bunch of tests taken that can be used to measure against future results."

"I'll look into it first chance I get," she told Finn.

He gave her a look. "You're just placating me, aren't you?"

Nik smiled up at him. "Is it working?"

"No," he retorted.

"Well, it was worth a try," she replied with a smile that Finn found was definitely wiggling its way under his skin no matter how much he tried not to let it. "Let's get back to the squad room and update that bulletin board," she said, leading the way to the car.

Chapter 18

It felt, Nik thought as the hours ticked away, like an exercise in futility.

The photographs and notations on the bulletin board were all neatly compiled and lined up in orderly columns beneath each victim's name. In anticipation of possibly finding even more victims—because there was always the outside chance that they would—the task force had made more room on the bulletin board. A second bulletin board was reserved in the stockroom just in case it had to be pressed into service in the near future, although neither she nor Finn, nor the rest of the task force, wanted it to come to that.

But by the end of an overly long day, nothing about the case became any clearer except that the person or persons they were pursuing were elusively more clever—for now—than they were.

"Let's call it a night, okay?" Finn suggested to the others.

"Don't have to twist my arm any, fearless leader," Harley said.

"Hey, I'm already gone," Ramirez told him, shutting down his computer.

"I've got a family that thinks I'm just someone their mother made up," Ed Walters, a third member of the task force, said. "It's as good a time as any to show them that I exist," the detective added as he gathered up the papers on his desk and put them together in some sort of a semi-orderly stack.

Finn noticed that only Nik didn't say anything in response. As he came closer to her desk, he saw she was writing illegible notes to herself on scattered pieces of paper.

"Hey, Kowalski," Finn said, raising his voice a little. He noticed that she still didn't look up. "Did you hear what I said?" he asked her. "We're tucking away our brains and calling it a night."

"Uh-huh," she murmured, still continuing to write. "Good night," she said as an afterthought.

Finn placed his hand on top of the pad she was writing on. Nik hadn't struck him as the old-fashioned type who still used paper and pencil, but obviously, she was.

Because his hand was in the way, Nik had to stop writing. Raising her head, she looked quizzically at the man who was standing over her.

"Go home, Kowalski," Finn told her.

"I will, I will," she assured him with a touch of impatience. "Just give me a few more minutes. I've got this thought running around in my head and I wanted to get it down before I lost it."

She had been working harder than any of the people who were officially attached to the task force. She needed to take a break.

"If you lose it, it'll come back to you," Finn assured her. "Rest first," he said. "C'mon, I'll take you home so you can get your beauty sleep and be fresh tomorrow morning."

She raised her eyes to his, actually seeing him as his words penetrated. Looking around, she realized that they were now alone in the back room. When had that happened?

"You think I need beauty sleep?" she asked Finn.

Heaven help him, he really didn't, Finn thought. If anyone didn't need sleep to be more beautiful, it was definitely Nik. But he also knew that he couldn't say that without sounding as if he was coming on to her. So, since he had to say something in response, Finn fell back on a half-truth.

"Everyone needs beauty sleep. Besides, the party's tomorrow," he added unnecessarily.

She had gotten so engrossed in her thoughts about the case, she had completely forgotten about that. She caught her bottom lip between her teeth. "Oh."

He didn't like the undercurrent he detected in her voice. She was going to beg off, he thought.

The moment that occurred to him, he realized that he didn't want her to beg off. For more reasons than just one.

"Yeah, 'oh.' And Uncle Andrew wanted me to make sure that you're going to be there," he informed her.

Nik highly doubted that. "From what've heard, these things usually have wall-to-wall Cavanaughs and 'friends of Cavanaughs' attending them. I sincerely doubt that he's even going to *notice* that I'm not there."

"Number one," he said, moving directly behind the chair she was on and turning it away from the desk that had been assigned to her, "the chief is the sharpest man I've ever known and he keeps track of *everything*. Number two, he specified that he wanted to talk to you personally."

"He did?" she asked. "Why would he want to talk to me?"

Finn paused, debating whether or not to say anything. He was tempted, but then he felt that her curiosity just might be what would get her to come tomorrow.

So he decided to be secretive. "I'll let him be the one to tell you."

It wasn't hard to read between the lines. "You think that's going to make me show up tomorrow, don't you?"

She saw laughter in his eyes and despite her best efforts to ignore it, she found herself drawn to him.

"Am I right?" Finn asked.

Nik pressed her lips together. She wanted to say no, but it wasn't in her to lie. So she said, "Maybe," and left it at that.

"Are you still willing to have me come to pick you up?" Finn asked.

Nik knew that if he didn't, she might be tempted to skip the festivities—especially once she started going over the various aspects of the case. If nothing else, she still needed to live up to her promise to Kim about finding the woman's daughter, hopefully alive.

"Sure," Nik responded. "What time will you be over?"

"Eleven o'clock okay with you?" he asked, peering down into her face.

One time was as good as another, she thought. "Sounds about right," she responded.

"All right, now that that's settled—are you going to get out of this chair, or am I going to have to push you all the way to the parking lot in it?" he asked her.

The image that created in her mind's eye made her laugh. "I'd really like to see that."

"Are you daring me?" he asked in a completely serious tone of voice.

She had a feeling that if she answered that question in the affirmative, the detective might just take her up on it. She had no desire to be gawked at while he wheeled her down the city street.

"No," she answered, "I think I'd better take a pass on that."

Finn nodded and then put out his hand to her. "Good choice."

She put her hand in his and allowed him to draw her out of the chair and up to her feet. For one second, the connection between them had a jolt of electricity zooming all through her veins. And judging from the look that she saw passing over his face, that same jolt passed through his as well.

Realizing that their hands were still connecting, she pulled hers away. "I can get downstairs on my own power," she informed him.

"Never doubted that even for a minute," Finn responded.

Nik bunched up another outfit she'd judged lacking and threw it on her bed.

Although she made it a point to put on a friendly face, the thought of being inside the Cavanaugh stronghold with so many Cavanaugh family members milling about made her feel somewhat nervous.

Not that she thought anyone would be judging her. Collectively they were far too nice for that. But although she could always put up a bold front, the Nik who existed inside wasn't nearly as confident as she pretended to be.

And what was this thing with the former chief specifically requesting her presence all about? Part of her did think that Finn was just making it up to get her to attend. But the other part worried that he *was* telling her the truth. That in turn left her wondering *why* the man was specifically making a point that she be there. Had she unwittingly done something wrong and now Andrew Cavanaugh wanted to dress her down for it?

Granted the man was no longer a part of the Aurora police department and hadn't been for a long time, but he still carried a great deal of sway over his children and his brothers, as well as *their* children. That made for a great many Cavanaughs who were all part of the force.

The truth of it was you couldn't really make a move in the police department without tripping over one of them, she thought as she discarded yet another outfit. She tossed it on top of the others as the clothes in her closet became fewer and fewer and the ones on her bed grew exponentially.

Nik blew out a breath, frustrated. Nothing looked right on her somehow. Outfits she'd always loved now failed to please her.

And she really wanted to look perfect.

Not going to happen, she thought. She went to stand in front of her all-but-barren closet.

"Well, you know that you're going to have to make a choice soon or he's going to come in and find you buck naked. That's *not* the kind of impression you want to give him," she told the frowning reflection staring back at her in her wardrobe mirror.

Glancing at her watch, Nik realized that she only had a few minutes before he got there. Her frown deepened. Knowing Finn, he would be perverse and arrive early.

Desperate, she grabbed a teal dress and light tan high-heeled sandals.

"Doesn't matter what this looks like on you, you're

wearing it," she ordered her reflection, wiggling into the dress.

She had just slipped on her shoes when she heard the doorbell ring. Habit had her glancing at her watch.

She was right. The damn man was early.

Cavanaugh had no respect for women, she thought to herself. Moving quickly, she secured the second strap on her shoes and hurried to answer the door.

Swinging the front door open, she accused, "You're early!"

"And you're...sensational," he said, substituting the word for the one he was going to say as the full impact of what he saw hit him. "Sensational" wasn't what he'd meant to say, but it was definitely what he felt the second he saw her. "Grumpy," Finn added after a beat, "but definitely sensational."

"Thank you—I think," Nik said, not entirely certain just how to react to the compliment and what followed in its wake.

Finn breezed by her response. "Sorry about being early," he apologized. "Do you need some extra time?" he asked. His eyes skimmed over her, all but feasting on what he saw. "Not that you look as if you need it," he added, unable to help himself.

"No," she said curtly, "I don't need any extra time. I had a feeling you were going to be early." She said it as if it was a failing of his that he would actually do something like that.

Finn took it all in stride. "So what's the problem?"

Was he actually being so thick? she wondered in disbelief. No, he was doing this to get to her, she decided. No one who looked like Finn did led a solitary life.

"The problem is," she told him, "it would have been nice not to have to rush."

His brother was right. Women were truly a mystery that couldn't really be unraveled. He knew that he definitely didn't understand what was at the bottom of her protest.

"Why did you rush if you thought I was going to be here at eleven?" he asked her.

"Never mind. It wasn't worth repeating the first time," she told him.

Finn totally agreed, but he felt it best not to say as much to Nik. Instead, he asked her, "Are you ready to go?"

"Just let me grab my purse and I'm ready," she told him.

He nodded. "I'll wait outside for you," he said, thinking it far more prudent that way than to stand around and possibly get into another discussion that went nowhere.

Because she'd been so stressed, it took her a minute to locate where she had left her purse. Finding it, she slipped the strap over her shoulder and took a deep breath.

This was the same man she had been working alongside for more than a week, she told herself. There was absolutely no reason to feel as if she was suddenly growing a squadron of butterflies in the pit of her stomach.

Taking another deep breath, she went outside.

Finn was standing less than two feet away from her door, waiting for her. The second Nik came out, he suddenly snapped to attention.

"I was going to go back into your apartment in a couple more minutes to see if you'd changed your mind again."

"I didn't." Was he telling her that he thought she was the type of person to go back on her word?

You're being paranoid, knock it off, she told herself.

"I was just trying to find my purse," she explained. "I

forget where I put it sometimes." And then, because she needed to stabilize herself, she turned it back around to him. "Why is it so important that I come?"

"I told you. I'll let Uncle Andrew tell you about that himself," Finn said.

She wasn't one hundred percent sold on that. "Are you being serious?" she asked. "Or is this just your way of making me attend?"

He led the way to his car. He'd made sure to park closer this time. "I wouldn't use deception," he told her. "You'll enjoy yourself," he promised. "Uncle Andrew does all his own cooking. The food's fantastic—even the simple dishes. And there's a pretty nice crowd, even if I do say so myself," he told her, holding the door open for her. Then, to ensure it all went well, he made the decision to open up to her a little. "I was where you are a few years ago."

How was that possible? she wondered. "Come again?"

He came around the hood to his side of the car and got in. He studied her for a second, his expression unreadable.

"I take it that you don't know the story about the previously unknown side of the family?" Finn finally asked her.

"The what?" She stared at him. He had to be putting her on and making this up. "You're kidding, right?"

He didn't answer until he snapped his seat belt into place. And then, wearing a totally straight face, Finn answered, "Nope. My late grandfather and Seamus were brothers. When their parents got divorced—back in the day when people really didn't do that very much—each parent took one of the kids. Seamus stayed here and Murdoch, my grandfather, went with his mother, who promptly did a disappearing act, I'm not really sure why," he confessed. "But I think it was because she didn't want her ex to find her."

He paused with his narrative, pulling out of her apartment complex before he resumed his story.

"It wasn't until Uncle Andrew decided to go looking for my grandfather to reunite Seamus and Murdoch that he stumbled across my side of the family. By the time that happened, my grandfather wasn't around anymore, but the kids he had—and *their* kids—were."

He laughed to himself as he thought about the coincidence. "Oddly enough that side of the family was into law enforcement just as much as Uncle Andrew's side, and gradually, over time, most of us resettled here to form the group of people that you are about to meet today."

Nik was still thinking about something he'd just said. "And you all *really* gravitated toward law enforcement?"

It seemed rather hard to believe, and yet, it was obviously true. It started her thinking about how certain traits ran in some families.

He nodded, saying what she was thinking out loud. "Funny how that kind of thing just seems to run in the blood," he told her. "Okay," he declared, "now you're all caught up."

"Hardly," Nik contradicted. "But it's a start. If I have any questions—"

"I'll be right there to answer them. And if I'm not, anyone else at the party can—unless, of course, you're talking to some of the really younger members of the family. Then you might not get an answer." A smile played on his lips.

"I'll be sure to ask only people over five feet," she told him.

"Good rule of thumb," he agreed.

She caught herself wondering if there were other rules she should know about and what they might be.

Chapter 19

"Maybe you people should think about renting a huge bus—or hold your parties in a stadium," Nik suggested.

They had arrived on Andrew's development and there were cars parked as far as the eye could see. The cars were on both sides of the block that went through the development as well as going down toward the park. From the looks of it, the cars were parked beyond that, too.

Nik stopped counting and turned toward Finn. "I thought you said we were early."

"Well, I thought we were," he answered. "I guess everyone else had the same idea. Tell you what, why don't I just let you off at the front door and then I'll look for somewhere to park?" He began to slow down as he approached the former chief's house.

Nik was surprised by his offer. She really had no desire for any special treatment. "Aren't you afraid I'll decide to take off once you drop me off?"

"I find that trusting someone puts them on their best

behavior," he told her and then spared her a quick glance. "And I trust you."

She studied his profile for a moment. He looked relaxed. She took that to mean he was telling her the truth.

"Nice to know," she commented. "But I'm not fragile. I can walk from wherever you finally find a space to leave your car."

Shrugging, Finn put his foot down on the accelerator again, pulling away from Andrew's front door. "Okay, but let the record show I did try to be a gentleman," he told her.

Finn began to slowly reconnoiter the area, making his way toward the park. As luck would have it, one of the residents on the next block who wasn't attending the party pulled his vehicle away from the curb. The second he did, Finn, worried about losing it, sped up and pulled into the newly vacated spot.

He glanced toward his passenger as he straightened his wheel. "Looks like you turned out to be good luck after all."

"First time anyone ever said that to me," she told him with a laugh.

He pulled up the parking brake and turned off the ignition. "Maybe other people just weren't paying any attention, Nikki."

Getting out of the car, she looked at him. "What did you just call me?"

"Nikki," he repeated, locking his car and pocketing his key. "That's your name, isn't it? I thought that since we're not working the case today, maybe I should call you by your given name."

She actually preferred him not using her surname. He just seemed to mangle it when he said it. But he still wasn't getting her name right. "That would be Nik," she told him.

He shook his head. "'Nik' is a guy's name," he told her. "It's also something that refers to a cut or scratch, neither of which begins to describe you. 'Nikki,' on the other hand, makes a person think of someone who's cute and who knows it," he concluded, looking at her.

"So I'm cute?" she asked, not sure if he was being serious or if he was just pulling her leg.

Finn nodded. The woman owned a mirror—she could make that determination for herself. "And you know it," he told her.

Okay, now she was sure he was pulling her leg, and while she liked compliments, she didn't appreciate being played. "There is no end to the lengths you'd go to in order to get me to attend this little party of yours, is there?"

His mouth began to curve, but he forced himself to sound stern. "I cannot confirm or deny your allegation," he answered in the deep, formal voice of a witness offering testimony behind closed doors.

She was about to tell him just what he could do with his confirmation when a blue sports car heading in the opposite direction began to slow down.

"Hey, you two out for a stroll?" Cullen Cavanaugh called out, rolling down the passenger-side window so that they could hear him.

"No, we're just walking back from where we parked my car," Finn responded. He saw the confused look on Nik's face. "In case you're wondering," he told her, "this annoying person is my brother Cullen."

Taking a closer look, she could see the resemblance. Nik raised her voice as she called back to Finn's brother, "You have my condolences."

"Hey, I like her, Finn," Cullen said. "Hold that thought," he told Nik. "I'll be right back as soon as I find a space."

"Ha! Good luck with that," Finn called back to his brother.

Picking up his pace, Finn took Nik's elbow without really thinking about it. He was leading her to Andrew's house.

Nik didn't pull away. Just for today, she was going to pretend that they were friends, not just two people joining forces for a common goal.

"Older or younger?" Nik asked, referring to Finn's brother.

"Younger," he answered, "but he acts like he thinks he's the older one." Suddenly realizing that he'd taken her elbow, Finn dropped his hand to his side. "Sorry," he apologized.

"Nothing to be sorry about," she answered.

"I was just trying to get us to the chief's house before Cullen found a space and had a chance to pounce on us," Finn explained.

That sounded a little strange to her, but then, Finn would know his brother far better than she did. "Does he do that often?" she asked, then added, "Pounce?" in case he didn't understand what she was asking.

"Cullen has this unabashed enthusiasm. Sometimes it gets to be a little too much," he told her. For now he didn't add that Cullen never met a woman he didn't like.

"You're being protective," she noted.

"I guess I am. Habit," he admitted. "I didn't mean to offend," he told her, referring to having taken her elbow that way.

They had reached Andrew's door. Nik stopped before it and flashed a wide smile at him. "You didn't," she assured Finn.

Her smile, as well as the very sound of her voice, seemed to nestle down in his very core. He felt a warmth spread out. He had no time to think about it because just then Andrew and Rose's front door opened.

An incredibly tempting, warm aroma immediately wafted out, creating an aura around the welcoming, very friendly figure who emerged and now stood in the doorway.

"Ms. Kowalski, you came," Andrew said, pleased as he enveloped her hand in both of his.

"Nik, please," she corrected. "And Finn made it sound as if I would be guilty of some sort of a grievous offense if I stayed away," she told him honestly.

"Not an offense," Andrew corrected. "But I admit that it would have been a huge disappointment if you didn't come. Please, come in, come in," he urged her.

Nik crossed the threshold, followed by Finn. "Finn also promised that you would explain why having me here was so important," she told him. "Because with all these people here—" she gestured toward the living room "—I really don't see how you'd even notice that I wasn't here, although Finn swore to me that you would."

Andrew looked puzzled at the much younger man. "You didn't tell her?"

"I figured it was your story to tell," Finn said with a nonchalant shrug.

"*Someone* tell me," Nik requested with a slight urgency.

"Let's get out of everyone's way," Andrew said, leading Nik over toward his kitchen. Finn followed in their wake.

She took in a deep breath. "That smells absolutely wonderful," she told Andrew.

"Thank you," he told her. He never tired of hearing

genuine compliments. "But I didn't bring you in here because I was fishing for a compliment. Besides, if anyone deserves a compliment, it's you."

Lost, she glanced at Finn, but he wasn't about to explain what his uncle meant. Nik looked back toward the older man. "I'm afraid that I don't understand, sir."

Andrew nodded and obliged her with an explanation. "My father was in a downward spiral after the mugging," he told her.

"I didn't realize that his wounds were that serious," Nik said, looking from Finn back to Andrew.

"They weren't," Andrew said. "At least not his physical ones. However, the wounds he sustained mentally were another story. Whoever mugged my father and left him in the parking lot broke his spirit. You saw him," Andrew pointed out. "After the attack he felt as if he had suddenly become a useless, helpless old man with no reason to continue living."

"When we spoke, I told him that wasn't true," Nik told him.

Andrew nodded. "I know, and by saying that, you managed to accomplish what the rest of us couldn't. When we said that to him, he felt we *had* to say that because he was the head of our family and we loved him. But you—you were a stranger to him as far as he was concerned. You didn't need to say that to him, which made your words carry more weight than ours did."

Andrew's eyes conveyed to Nik just how deep the gratitude he felt went. "That story you told him about your uncle Walter—that *really* got to him. He started slowly coming around right after you left." Andrew smiled. "Thanks to you and what you said to him, we have that dour, cranky old man back."

"Hey, who are you calling cranky?" a deep, gravelly voice behind Nik said.

When she turned around, Nik saw that Seamus Cavanaugh had come into the kitchen to join them. Just like his son's did, Seamus's eyes crinkled as he looked at Nik.

"Well, if the shoe fits, Dad—" Andrew began.

"I can kick your behind with it," Seamus told his oldest son. And then he turned to look at the young woman he credited for his renewed lease on life. "See what I have to put up with?" he asked Nik. "If I don't crack the whip around these kids, they give me no respect." And then Seamus surprised Nik, as well as Andrew and Finn, because he put his arms around her and hugged her hard. "I hope you don't mind indulging an old man by allowing him to give you a hug."

"What old man?" Nik scoffed, her voice all but muffled against the man's barrel chest. "I don't see an old man around here," she said. "All I see are three very vibrant men. Or at least two," she amended, glancing toward Finn as if she was having second thoughts about including him in the initial group.

Seamus chuckled as he released Nik. "She's a spitfire, this one is, Finley," he said to Finn.

"Well, she is something, I'll give you that," Finn agreed. "Although what that is I can't say I'm exactly sure."

Seamus looked at her wistfully. "Ah, if I was just thirty years younger," he lamented.

Andrew cleared his throat. "How many years did you say, Dad?"

The subject of age was still a sore topic for the older Cavanaugh. "All right, maybe forty. But like the lady said, I've got a young heart," Seamus told Andrew, winking at Nik.

"You three going to stay huddled in here all night, keeping poor Nik here practically a prisoner?" Rose asked, walking in on her husband, her father-in-law and Finn. "C'mon, girl, time to make your escape now before these two succeed in talking your ears off," she said to Nik, nodding toward her husband and father-in-law. She put her hand out to pull Nik away.

"Her ears are safe, Rose," Seamus assured his daughter-in-law. "I wouldn't do anything to harm so much as a hair on that pretty girl's head. I owe her," the senior Cavanaugh said, his eyes meeting Nik's. "Why don't you and Finn go out there and talk to people your own age while Andrew and I here reminisce about what that was like."

Rose laughed at her father-in-law's choice of words. "What's to reminisce about? You're younger than any of us, Seamus."

Her father-in-law chuckled in response. "I am, aren't I?"

Finn then took his opportunity to finally lead Nik out into the living room.

"You really did bring Seamus back, you know," he told Nik once they were clear of the kitchen. "I know for a fact that the chief was really worried about him. He was afraid that his father was never going to be able to come around and shake himself free of his depression. Whatever you said to Seamus that day I brought you over, it wound up snapping him out of that really black funk.

"Not just that," he continued, "but I think his memory's coming back, too. I'm going to wait a little longer before I try to question him, but with any luck," he said, "he might be able to actually tell us what happened before he was knocked out—and give us a description of the guy who did this to him and stole his car."

Finn brought her over to one of the tables that Andrew

had set up in the living room, and there were more on the patio. Each was laden with appetizers and different sorts of snacks.

"Thanks to you, we might actually be able to pull together all those elusive threads and make some sort of sense out of all this—or as much sense as something like this can make," Finn amended. He wasn't one to allow himself to get carried away until after everything finally fell into place.

"Well, whatever effect this finally has on the case we're working, I am *really* glad I could help bring the chief's father around. Your—" she paused a moment to get the wording just right "—grand-uncle is a really sweet man."

"You know, I don't think I've *ever* heard Dad referred to as 'sweet,'" Brian Cavanaugh said, coming up just in time to hear the last thing that Nik had just said. "I guess it takes an outsider to see those 'hidden qualities' about him," he said with an appreciative laugh.

"Not just any old outsider," Skylar Cavanaugh said, joining the small group. "But a very special one. Hi, I'm Skylar and from what I've heard, Uncle Andrew and Aunt Rose are ready to nominate you for sainthood."

"I really didn't do anything," Nik protested. "I just told Seamus about my great-uncle."

"Well, whatever you did," Sean said, overhearing her protest, "it certainly helped. Let me give you a little tip here," he said, coming up to her side. "Take the compliment and say thank you. We're not known for giving empty praise, trust me," he told her. "And, on behalf of this motley crew—" he nodded at the people in the immediate area "—thank you. Now, go mingle and eat. Food goes fast here. They might not look it, but it's like having a convention of shrews—not because of their temperaments but because they could all probably eat their own weight in food. Andrew's food is really excellent—the man doesn't know how to make anything that doesn't taste wonderful—and it also doesn't last long with this crowd," Sean told her.

"Hey," another member of the group called out. His face looked vaguely familiar to her, but she didn't immediately recognize him as he joined them. She looked toward Finn quizzically.

"That's Duffy," he whispered in her ear. "He's in Homicide."

She pressed her lips together. So many different names were floating around in her brain. She was afraid of making a mistake and calling someone by the wrong name. She assumed that they would take it in stride, but you just never knew.

"You know, you people should really all have name tags," she told Finn. "So we outsiders wouldn't feel so lost."

"We're seriously thinking about it," Finn answered. "Of course, being able to identify us *without* name tags points out just how keenly developed your sense of observation really is."

Nik laughed. "As long as there's no test at the end of the evening."

"Oh, didn't I tell you?" he asked innocently. "You have to pass a test before you're allowed to leave the premises and go home."

Nik slanted a look at him. He was kidding, she thought. Or at least she hoped he was.

Chapter 20

"You know, for someone who was really dragging her feet about coming to the chief's gathering, I've got to say I was surprised. You practically closed the place down," Finn said late that evening when he finally brought Nik to her door. "Another fifty-three minutes and it would have officially been tomorrow." He didn't bother hiding the smile on his lips, which underscored how pleased with himself he was for convincing her to come.

Nik fished her key out of her purse. She saw no reason to deny what was so obvious to both of them. "I had a very good time."

"No, really?" Finn asked, looking at her with widened eyes as he put his hand to his chest. "I couldn't tell," he said, deadpan.

"Very funny," Nik countered. "And you were right," she said, giving him his due. "I found them all to be very nice, warm people." Cocking her head, she peered up at his face. "Are you sure that you're related to them?"

"Why?" he asked, feigning surprise. "You don't think I'm a nice, warm person?"

Unlocking her door, Nik turned toward him. "I think that you're a sharp detective," she told Finn, keeping a straight face.

"That's not what I asked," he pointed out.

Turning the doorknob, she pushed the door open. This was fun, she thought. Moreover, she realized that she was really reluctant to see the evening end, even though it was getting really late.

"No," she agreed, "but it's what I answered." She paused for a second, then decided to dive right in before she lost her nerve. "Would you like to come in for a nightcap?" Nik stepped inside her apartment and waited for him to respond.

He didn't even have to think about it. He'd found himself growing more and more attracted to her over the course of the day and the idea of prolonging this situation even a little longer appealed to him.

"All right," he said, coming inside, "but in my case, I think we should make it coffee. I still have to drive home. I find that the trip is best made sober."

Nik looked at him in surprise. She'd been with him or near him for most of the whole day. She hadn't seen Finn overindulging—except when it came to Andrew's chicken. "You didn't have that much to drink."

"No," he admitted, "and I'd like to keep it that way. Worst-case scenario is being just a drop over the legal limit and then winding up being pulled over because I swerved to avoid a dog running out into the street." He saw the skeptical look on her face. "It's been known to happen," he assured Nik. "The dog," he clarified, "not the rest of it."

She didn't feel that his protest carried any weight.

"You're a Cavanaugh," she said, walking into the kitchen. "They'd cut you some slack."

"No, they wouldn't," he contradicted, "*because* I'm a Cavanaugh. We're the ones who are supposed to set an example."

She measured out the proper amount of coffee to make Finn a really strong cup. "Wow, you know, I never really thought about what it had to be like on your end."

Watching Nik move around in her kitchen, he smiled as he made himself comfortable on her sofa. She was still wearing that dress she'd had on at the party. He took a longer look at her dress, and noticed how the fabric clung to her body as she moved. In the background, the coffee maker was making percolating sounds as it brewed his coffee.

"Yup. There is no coloring outside the lines for a Cavanaugh," he told her.

The moment the coffee maker had finished, she poured the end result into a mug and brought it over to him. Having watched him get coffee for the last week, she knew the way he liked it.

"You will forgive me if I don't shed any tears," she said, sitting down beside him on the sofa.

"I'll let you slide," he told her with a laugh. He took a long, healthy swallow from the mug, then looked at Nik and asked, "So, what did you think? Now that you got to meet everyone outside of their usual work environment, what's your opinion?"

"That's easy," she told him. "I think you're very, very lucky to have a family like that. Most people aren't so lucky," she confided.

"I know, but there were times when I really didn't think so—even before Uncle Andrew came along and 'discovered' my side of the family and brought us all together." He took another long swallow, remembering parts of his adolescence. "When you're growing up, you don't exactly crave rules and regulations, or having to toe a line."

"Oh, I don't know." She watched him finish up his coffee and caught herself wondering if the liquid had made his lips warm. "Deep down, I think that kids do crave those regulations. Regulations make you feel as if there's structure to your life, not to mention that rules make you feel as if you're protected."

Finn was certain that he heard something in her voice. He set down the empty mug on the coffee table. "You didn't feel like you were protected growing up?" he asked.

She realized what Finn had to be thinking. "Don't get me wrong. My dad was always a great dad and he went out of his way to make sure that my sister and I had everything we needed or wanted, but…" Her voice trailed off.

"But?" he repeated, waiting for her to finish her thought.

Putting her long-ago fears into words almost made them sound silly now. But he was waiting, so she finished what she'd started to say. "But sometimes I worried about what would happen if my father wasn't there."

She half expected him to laugh at her. But he didn't and she found herself being grateful. "You mean if he died?" Finn ventured. "Was your father sick?"

She shook her head. "No. I used to worry about what would happen if he suddenly decided to take off the way my mother had." If nothing else, Finn would probably think that she was being unduly paranoid.

"Did he ever give you any cause to think that way?" Finn asked.

She should have never opened her mouth and had no one to blame for this but herself.

"No, he made me feel very loved," she admitted. Embarrassed, she looked at the empty mug on the table, avoiding Finn's eyes. "How did we suddenly get so serious?" she asked, shrugging off the moment. She hadn't thought about having her father leave her in *years*. "Must be the smell of your coffee," she said. "That's what did it. It's really strong and it got to me."

"Right," Finn said, agreeing with her, or pretending to. She could tell he wasn't being serious, even though he said, "That's got to be it."

Nik looked at him skeptically. "You're being just too agreeable," she told Finn. "So stop it. That's not like you."

He looked at her innocently. "I could snap at you if you like."

"There you are, being agreeable again." And then she laughed, the serious moment evaporating just like that. "You must think I'm crazy."

"I don't." His eyes swept over her. She was sitting very close to him and he could feel himself reacting to her. But this time, there was no one around who could help him camouflage it. Heaven help him, he could swear that the perfume she was wearing was filling all his senses. "That's not exactly the thought that occurs to me when I look at you."

She raised her chin. "All right," she said, bracing herself. "Just what *does* occur to you when you look at me?"

His voice was low, seductive and arousing as he answered her. "That you're a smart, beautiful woman who's incredibly loyal. You have a way of tapping into people's thoughts and minds. You certainly got to my grand-uncle when no one else in the family could."

Each word he uttered felt as if he was making verbal love to her. Nik had to remember to breathe.

"Funny," she finally said, "I wouldn't have guessed that from the way we talked to one another."

"I guess I'm really good at keeping my thoughts hidden," he told her, his words all but undulating along her skin.

He was sitting so close to her that when he exhaled, his very breath seemed to caress her. Though she was trying to steel herself off, she could feel herself tingling all over in response. Could feel herself *willing* him to move in even closer and take this—whatever *this* was—to the next level.

As if sensing her thoughts, Finn gently cupped her face with his hand and then, almost as if moving in slow motion, he brought his mouth down to hers.

When his lips touched hers, Nik could have sworn that she had instantly felt an explosion going off inside of her.

Or maybe not an explosion, but fireworks, she amended. The kind of fireworks that went off lighting up the sky on the Fourth of July.

In less than a blink of an eye, Nik found herself erasing the tiny distance that still remained between them. Her eyes on his, she laced her arms around his neck, and gave herself permission to get completely lost in the sensation that all but swallowed her up.

She could feel her heart racing, as if it was radiating and smiling in warm anticipation.

And then, as he kissed her again and again, Nik felt his mouth curving against hers. Was he smiling—or laughing at her? She really couldn't tell.

Drawing her head back to look at him, she searched his face. "What?"

"Your coffee's definitely got a big kick to it," he told her.

"Too strong?" she asked, thinking that perhaps she had misread the signs and wound up coming on too strong.

"No," he whispered, the sound of his voice seducing her. "Just right," he assured her, lowering his head once more and kissing her again.

This time, when the fireworks began exploding in her veins—and they did, instantaneously—she just went with them. She couldn't hold back but reveled in the way he made her feel.

Deep down, she knew that she should listen to the little voice in her head that was telling her to back away—but she didn't want to. Yes, there was a line that needed to be drawn between them, a line in the sand that they each had to stand behind, but right now, she had absolutely no desire even to acknowledge that such a line existed.

Nik kissed him harder.

This was truly a first for him. Finn felt overwhelmed. When he had leaned in to kiss her, he admittedly had wanted to recapture, just for a moment, that sensation he had felt the last time he had kissed Nik.

He wasn't prepared to be knocked over like this.

And he definitely wasn't expecting to have ravenous desire exploding in his veins like this. He felt more alive than he had ever felt before.

His breath caught in his throat, feeding on what was going on between them. He kissed her again.

And again.

Each time he did, he felt even more intoxicated than he had just a moment before. She was making him feel drunk and he hadn't indulged in a single drop of alcohol, not in hours.

He threaded his fingers through her hair, holding her to him. "If they ever found a way to bottle you, that person would definitely become a millionaire a thousand times over," he breathed against her lips.

Her head was spinning so hard, she was losing her grip on everything except for what has happening right here, right now. Nik knew she was completely losing control. Rather than be afraid, she reveled in the wild, heady feeling.

All up and down along her arms, she could feel goose bumps forming, even as her flesh heated in response to his kisses.

Her breath continued to grow shorter and shorter, her pulse heightening as he slid his fingertips along her curves, feeding her ravenous desire.

Her breathing was raspy.

When he kissed Nik's throat, Finn felt her pulse throbbing beneath his lips. That only increased his own desire to almost unmanageable proportions. He struggled to rein himself in. He didn't want to go too fast, didn't want to make her feel that if she wanted to, she couldn't put a stop to what was happening at any given moment—even though he fervently prayed that she wouldn't want to.

Her heart was slamming against her ribs. The eagerness that was possessing her was growing to outrageous proportions.

Every movement he made with his hands, with his lips, all just fanned the flames of desire that were all but burning up her very insides.

Unable to hold back any longer, Nik pulled at the buttons on his shirt, working them free of the holes that were holding them in place. The second the last button had been freed, she was pushing Finn's shirt off his shoulders. Her fingers moved possessively along his naked flesh.

And then her lips replaced her fingers, working a hot network of heated kisses along his bare skin.

Nik had opened the floodgates. Finn followed suit, making love to every part of her body slowly, tenderly, working hard to hold himself in check as much as humanly possible.

But it wasn't easy.

When she pressed her body against him, Finn worshipped her with his lips and tongue, anointing every part of her even as he drank her in like a man who had been lost in the desert counting the seconds as he waited for that very first drop of rain.

She felt his hands on her, felt her own clothes disappearing from her body. Each time Finn touched her, she moaned, twisting hard to absorb the feel of his hands on her body. A fire had been lit in the very core of her. Breathing hard, dragging air in, she reached for him, eager to return the favor.

Neither one of them remembered how they found their way to the carpeted floor, but when they did, they took advantage of the position. They feasted on their freshly nude bodies, making love to every part and creating a desire that refused to be contained.

And then they were finally positioned for the final act of lovemaking.

Nik felt she could barely control herself. Fire was licking at her limbs as she arched her back, moving urgently beneath him. Desperate to receive him yet wanting to sustain this wild, wonderful feeling just an instant longer.

Balancing his weight on his elbows, Finn looked down into her face and caught himself thinking he had never seen anything quite so beautiful as the expression he now saw on her face.

Again his breath caught in his throat, this time as he positioned himself over her body and then slowly, increment by tiny increment, lowered himself until they became one joined unit.

The second they were united, he began to move. Slowly and then increasingly faster, as if there was some sort of race they needed to conquer, some sort of finish line they needed to cross.

When the explosion finally came and enveloped them in its euphoric cloud, she had to bite her lower lip to keep from crying out.

The ecstasy was overwhelming.

She could feel it flowering all through her, filling up every inch and hovering inside of her until finally, it floated away, leaving them both spent and trying to catch their breaths.

Eventually the sound of heavy breathing leveled off and she felt his body sink down against hers before he moved over to the side, giving her a little breathing space.

"Wow," he whispered against her hair.

He tried to pull air into his lungs and it took him almost a full minute before he was able to successfully do that.

"Is this the way all the parties at the chief's house end?" she asked.

He raised himself up on his elbow to see if she was being serious. The glint in her eyes gave her away. He smiled.

"As a matter of fact, they don't," he answered, "but this definitely earned my seal of approval."

"Really," she said, the corners of her mouth curving in a satisfied smile.

His eyes crinkled in the corners. "Really," he answered.

"Well," she replied, beginning to weave a small network of kisses along his neck and jawline, "then maybe we can do it again."

"When?" he asked, feeling his blood beginning to accelerate and rush, full force, through his veins all over again.

"Now," she breathed.

And then there was no more space for any words. They were far too busy undertaking an encore performance to say anything more.

Chapter 21

The scent of fresh, strong coffee brewing wafted in from the kitchen and wrapped itself around him. As the aroma slowly penetrated his brain, it gradually nudged Finn into a state of consciousness. As a rule, he wasn't a morning person, but the nature of his work had made him become one.

Finally awake, Finn focused on his surroundings. That was when he realized that he had never gotten around to going home. After that final time that he and Nik had made love, he'd been just too exhausted to move. So he had slipped his arm around her, held Nik to him, and silently promised himself that he would get up and leave. He just wanted to rest for five minutes.

When that had passed, he gave himself another five minutes. And then five more after that until eventually, he ran out of minutes and just drifted off to sleep, still holding Nik.

The ultimate result of his nocturnal activity was that he wound up sleeping far more soundly than he had in years.

But now he was awake with questions forming in his

brain at what felt like the speed of light. He threw on his clothes and followed the scent of coffee back to its origin. The kitchen.

He saw that Nik was awake and already dressed, wearing jeans and a blue pullover sweater that had managed to lose its shape somewhere along the way. Her feet were bare. She was petite. He hadn't realized that Nik was as short as she was.

Why that made him smile made no sense to him, but it did.

"Why didn't you wake me?" he asked, walking into the kitchen.

She hadn't heard him entering and he'd caught her by surprise as she swung around to look at him. "You looked so peaceful, I didn't want to disturb you." She thought of all the work they had put in. "It's been a rough week."

"The last twenty-four hours weren't too bad," he told her with a wicked grin.

Getting their cups ready, she looked at Finn over her shoulder. "No, they definitely weren't that," Nik agreed.

Coming up directly behind her, he wrapped his arms around Nik. He breathed in the coffee as well as her scent. It was hard to say which he craved more. He decided the coffee came in second.

"So," he began, continuing to hold her, "how's the rest of your Sunday shaping up?"

Nik turned around in the circle of his arms, smiling up into his eyes. "What did you have in mind?" she asked him. She had no sooner asked her question than his phone rang, vibrating in his back pocket. She suppressed a sigh. "Hopefully your plans don't include answering your phone," she told him.

"Maybe it's a wrong number," Finn said.

She laughed softly. "What are the odds?" she countered as he took it out. One look at his face as he glanced down at the screen answered her question for her. "My guess is that it's nil."

"This is kind of early for you, isn't it?" he said to the person on the other end of the call. "Uh-huh. Uh-huh," he said, listening. After another beat, he said, "Thanks for letting me know."

Ending the call, he slipped his phone back into his pocket. He could see that Nik was all but jumping out of her skin, waiting for him to explain. Rather than play out the moment, he filled her in. "That was my cousin-in-law. She's on duty today at the morgue."

She wasn't sure what he was telling her. "Are you bragging or looking for some sympathy for her?"

Rather than banter, he gave her a direct answer. "She just finished up doing all those extensive tox screens on the victims," he told her.

Nik could feel her pulse jump. This was it, she thought, instantly becoming serious. "And?" she asked. "What did she find?"

"Just what we suspected," he told her. "All the victims had at least traces of Rohypnol in their blood, if not more."

"Well, that would explain why none of the victims fought back. They weren't able to," she said angrily. There was fire in her eyes as she looked up at Finn. "We've got to catch that worthless scum," she cried with feeling.

"We will," he promised. He glanced over toward her kitchen. "How about I make us some breakfast and then we'll go to the squad room to work these cases from the beginning? Maybe we can figure out who the killer is. It's Sunday so it should be quieter—"

"Hold it, back up," Nik said, holding up her hand like a traffic cop to get him to stop.

"Look, if you don't want to go in," Finn told her, "I under—"

Shaking her head, Nik interrupted him. "That's not why I'm telling you to stop. Did I hear you right?" she asked. "Did you just offer to make breakfast?"

He didn't understand what the big deal was. Why did she look so surprised at his offer? "Yes, so?"

She was still having trouble wrapping her mind around this. "You *cook*?"

He looked at her. Why was she having such a problem with this? "I just offered to make breakfast so I would have thought that was self-evident. Yes, I cook. I'm a Cavanaugh," he told her. "Like law enforcement, it's in our blood." Maybe she was expecting something outstanding, he realized. He was quick to set her straight. "I don't do anything overly fancy, but it's enough to keep me alive. Why?" he asked, looking at her expression suspiciously.

"I'm just surprised, that's all," she confessed. "Most men I know have trouble with the concept of boiling water and which way to turn the little dials on the stovetop."

Just then, his cell rang again, interrupting her.

Nik looked at the offending gadget, bemused. "Did your cousin-in-law forget to tell you something?" she asked as Finn pulled out his phone again.

"Cavanaugh," he announced, answering his cell. The look on his face quickly turned grim. "Got it. I'll be there."

"Be where?" Nik asked, her heart sinking as he ended the call.

"Looks like breakfast is going to have to be to-go," he told her. "Another body just turned up. This victim was found in an alley just two blocks away from a popular night spot called Good Times." His expression became even grimmer as he added, "Suffice to say that our victim didn't have one."

"Same as the others?" she asked, although she felt she already knew the answer to that.

He nodded, confirming her suspicions. "Sounds like it." He watched as Nik went to her refrigerator and took two packaged items out of her freezer. Removing them from their packaging, she popped both items into her microwave and pressed the appropriate buttons. "What's that?" he asked.

"That," she told him as she poured coffee into two thermal mugs and twisted on their lids, "is my answer to breakfast on the run." The microwave bell dinged. "It's not half-bad," she assured him.

"Not half-bad," Finn echoed, shaking his head. "Now, that's a ringing endorsement if I ever heard one," he said, amused.

Nik shrugged. "Sorry, best I can do on short notice," she told him, wrapping up the heated breakfast servings and tossing each one into a paper bag.

Well, at least it smelled appetizing, he thought. "Your 'best' is definitely good enough for me," he told her.

Finn grabbed his coffee container and followed her out the door.

Bemused, Nik gave him an uncertain look as she locked up her apartment.

"You know, you're like a whole different person today. Did you have some kind of an epiphany yesterday?" she asked.

His grin immediately burrowed straight down into her bones.

"As a matter of fact, I did," he told her. Switching subjects, he said as he got into his car, "And if they ask, I called you when I got this message and swung by to pick you up."

In her opinion, he was being unusually deceptive.

After all, it wasn't as if they were coworkers. "Okay, but why? Don't want anyone to know we spent the night together?" she asked, getting in on her side. She deposited her packed provisions on the floor.

"I figured that you wouldn't want anyone to know," he told her, then added, "I was just looking out for your reputation."

"I can look out for my own reputation, thank you," she told him. And then, feeling like that sounded a little too defensive, she softened. "But that was a nice thought on your part."

"Hey," he said with a good-natured shrug, "I'm a nice guy."

"Yes," she agreed, turning toward him and smiling, "you are."

Harley, who had called him about this latest murder, and Ramirez were already on the scene when he and Nik arrived.

Finn lost no time in getting out of the car and crossing over to his men, who were still standing over the victim.

"What can you tell us about this one?" Finn asked Harley.

Nik was right behind him. Pity filled her as she looked down at the dead woman. Pity and anger. Like the others, the victim had been stabbed through the heart. How could anyone *do* this to another human being?

"Just that she seems to fit our killer's 'type,'" Harley answered. "Dressed up, young, pretty and—" he hesitated before adding the final identifying piece "—stabbed through the heart." And then he pointed out something different. "Her clothes are all rumpled."

Finn nodded as he noticed. "Like she was dressed in a hurry."

"Or redressed," Nik pointed out.

Ramirez picked up on her tone. "You think someone interrupted him?" he asked, looking from Nik to Finn.

"Either that or he's getting sloppy." Squatting down, Finn looked more closely at the young woman's face. "She looks as if she was just killed."

"Good call," the medical examiner said, coming up to join them. Finishing a notation, he handed his notebook over to his assistant. "According to the liver temperature I just took, this one has been dead between four to six hours."

Nik glanced at her watch and then looked at the dead woman on the ground. Finn had a feeling he knew what she was thinking. That they had been making love around that time. He refused to allow his mind to go there. Last night had been special and that was the only way he was going to look at it.

"Did she have any ID on her?" Finn asked, looking at the two members of the team who had gotten there ahead of them.

Ramirez shook his head. "None. Just like the others," he added. But there was something and he pointed it out to the head detective. "There's a stamp on her hand. It's faint, but if you shine this light on it, you can just about make it out."

Demonstrating, he aimed the small flashlight he was holding on the dead blonde's hand. The outline of a club logo became visible.

"You're right," Nik cried, crouching down to get a better look. "She was at Good Times."

Finn looked toward Ramirez. The latter nodded, answering the unspoken question. "Already got a call in to the owner," he told Finn. "He should be coming in at any minute. One piece of good news," Ramirez volunteered. "The club was robbed eight months ago."

Mystified, Nik shook her head. "Just how is that good news?" she asked.

"Because after that happened, the owner put up a couple of surveillance cameras *inside* his club as well as out front and in the back," Ramirez told them. "We get to see the customers up close and personal for once."

"Maybe this time we'll catch a break," Finn said.

"It'll be about time," Harley said, adding his voice to that of the others as he crossed his fingers and held them up.

Jacob Hollander was a self-made man who made it clear that he did not take kindly to anyone trying to undo what he had managed to do. He arrived looking disgruntled, but once the situation was made clear to him, he seemed more than happy to cooperate with the police and get the killer off the streets.

Inside the club, he answered all their questions, then added, "I'll do whatever you want to help you catch this guy. I can't afford having people stay away because they're afraid that they—or their dates—are going to be that guy's next victim." He looked at the detectives hopefully. "Is there any way this can be hushed up?"

"These things are never hushed up," Finn told him in his no-nonsense voice. "But your cooperation will hopefully go a long way in getting this killer off the streets. I hear you have surveillance cameras—"

"I sure do," the owner said, interrupting him.

Finn nodded. "We're going to need to see those videos and we're also going to need to go over all of your credit-card receipts from the last twenty-four hours."

"There are a *lot* of receipts," Hollander warned. He smiled. "Business has been really good lately."

"And, with any luck," Finn said, "we'd like to keep it that way."

"Amen to that," the club owner said with feeling. "Let me just go get those for you," the man said, beginning to retreat to his office.

"Harley," Finn said to the detective closest to him as he pointed toward the owner, "go help him bring those receipts and videos here."

Nik waited until after Harley had left with the club owner. "You don't trust him, do you?" she asked.

"Right now, I'm not sure I trust anybody," he answered, then amended with a smile, "Present company excepted, of course."

"Of course," she echoed. "But why don't you trust the club owner?"

Finn shrugged. "I get the feeling that he might be trying to shield someone. He just seemed a little too eager to help, that's all."

She granted that the man did seem eager, but there could be another reason for that. "He might be on the level. You know that it's in his best interest to help catch this guy."

"I'm not denying that," Finn said. "I'm just being skeptical. It's in my nature."

And it was a very confusing nature that he had, she thought. "You, Finley Cavanaugh, are a very complex man," she told him.

He flashed her a small smile. "Never said I wasn't," he reminded her.

"That you didn't," she agreed, nodding.

Harley came back, followed by the owner. Both men were carrying large boxes that were overflowing with receipts as well as surveillance videos.

"Like I said," Hollander told Finn, "Saturday night is one of my busiest nights. Maybe even my busiest, although it's neck and neck with Friday night."

Finn took the box from the owner. "We'll find a way to manage," he said.

Hollander nodded. "I'm going to need a receipt for all of this," he told Finn before the latter could take another step toward the front door with the box.

"Sure thing," Finn said, temporarily setting down the box he had been holding. "Harley, take that box and put it into my car." He turned toward the club owner. "You have a release form on you?" he asked. He half expected the owner to stutter and say that he didn't. Instead, Hollander took out two sheets of paper and placed them in front of Finn.

"There you go," the owner said. "This is for the first box, this is for the second."

Finn signed his name to each sheet, quickly glancing at them before he signed. When he finished signing his name to the second paper, he handed both over to the owner. He eyed the man knowingly.

"Something tells me you've been through this before," Finn told him.

"Not me. A cousin of mine was, though. He wound up losing his property. Taught me to be extra careful with what I handed over to anyone. When can I have the receipts and videos back?" he asked.

"You'll get them as soon as we're finished with them, Mr. Hollander," Finn told him crisply. He glanced at Nik. "Ready to go?"

"You have no idea how ready I am," she told him. There was something about the owner that made her feel uncomfortable, although she couldn't put her finger on exactly why.

Maybe she just needed distance from the man to figure out the reason.

Chapter 22

"You know, I am strongly considering billing the Aurora Police Department for a pair of glasses because I'm definitely going to need them," Nik told Finn almost twelve hours later. She looked away from the viewing screen and blinked several times, trying to get her eyes back into focus. "I think that I'm beginning to see double."

"Nobody's twisting your arm to do this," Finn reminded her. He had been doing his own viewing just as long today. "You volunteered."

She sighed, knowing that she had been the one to offer to help. Finn was right, but that wasn't the point, she thought.

"The least you could do is be sympathetic," she said.

"I am being sympathetic," he told her. "I'm telling you that you don't have to keep doing this if you don't want to."

Nik frowned. "You know I'm not about to stop."

He raised one inquisitive eyebrow as he spared her a look. "Doing it, or complaining about it?"

"Very funny," she murmured as she went back to flipping through the various camera videos. All the people's faces were beginning to meld together.

"Hey, maybe you guys would rather be looking through this pile of credit-card receipts," Ramirez said, raising his voice so that Finn and Nik could hear him from where he and Harley sat.

"Hey, in case you haven't noticed, I'm not the one complaining," Finn pointed out.

Harley grumbled under his breath as he continued plowing through his share of the credit-card receipts. "I thought this was supposed to be a paperless society," he complained.

"That's the rumor," Finn told the other detective as he watched another set of surveillance videos whirl by in fast-forward mode.

"So *why* am I wading through a ton of paper?" Harley asked.

Nik looked up at the three detectives. "Rumor has it that rumors aren't always true," she quipped.

"Was that a joke?" Ramirez asked, his dark eyes looking at Finn, then over toward Nik. "Did your volunteer over there just make a joke?"

Finn kept a straight face as he glanced toward Nik. "Did you, Kowalski?"

"Maybe," she responded with a shrug. "At this point I'm too tired and punchy to know." She leaned back in her chair, stretching. Even her eyelids hurt. "Why don't we take a break and send out for dinner?" she suggested, watching Finn hopefully.

"Sounds good to me," Finn said. "Since this is your idea, what's your preference?" he asked Nik.

Nik suddenly sat up. "Hold it!" she cried, her eyes widening.

Finn exchanged looks with the other two men in the room. "I haven't picked up the phone yet," he told Nik.

"No, not the phone," she insisted, still not taking her eyes off the screen in front of her. "Look!" She jabbed her finger at one of the frozen images on the monitor.

Getting up, Finn walked around her desk and stood behind her. The images appeared fuzzy to him. "Okay, what am I looking at?" he asked, keeping his expectations low.

They had all been at this for hours now without any viable results. So far, the searches had been no different from all the other ones they had conducted involving the mysterious killer.

"Don't you see it?" she demanded. "That's her," Nik cried.

"Who? The victim?" Finn asked, leaning in for a closer look at the monitor. Out of the corner of his eye, he saw both Harley and Ramirez stop what they were doing. They were waiting for some sort of a response from Nik. They were all looking for a breakthrough in this frustrating case.

"No, it's Marilyn," Nik told Finn. She looked at him over her shoulder. "My friend's daughter. The woman I was looking for when I first met you," she clarified in case he wasn't following her.

"I remember who Marilyn is," he said. He squinted, looking more closely at the frozen images, trying to make out their features. "Rewind that," he told her.

The images came to life. Marilyn was dancing with

someone, or at least she was doing something that he thought *passed* for dancing.

"Again," Finn told her. He leaned in ever closer, staring hard at the images. "Is that—?"

Nik anticipated his question and nodded. "I think she's dancing with that doctor," she said. She paused before saying his name. "Dr. Garrett."

Finn didn't want to get ahead of himself. They were beyond tired at this point.

"Well, there really is no law against that," Finn said, moving back to his desk again.

But Nik hardly heard him. Something else had caught her attention. Or rather, some*one* else. This time, she rewound the video before she said anything. And then she rewound it again.

The repetitious sound caught Finn's attention, as did the expression on her face when he looked up at her. Without a word he got up again and came up behind her.

"What did you find?" he asked.

She raised her eyes to his. "I think I just found our latest vic," she told him, her voice trembling.

"You did what?" Ramirez asked, stunned.

He pushed his chair back so hard, it nearly fell over. He hardly noticed as he came over to take a look at Nik's screen. Harley was quick to join Ramirez, as well as Finn, who was still standing there. All three detectives hovered over Nik, jockeying for position to get a closer look at the video Nik had found.

"You sure that's the doctor with Marilyn?" Finn asked her. No matter how he concentrated, the image on the monitor was really difficult to make out.

Rather than say anything, Nik took out her cell phone. She flipped through the photographs she had stored on it until she found the one she was looking for. Once she did, she held up her phone for Finn and the other detectives to look at.

"This is Dr. James Garrett," she announced. "I found his photograph on his hospital's website, along with a lot of glowing words. Seems that Dr. Garrett has quite the following." She looked at Finn. "Apparently a lot of his patients are crazy about him."

Finn appeared dubious about the testimonials, but that still didn't mean the man was guilty of anything other than being a very handsome man. "Even if he hoodwinked all those patients, that still doesn't qualify as a crime."

"No," she agreed, putting away her phone, "but being with Marilyn *and* our latest victim is definitely a reason to really start looking for the man, if only to question him more closely. It's just too much of a coincidence that he's Marilyn's doctor as well as the doctor for that young woman who was killed last week." She had a feeling that the list of the doctor's patients didn't end there.

"No argument," Finn agreed. "Harley, find out the make and model of the good doctor's car—or cars." He had a feeling that the doctor was vain enough to have more than just one fast car to feed his ego. "Ramirez, get me the doctor's home address. And, if for some reason, he turns out not to have been there for a few days, I want an APB put out on this guy as soon as possible."

As the two detectives scattered to fulfill their assignments, Finn turned toward Nik.

"Good work," he told her. But rather than smile at the compliment, she seemed rather preoccupied. Something was off, he thought. "For someone who just might have tracked down a cold-blooded killer, you don't look very happy."

"Well, I am glad that Marilyn's still alive," she told

Finn. "But the fact that she was there last night with the dead girl raises a whole bunch of questions," she confessed, "and I've got this uneasy feeling that I won't like the answers."

It didn't take a genius to know what was bothering her, Finn thought. "You think she's involved with the murders in some way."

"Well, what else can I think?" Nik asked.

Because of the evening they had spent together, he saw her in a completely different light now. His heart went out to her. She really looked distressed, he thought. He actually agreed with Nik's take on it, but for her sake he tried to come up with something that she could hold on to until the verdict was in.

"Well, there's a chance she might be doing this against her will," Finn pointed out. "The killer might have threatened her."

Nik looked at him, surprised that Finn would come up with a possible alternative to what seemed like a pretty straightforward scenario. "Who are you and what have you done with Finn?" she asked him.

Finn shrugged. "Maybe I'm just giving your friend's daughter the benefit of the doubt," he told her. "It is possible," he pointed out.

"Like I said, who are you and what have you done with Finn?" she repeated, a sad smile playing on her lips. "Because that doesn't sound like you."

Finn laughed quietly in response to her take on the situation. "I'll let you know when I have an answer to that."

"I've got the doctor's address, boss," Ramirez said, coming back into the small room. "Get this," he said by way of preparing Finn for the bombshell he was about to drop on him. "Seems our suspect likes to move around a lot. According to what I found, the man doesn't stay at any one address for more than a few months or so. Once the time is up, he clears out."

Finn frowned, looking at the sheet Ramirez brought to him. "Wonder why that is," Finn said.

"Maybe he's afraid there might be evidence on the premises that could convict him so he wants to distance himself from it," Ramirez said. "Seeing the type of property it is, the landlord would be quick to have the place cleaned up and prepped for the next tenant. He wouldn't want to lose any money," the detective said with conviction.

"It was a rhetorical question, Ramirez," Finn told the other detective. He looked down at the sheet. A low whistle escaped from his lips. "This his latest address?" he asked, pointing to it.

Ramirez glanced down at what Finn was pointing to, then nodded. "Yes, provided that he hasn't moved yet," he qualified.

Harley walked in just then. "I've got the make and model of those cars you wanted—you were right, the doctor does have more than one." He came over to Finn and laid the paper down in front of him. "Did you know that your cousin's working in the computer lab today? Doesn't she ever go home?" the blond-haired detective asked, curious.

"On occasion," Finn answered, then added, "But to my knowledge, not very often." He made a mental note of the two license plate numbers as well as the types of vehicles they belonged to. "Have that APB put out on both these two cars—no telling which one he'll be driving." He turned toward Nik. "You feel up to taking a little road trip?" he asked.

"To Dr. Garrett's latest residence?" She guessed at their destination.

Finn nodded. "Who knows, we might even get lucky and find him in."

But Nik was rather skeptical as she walked with him toward the elevator.

"This is Sunday night. He might want to go to one more club before the weekend's over—the body count is clearly going up," she pointed out. "And, if you notice, he has a pattern. He goes to a high-end, fancy restaurant if he has an 'urge' for female companionship Monday through Thursday, but Friday and Saturday, he switches to a nightclub."

Finn looked at her as they got on the elevator. "So what are you saying? You think that Sunday is his day of rest?"

She wasn't sure yet. "It might be." The elevator came to a stop and they got off. "Let's give that address Ramirez found a try."

The address took them to the most expensive area in Aurora. Each of the homes had a uniqueness about them—no two structures were alike.

Finn pulled up in front of a huge building that was definitely meant to impress the beholder.

Nik hadn't even known so-called houses like this existed. "This looks like a mini-mansion," she commented, getting out of the car. "I guess being a good-looking surgeon seems to be paying off."

"Guess so," Finn agreed with no emotion. He rang the doorbell, but there was no answer. He rang it again, and then knocked on the door on the outside chance that there was someone inside. Or, if there was someone inside being held against their will, hearing that there was someone at the door might give them the courage they needed to yell out for help.

He listened, but there was no sound coming from inside the house, no indication that there was anyone on the premises at all.

"Maybe he is out clubbing," Finn said to Nik as they turned away from the front door.

They noticed that there was an older man out walking his dog. The man saw them at the same time and eyed them with unabashed curiosity.

"You two looking for that young doctor?" he asked.

"Yes," Finn responded. "Do you know where he is?" To encourage the man to give him an answer, Finn took out his ID and held it up. "I'm Detective Cavanaugh with the Aurora PD. Would you know where Dr. Garrett is tonight?"

"Henry Anderson." The little man introduced himself, shaking each of their hands. "Why, what did he do?" Henry asked, coming alive right before their eyes, curiosity all but radiating from his body.

Finn held back the reason for their search. "We're just looking to ask the doctor a few questions. He might have been a witness to a robbery," Finn explained, saying the first thing that came to his mind.

Anderson's high forehead furrowed. "A robbery around here?" the man asked, looking around as if he expected to see the robber suddenly pop out from behind the bushes.

Finn didn't answer him. Instead, he asked, "Would you happen to know where I could find the doctor?"

The dog walker shook his head. "Beats me. He might be at his new house," he said out of the blue.

"His new house?" Finn repeated, surprised. Then what Ramirez said was really true, he thought.

"Yeah, I saw this big moving van pull up early this morning," the man told them. "Five big, burly guys got out and moved all this stuff out of the house and into the truck in about three hours. Never saw such big men move so fast. They were going like a house afire." The man laughed at his own choice of words. "Not the right things to say around here, I guess, seeing like it always seems to be fire season these days, but you get my drift."

"The doctor moved? Seriously? Today?" Finn persisted, trying to get the man back on point and go on with his story.

"That's what I just said," Anderson told them. "It was kind of funny, if you ask me, seeing as how he was only here for about three months." The dog walker shrugged. "I guess the house just didn't suit him," the man said as if he was making some sort of a revelation. "He said he was looking for something bigger when I asked him." The little man shook his head. "He seemed kind of annoyed that I was questioning him. Oh, the doctor did smile a lot, but he wasn't all that friendly if you ask me."

"Did he happen to mention where he was moving to?" Nik asked the gossipy man.

But the dog walker shook his head. "Like I said, I asked, but he didn't tell me. Like it was some kind of a secret. All he did say was that the new house cost more, but the view was better."

The man pursed his lips, as if the answer didn't sit well with him.

He gestured around the area. "If you ask me, this view is really magnificent. But I guess there's just no pleasing some people," he sniffed. "The doctor struck me as that kind of a guy, never really satisfied." His dog, a rather heavyset Pomeranian, was tugging harder on its leash, trying to get his owner to go. "All right, all right, Delilah," he said with a laugh. "My dog doesn't like me socializing. She seems to feel it takes attention away from her. Or at least that's what her therapist says."

Not that much surprised Nik these days, but she had to admit that certainly did. "Your dog has a therapist?" Nik asked, staring at the animal.

"Yes." The owner lowered his voice. "I know I'm indulging her but she seemed so unhappy. She's more adjusted now that she's been seeing Dr. Weston three times a week. Worth every penny, too," he declared happily. "Hey, if you find Dr. Garrett, tell him Delilah says hi." He smiled down at the dog. "She had an affinity for him. So did all those women he brought home. But if you ask me, the man had no sticking power. Never saw the same woman twice."

"You saw him bringing home women?" Finn asked.

"Delilah requires a lot of walks," Anderson said a little defensively.

"Would you mind giving me your number?" Finn asked the man. "I might need to speak to you again."

The pleased look on Henry Anderson's round face told them that he was only too willing to oblige.

Chapter 23

Finn waited in the squad room for some sort of notification that at least one of the doctor's very expensive cars had been sighted. He waited until after 9:00 p.m., but the APBs that had been placed on both vehicles yielded no response. Frustrated, Finn decided to call it a night. He left the orders in place and told Nik he was taking her home.

"Would you like to come in?" she asked him when he brought her to her door.

Finn hesitated taking her up on the invitation. "I'm not exactly sure I'd be very good company tonight," he told her.

Nik unlocked her door. "Let me be the judge of that," she responded. Leaving the door open wide, she walked inside and said, "I have wine, beer, coffee and a couple of diet sodas. Take your pick."

After a beat, he crossed the threshold and followed her in.

"Diet sodas?" he repeated. Finn looked at her. She had to be one of the trimmest women he knew. "Why would you need diet sodas?"

"I like the taste," she answered.

"Okay, that makes sense. I'll have a beer," he told her, closing the door behind himself.

"One beer coming up," Nik responded, going to her refrigerator. Fetching a bottle, she twisted off the cap and placed the open bottle next to a tall glass on the coffee table. "Glass or bottle, take your pick," she said, gesturing toward the items.

"I'll rough it, no need to dirty a glass," Finn said. He made himself comfortable on the sofa.

"Very thoughtful of you," Nik responded with a smile, sitting down next to him on the sofa. Leaning forward, she studied the expression on his face. He was still upset that Garrett hadn't been located. "We have one of the best police forces in the country," she reminded him. "Someone is bound to locate one of his vehicles and find him."

He agreed with part of her statement. "What I'm afraid of is that they'll locate the car—or cars—in a landfill and that for whatever reason, Garrett'll take his killing spree to another city or maybe even another state."

She knew how destructive negative thoughts could be. She'd been there herself. "You have to think positively, Finn."

"Okay," Finn agreed, tipping back the bottle for another long drag of the amber liquid, "I'm *positive* that Garrett'll take his killing spree to another city or state."

She frowned, moving in closer to him so she could examine his expression. "Are you sure you're a Cavanaugh? I hear they're very optimistic by nature. *You* are not even being remotely that."

He shifted, about to get up. The almost-empty beer

bottle was still in his hand. "Maybe I'd better leave. I'm bringing you down."

But Nik placed her hand on his chest, pushing him back into a seated position. "I've got a better idea. You stay and I'll try to bring your spirits up."

The corners of his mouth only curved slightly. "Right now, Nik, I don't really think that's doable," he warned her.

Her eyes met his, a confident smile on her lips. "I told you I'm Polish, didn't I?"

"Yeah." He laughed under his breath. "I got that from your last name."

Undaunted, she continued. "I also told you that Polish women are known for their stubbornness," Nik reminded him.

"Nik—" he began, trying to tell her that right now, she was just butting her head against a wall.

Nik wouldn't let him finish his thought. "Shh," she said, placing her fingertip against his lips and prohibiting any more words from emerging. "You're interrupting my concentration," she whispered just before she brought her lips up to his.

His mouth curved just before she kissed him. "Anyone ever tell you that you're incorrigible?"

"Oh, on the contrary, I'm very corrigible," she whispered against his lips, her breath tantalizing Finn.

He didn't wait for her to kiss him. Instead, he pulled her onto his lap and did the honors himself.

Within less than a minute, Finn was getting himself lost in the sweetness of her mouth, in the warmth that just being with her like this generated in his chest.

For the remainder of the evening, neither one of them spared a single thought about the case, or about the cold-blooded killer who seemed to revel in killing innocent young women.

They didn't think at all, they merely appreciated just how heated their blood became as each sought sanctuary within the other's arms.

For the rest of the evening, nothing else existed for each of them except for the other.

When Finn woke up the next morning, he found that Nik was still in bed beside him. Despite everything currently going on and the body count that was piling up, he couldn't help thinking that this was the way he wanted to wake up every morning: lying in bed beside a woman who had accidentally crossed his path, a woman who he found himself falling in love with.

The realization took him by surprise, startling him. He let the thought settle in…and found himself smiling. It felt right.

As Nik, still asleep, stirred against him, Finn felt almost a reluctance to get up. But he knew he had to. Not just get up, but go home as well, so he could get a change of clothes. He knew if he turned up in the same shirt and slacks he'd already worn two days in a row, it wouldn't go unnoticed, even if no one said anything.

As he began to slip out of bed, he saw Nik's eyes open. She grabbed his arm, holding him in place.

"Much as I'd like to lie here," he told her, "it's Monday and I've got to go home first to get a change of clothes before going in to the precinct. People are going to notice my turning up in the same outfit two days running."

She bolted upright, but instead of commenting on what he'd just said, Nik looked at him and cried, "The moving van."

He had no idea what she was talking about. "Come again?"

"The moving van," she repeated in a more urgent voice.

It still wasn't making any sense to him. "What about it?" he asked.

"We've got to talk to that dog walker. Anderson," she said, suddenly recalling his name. "Someone like him thrives on absorbing every detail."

Maybe he was still half-asleep, Finn thought. "And?" he asked.

She'd woken up with this thought taking shape in her mind. Nik realized she was talking too fast and slowed down. "Anderson would have noticed the logo on the moving van. If we can track it down, they'd have the address where they took the doctor's furniture," she declared.

Now he understood where this was going. "And we would find out where he moved to."

"Yes," she cried, throwing her arms around his neck and hugging him. Just as quickly, Nik released him. "Get out of bed and make that call," she said, kicking off the covers on her side of the bed.

He reached for the cell phone he'd left on the nightstand. "Anyone ever tell you you've got the makings of a general?" Finn asked with a laugh.

Nik grinned. "I believe you just did." She pointed to the phone he had in his hand. "Call. I'll make us some breakfast to-go again."

Finn laughed as he shook his head. The woman really did enjoy giving orders, he thought affectionately. He called the number that Henry Anderson had given him.

After four rings, Anderson's phone went to voice mail. Given the hour—7:00 a.m.—Finn had to admit that he wasn't all that surprised.

* * *

"He's not answering," he told Nik when he came out to the kitchen several minutes later. "Listen, I'm going to go home and get a change of clothes," he said, repeating what he'd initially told her when she woke up. "I've had these on since Saturday and I'm going to start smelling gamy."

She pretended to sniff the air around him. "Not yet, but it wouldn't hurt to change. I'll come with you," she told him. She poured coffee into the two thermal containers they'd used the day before. "We can go to the precinct from there. Maybe someone made some progress since we left."

He picked up one of the containers. "You really are optimistic, aren't you?"

She didn't say anything, but her eyes seemed to smile at him as she handed Finn the breakfast she'd wrapped up and placed in a bag for him. "Let's go."

After swinging by for what amounted to a five-minute stop at his place so he could change his clothes, Finn tried Anderson's phone again. The result was the same. It went to voice mail.

"Maybe the man's a heavy sleeper," Nik mused. "Being the neighborhood busybody must take its toll on him."

"How do you feel about going over to his house in person?" Finn asked. In addition to his phone number, Anderson had also told them where he lived. The older man had seemed eager to show the place off, but at the time they had begged off.

"Sure, why not? It'll give the older man something to talk about for the next month, not to mention telling people that the police department sought his help to apprehend a dangerous killer," she said.

Finn laughed. "You're probably right."

She thought of the look on Anderson's face. "I know I am."

Henry Anderson did not look like a happy man when he responded to the knock on his door. They could hear him muttering as he approached, not to mention hearing his dog barking up a storm the moment they knocked.

"I'm going to call the police!" Anderson threatened as they heard him flipping open not one but two locks on his door.

Finn raised his voice. "I am the police," he said authoritatively just as Anderson pulled open the front door.

The annoyed look on the man's florid face instantly vanished when he saw who was on the other side of his door.

"Oh, Detective, I didn't know it was you," Anderson said solicitously. "Come in, come in," the old man urged, swinging his door open all the way and gesturing into his house.

"No, that's all right," Finn told him. "This will just take a minute of your time." He looked into Anderson's eager face. "You said you saw movers loading up the doctor's furniture."

The balding head bobbed up and down. "I did, and if you ask me, they wouldn't be the people I'd use. I saw them drop a couple of pieces and that bed frame they carried out, granted it was really heavy, but they almost—"

The man sounded as if he would go on forever. "Did you happen to see the logo on the truck?" Finn asked, interrupting Anderson's narrative.

His bushy eyebrows drew together, almost touching as he stopped to think. And then he smiled broadly as he remembered. "It was a lightning bolt!" he declared in triumph.

"A lightning bolt," Finn repeated, waiting for more.

Anderson nodded. "Yes, on account of their name," the man informed them proudly. He beamed, remembering the wording on the side of the van.

"And what was that?" Nik asked, suppressing the urge to jump down the man's throat and pull out the words.

"Lightning Movers," Anderson answered. "It was written in bright yellow letters directly under the lightning bolt. A little overkill if you ask me," he told them disdainfully. "But then, I guess that—"

"Thank you," Finn told the old man, shaking his hand. "You've been a great help."

Anderson looked almost disappointed that his moment in the spotlight was over. "Are you sure you won't come in?"

"No, we really have to be going. Thanks to you," Finn told him, backing away. Nik was already ahead of him. "We have a destination."

"Hey, anytime I can be of more service, just let me know," Anderson called out to them.

"We'll do that," Finn answered, feeling that it was only fair to let the man down gently.

Finn and Nik hurried to put distance between themselves and the man standing and waving in his doorway. They quickly got into Finn's car.

"Let's hope Harley was right," Finn said, starting up his car.

He'd lost her. "About what?" she asked as they made their way out of the elegant neighborhood.

"About Valri practically living in the computer lab," Finn answered.

They were on the main thoroughfare now. "What do you need her to check out?" Nik asked.

"Lightning Movers. I need the address of the company plus their hours of operation." He glanced at the clock on his dashboard. "They might not be open at this hour."

"Oh, hell, you don't need Valri for that. I can check that out for you," Nik told him, typing in the moving company's name into the search engine on her phone.

Because he didn't have a destination yet, Finn drove toward the precinct.

"Well?" he asked as she typed.

She had just finished inputting the name, and was scrolling through the information that had come up.

"It says here that their office opens at nine on Mondays. They open at eight all the other days of the week— except for Sundays," she added. "Looks like they're closed Sundays."

Finn nodded, continuing toward the precinct. "Okay, we'll stop by the precinct, see if either Harley or Ramirez have any updates, then tell them about what Anderson had to tell us."

Nik could feel excitement mounting as they drove. "This is like a giant jigsaw puzzle, isn't it?"

"Yeah," he answered, nodding. "Except nobody dies in a jigsaw puzzle if you can't get all the pieces to fit together," he pointed out grimly.

She thought of the women who had already died, and then she thought of Marilyn, who may or may not still be alive—her fate was still unknown. "Yes, there is that," she agreed quietly.

"I was just going to call you," Ramirez said, rising to his feet the second that he saw Finn and Nik walking in.

Finn searched the other detective's face, wondering

if this was good news or bad that Ramirez was going to relay.

"About?" he asked.

Harley broke in, not allowing Ramirez to finish. "We were combing through some of the old open cases on the books, trying to see if there were any similarities to our case."

"And?" Finn asked warily.

"We found five women who were killed the same way that these latest victims were. The killer used the same MO," Harley said. "They were all young women, each dressed up for a night out on the town, except that it turned out to be their last night out on the town," he added grimly.

"Why didn't we find these other victims before?" Finn asked.

Ramirez shook his head. "It turns out that these five women were killed in or around Palm Springs approximately two years ago. It was a spree, and then it apparently stopped."

"Find out just when Dr. Garrett transferred to Aurora Memorial," he said to the two detectives. "Text me the answer as soon as you find out."

Ramirez looked at Finn. "Where are you going to be, boss?"

"Kowalski and I are going to go talk to the moving company that moved Dr. Garrett to his new residence and find out exactly where that is. With any luck, we'll find the cocky SOB there and bring him in." He looked at Nik. "You ready to go?"

"I thought you'd never ask," she said, falling into step beside him as they left.

Chapter 24

Armed with the address that the assistant working in Lightning Movers' tiny general office had been persuaded to give to him, Finn drove himself and Nik to Dr. Garrett's latest place of residence. It was located in an even more exclusive neighborhood than the previous one.

There appeared to be no one around walking a dog, jogging or even driving anywhere.

"Wow, that's his new house?" Nik said, craning her neck to get a better view of the large, three-story building. She turned toward Finn. "It looks more like a castle than a house."

"A castle that comes with its own evil ogre," Finn said under his breath.

Pulling up in front of the towering wrought-iron gates, Finn parked along the curb, then got out of his car. Nik was already out on her side.

Inspecting the gates, he didn't see a buzzer to press in

order to announce himself and gain access to the front door. "Talk about not wanting to be disturbed," he said to Nik.

Because there didn't seem to be a way in, on a whim, she tugged on one of the gates. It gave way and opened. Nobody could have been more surprised than she was. "I guess he didn't have time to install a security system," she said to Finn.

"I guess not," Finn responded, pushing the gates farther apart. Then they walked onto the property.

"This doesn't seem right," she said, looking around as they approached the house. "Did he know we were coming?"

"Doesn't seem likely. My guess is that the good doctor would have had the gates wired in that case," Finn said.

Taking in everything, he quickly circled the perimeter of the house. Nik matched him step for step, being his second set of eyes.

"It doesn't look like there's anyone home," Finn concluded when he had made a full circle all around the structure.

"Not on the ground floor at any rate," she agreed. As she watched, she saw Finn take out his phone. Her curiosity aroused, she waited to hear him talk to someone before asking questions.

"Ramirez, I want you to get a search warrant for the address I'm about to give you. It's the doctor's new den of inequity," he said, then rattled off the address to the other detective.

Ramirez's voice carried on the phone. "We need probable cause, boss," the detective reminded Finn.

"Probable cause is that both the missing woman and the dead woman we found yesterday were last seen in this guy's company. We need to find this creep *now*," Finn insisted.

"You don't have to convince me," Nik heard the other detective say.

She waited until Finn put away his phone. "So what do we do until Ramirez gets here with a warrant?" she asked.

He looked up at the towering structure. "We hang around and make sure that if someone *is* in there, they don't try to escape."

She nodded, going back with him to his car. "Too bad I didn't bring a deck of cards," she said, resigning herself to a possibly long wait. She really hated wasting time.

Ramirez and the warrant were there less than an hour later. Harley had come with him.

Taking the warrant from Ramirez, Finn quickly headed back to the front door. "Okay, let's search the place," Finn declared.

They hadn't seen anyone leave the premises, but he pounded on the door anyway. There was still no response. It really did seem like there was no one home.

"Are you going to break the door down?" Nik asked just as Finn seemed to be getting ready to do just that.

"There's nobody home," he told her. "You know a better way to gain access?"

"Maybe," she answered, surprising him. "Just let me give this a try."

Finn scowled. Before he could ask her what "this" was, Nik had dropped down to her knees in front of the door's lock. She started using something she had pulled out of her wallet. Finn moved closer, watching her. Before he could say anything, he saw that she had managed to jimmy open the lock. She turned the knob and pushed open the door. Then, holding on to the doorknob, she got back up to her feet.

"You're really handy to have around, Nik," Harley told her, genuine admiration in his voice.

Finn was staring at her. "Where did you learn how to do that?"

"That's a little something my father taught me," she said in an offhanded manner. "He said it might come in handy someday if I locked myself out of somewhere important," she explained.

Finn wasn't a hundred percent convinced of the veracity of her story. "When this is over, I think we should have a little talk regarding your background and your family," he said as they all crossed the threshold and entered the house. Once inside, Finn raised his voice and called out, "Aurora PD. Anyone here?" No one answered.

Going to the bottom of the staircase, he called up the stairs with the same exact result. No one answered him and there was absolutely no sound coming from any other part of the rambling house.

If this was Garrett's new residence, it didn't look as if he was anywhere on the premises.

"All right, you know what to do," Finn told the other two detectives behind him. "See if you can find anything that could tie Garrett to any of the dead women we've recently found. A photo, an article of clothing. Anything that doesn't belong. Who knows, he might have gotten sloppy, which means we get lucky."

The detectives began to head in different directions, one taking the top floor, the other the second floor.

"What do you want me to do?" Nik asked Finn.

For a second, he'd almost forgotten she was here. "Raise your right hand."

Nik looked at him, a little bewildered as she did what he told her.

His voice took on a formal tone as he said, "I hereby appoint you to the post of temporary rookie with the Aurora Police Department with the understanding that you are exclusively attached to only this investigation. You can put your hand down," he told her, then said in his regular voice. "Now you can help with the search. If you find anything," he went on, "I want to know the second you do."

"You got it."

Two hours of methodical searching yielded absolutely nothing that was useful in the slightest way. They had all come up empty.

"I don't get it," Harley complained as he joined the others on the first floor. "There are no personal effects, no photographs, no souvenirs to commemorate his kills. Nothing. This might as well be a movie set," he told the others in disgust. Shaking his head, he repeated, "I don't get it."

Finn saw Nik working her bottom lip, the way she did when she was thinking. She looked as if she was going to bite clean through it. "What are you thinking?" he asked her.

"Maybe he has a storage unit somewhere where he keeps all that kind of stuff," Nik mused. "This way, when he moves from house to house, he doesn't have to pack that up—or run the risk of one of the movers finding it. Everything is tucked away," she concluded, looking at Finn. "Nice and safe."

That had to be it, Finn thought. There was no other explanation. "You know, the way your mind works is beginning to worry me," he told Nik. He was only half kidding.

She wasn't sure if he was being serious, but she was taking no chances. "It shouldn't," she told him. "I like to read murder mysteries in my free time."

Finn turned toward the other two detectives. "Okay, see if either one of you can find a key to this possible storage unit."

Nik had one more idea on the subject. "It might not be here," she told Finn. "The doctor might have it on his person. You know, keeping the 'stuff that dreams are made of' close," she said, theorizing.

"Makes sense," Ramirez said, rolling over the possibility in his head.

They searched the various rooms anyway, just in case Garrett didn't have the storage unit key—if he even *had* such a unit—with him.

They came up empty.

Finished going through the rooms, Finn said, "Harley, I want you and Ramirez to watch the premises. My guess is that he's got to come back to his new 'home' sooner or later. According to the most up-to-date information about the good doctor, he's going to be returning to work in a week. I've got a hunch that he's going to want one or two more women to pay the ultimate price for knowing him before he puts a lid on his bloodlust, at least until the next time," he said, thinking of what had been discovered about a possible previous killing spree.

"Sure thing," Ramirez agreed just as Finn's phone buzzed, announcing an incoming text.

Finn quickly scanned his screen.

"Anything good?" Nik asked, forgetting protocol and standing on her toes to get a better look at Finn's cell phone.

There was a grim smile on his face as he put away his phone. "That depends on your point of view." He looked at the other two detectives, letting them in on the text as well. "Garrett's Porsche was just spotted parked in the vicinity of The Greek Isles Restaurant."

Nik was ready to fly out the door. "I take it that's our next stop."

Finn nodded. "We'll set up surveillance near where his car is parked." His eyes shifted to Harley and Ramirez. "You two do the same across the street from this house. The bastard's luck can't last forever," he said as he strode out of the mansion, Nik following behind.

"Hang on," he told Nik as he started up his car. His adrenaline was amped up. "I want to get there before he has a chance to take off."

"Don't you have an officer on the premises?" she asked him. Worst-case scenario, the officer could follow the doctor's vehicle.

"I want to be there," Finn insisted.

The car revved to life in less time than it took to say the words. Nik braced her hand against the dashboard, her heart racing.

"You weren't kidding about hanging on," she told him. "Birds have slower takeoffs than you just executed."

She thought she saw a glimmer of a smile on Finn's lips, but he didn't say anything in response. He just focused on the road and drove. Fast.

"That has to be some kind of a record," she told him as he pulled into the parking lot across from the restaurant less than ten minutes later.

Her heart was still pounding. Nik scanned the area and although she saw the Porsche parked several yards away, she didn't see the patrol car.

She said as much to Finn.

"That's the whole idea," he told her. "I don't want to scare Garrett away." Turning off his own car's lights,

Finn sat back in his seat. "Hope you're in the mood to wait," he told her.

"If it means dragging this guy off the streets and into the police station, hell, I can wait all night," she told him.

That's what he'd figured she'd say. "Let's hope we don't have to."

But they nearly did.

Finn had begun to give up hope, thinking that for some reason Garrett had decided to abandon his car and use another vehicle to make his exit, when he felt Nik suddenly stiffening and coming to attention right beside him.

"We're in business," she told him, whispering the words as if she was afraid that the doctor might overhear her. "Over there," she said and pointed, just in case Finn didn't see the threesome in the distance. They appeared to be approaching the doctor's Porsche.

From where he sat, Finn could make out a well-dressed, handsome man and a slightly shorter, attractive blonde woman, each with their arms around another woman, who was between them. The woman would have surely fallen to the ground if they weren't actively guiding her toward the newly waxed, gleaming white vehicle parked several yards away from them.

"That's them," he confirmed. "And they've got another candidate."

Finn was immediately out of his car. Nik lost no time in joining him. Striding ahead, Finn reached the threesome first.

"Is there a problem?" he asked, sounding helpful as he indicated the woman between the couple. The former looked as if she could hardly walk without help from her human bookends.

"I'm afraid that my fiancée's sister has had a little too

much to drink," Garrett told the so-called Good Samaritan. "Thanks for your kind offer, but we won't be needing any help. I'm a doctor," Garrett announced proudly. "We'll just get her home and into bed. I'm sure she'll be fine by morning," he told them with confidence.

"My guess is that if I let her go with you two, she'll be dead by morning," Finn said.

"That's absurd," Marilyn protested, her voice cracking. She looked very unsteady as she tried to hold up the other woman. "What are you talking about? Please get out of our way," she demanded. She looked nervously at the man who was helping her hold up the barely conscious woman between them.

That was when Nik stepped out of the shadows. "He can't do that, Marilyn. And you don't have a sister," Nik said with finality.

Fear and horror washed over Marilyn's already ashen face. "How do you know my name?" Marilyn cried.

"Look, the longer we delay getting this poor girl home, the worse off she is probably going to be." The doctor's voice hardened. "Now, good intentions or not, I want you to step aside, do you hear me?" he demanded.

"Afraid I can't do that, Dr. Garrett," Finn told him. "I suggest that you let her go," he ordered, drawing out his service weapon from the holster at his waist. "*Now*, before things get any worse."

Garrett's face darkened. Shouting out a curse, he shoved the woman he'd chosen to be his next victim, pushing her straight into Finn. The latter made a grab for the falling woman with the intent of placing her on the ground and giving chase after the homicidal physician. But he found he didn't have to. Executing what he could only later refer to in his report as what looked like an intricate dance move, Nik whirled around, knocked the doctor off-balance and wound up tripping him. He went down with the full force of his weight, hitting the asphalt hard and screaming obscene curses at her.

The next moment, Finn was cuffing him and the doctor was swearing that Finn was going to live to regret ever having been born.

Finn didn't even bother answering him.

"You, too, honey," he said to Marilyn as he restrained her and snapped a pair of cuffs on her. "You're not going anywhere, either, except to jail along with your boyfriend here." Pulling out his cell phone, he handed it to Nik. "You get to call for backup," he told her. "Just press two," he instructed, raising his voice over Marilyn's anguished sobs and Dr. Garrett's very vocal predictions of what the doctor was going to do to him to make him regret ever being born once the charges against him were dismissed.

The only one who was quiet at this point was the unconscious, drugged woman on the ground.

Nik did as Finn instructed and pressed the number two on his phone. The second she heard Ramirez answering, she immediately told the other detective, "We got him. I mean, Finn got him," she amended. "Garrett was about to kill another woman," she said, her voice filled with emotion. "Send an ambulance and backup to the parking lot across the street from The Greek Isles Restaurant. Fast," she stressed.

Finished, she held out the phone to Finn. She could feel her heartbeat all the way into her fingers.

"A little busy here at the moment," Finn told her, as he passed on taking the cell from her and talking to Ramirez. "You said it all, anyway."

"Look, garbage-for-brains, unless you release me immediately, you are going to regret the day you were ever born, do you understand?" Garrett threatened.

"I don't think so," Finn replied in a voice he figured the doctor would find maddeningly easygoing.

Marilyn, meanwhile, was crying. "Let me go," she begged frantically. "Please let me go." Her head whirled as she looked from Finn to Nik. "My mother doesn't know where I am. I have to go see her," she insisted.

"Damn straight you do, but not until this is over," Nik said. Thinking of how Kim was going to take this, it hurt her to say what she did to Marilyn, but there was no other choice in her opinion.

"But I didn't do anything," Marilyn cried. "Not on my own. Not because I wanted to," she insisted. "He *made* me help him. He said that if I didn't, he'd kill my mother in her sleep. I knew he would! Don't you see, I had to help him. I had no choice!" she shouted.

Finn saw Nik's eyes go cold as she looked at the woman she had searched for and he had to admit that he was impressed. And proud of her for not allowing herself to be manipulated.

"You *always* had a choice," Nik said to Marilyn.

"I didn't, I didn't," Marilyn insisted.

Her voice broke as Garrett cursed at her roundly, saying things that made her mouth drop open.

In the background, Finn heard the sound of approaching sirens. They grew louder as they came closer.

"None too soon," he commented to Nik. He expected her to say something in response. But she didn't and the look on her face grew exceedingly grim.

Chapter 25

It had been a long day and an even longer night. Nik felt as if she had been through a twenty-five-mile forced march through the desert in the middle of an extremely grueling heat wave.

But when it was all over, she told herself that it was all worth it.

Or at least a large part of it was. In the end, after questioning the homicidal doctor and his utterly clueless, hysterical accomplice in separate interrogation rooms, Finn, Nik and his task force got what they needed to build an airtight case against Dr. James Garrett. Marilyn talked nonstop once a deal for a more lenient sentence was dangled in front of her. With her evidence, Finn was confident that the psychopathic physician would never prey on another woman again, and never cause another family the kind of grief that his previous killing sprees had created.

"This is a huge win," Finn told Nik after Garrett and

Marilyn were taken away, and he and Nik finally went back to their desks in the robbery squad room. He smiled to himself. "I knew Garrett would talk. By definition, serial killers are all self-centered narcissists who think they're completely superior to the people they prey on. They can't help talking about what they've done. All we needed was to find the right way to tap into that. And you did it." He sat down on the edge of the desk she was using, smiling broadly at her. "You got Marilyn to talk, to tell you how Garrett coerced her to help him get to those women and have them lower their guard just enough so that they could be charmed by him.

"And," he continued, attempting to get her to snap out of what he took to be a depressed funk, "if it wasn't for you getting Marilyn to open up, we would have never known just where he had that storage unit of his. It would have taken us forever to find the one he frequented. This whole area is full of storage units." He shook his head, thinking about that. "If you ask me, Californians have way too much stuff."

"No argument there," Nik agreed quietly.

Finn paused, studying her face. Nik's eyes looked incredibly sad to him. He had a feeling he knew why. "You're thinking about your friend, aren't you?"

Nik blew out a long breath, trying not to dwell on what she had done—and what she still needed to do.

She raised her eyes to his. "Actually, I'm thinking about the fact that I have to tell a woman who asked me to find her missing daughter that her daughter isn't missing, but she's an immoral accomplice who was helping a sick individual lure who knows how many women to their deaths. How do I do that?" she asked Finn. "How do I tell her that?"

He took Nik's hand in his and held it for a moment. "We do it together," Finn told her.

She shook her head. This wasn't right. "I can't ask you to do that."

"You're not asking," he gently pointed out. "I'm offering." Finn rose from the desk, still looking at Nik. "What do you say we get out of here and go have a drink at Malone's?" he suggested.

She didn't think she would be up to that, not after she finished facing Marilyn's mother. "If it's all the same to you, I'd rather just go see Kim and get this over with, then go to my place." She watched his face for a reaction.

Finn nodded. "Yes, that's doable, too. C'mon, let's go and get this over with."

She knew that he was as wiped out as she was. And for Finn, this had turned into a complete victory. Even that last would-be victim they had gotten away from the doctor before he was able to give her another dose of Rohypnol, a lethal one this time, was going to make it according to the ER doctor. Finn should be out celebrating right now, not coming with her and holding her hand.

"You don't have to do this," she told him.

"Sure I do, 'rookie,'" Finn told her with a smile, putting his arm around her shoulders as they walked out of the squad room. "We're in this thing together, remember?" he reminded her.

She remembered, all right. Remembered the exact wording he had used when he'd allowed her to work on the case with his team.

"Just until the case was over," she said, quoting his words when he'd "sworn" her in.

"Well, I'm thinking we need to extend that time frame just a little longer..." he replied loftily. Finn left his statement hanging.

That was when she realized that she loved him—and that she was in deep trouble because there was nothing she could do about that.

It was very late when they arrived at Kim Palmer's house. As Finn brought his car to a stop, Nik was tempted to tell him to turn his car around and return in the morning. But she also knew that this would just be hanging over her head, growing bigger and bigger. Besides, she'd still have to face it in the morning, so she kept silent. Getting out of the vehicle, she went up to the front door and forced herself to knock.

Rather than endure a muffled exchange through the door, Nik saw it suddenly opening before she had a chance to knock a second time.

One look at her friend's face told Nik that Kim Palmer knew everything.

And she wasn't happy about it.

"You!" The single word came out sounding like a shrilled curse. Kim's dark eyes darted back and forth between Nik and Finn. "How could you?" she angrily demanded. "How *could* you?"

Nik started to open her mouth to defend herself, although she had no idea what she was going to say. She felt Finn's hand on her arm, exerting just enough pressure to make her hold her piece.

Instead, Finn spoke to the angry woman in the doorway. "I'm assuming that your daughter used her one phone call to call you."

"Of course she called me," Kim snapped. "I'm the only person who didn't betray her."

"No one's being betrayed," Finn told her, enunciating each word in a quiet voice in order to get the woman to calm down. "The truth of it is your daughter acted as a panderer and lured unsuspecting women to their deaths by bringing them to her boyfriend and turning them over to him."

"Boyfriend," Kim scoffed. "He wasn't her boyfriend. What kind of a man threatens to kill someone's mother if she didn't do what he told her to?" Kim shouted. "Marilyn was just trying to protect me," the woman insisted, almost beside herself.

Finn began to answer Kim, but Nik held up her hand, stopping him. She wanted to answer Marilyn's mother herself.

"Marilyn was just trying to justify herself to you, justify the horrible things she had done. Kim, she was desperate to get Garrett to stay with her. She wanted to prove to him that she was indispensable. Marilyn was convinced that as long as she helped Garrett satisfy his bloodlust, he'd keep her around—instead of the alternative," she concluded grimly.

Kim's eyes widened with fearful disbelief. "Which was?" she asked.

Nik's eyes met hers. "I think you know the answer to that," she told the woman. When Kim continued looking at her, waiting even as she trembled, Nik answered her. "He would have killed her, too. Just as he had his last 'assistant.'"

"What are you saying?" Kim asked in a shaky, disbelieving voice. The woman seemed to all but fade into herself, looking fearful.

"She's telling you that Garrett had done this before," Finn told Marilyn's mother. "We dug through open case files in Palm Springs and we found that Garrett conducted the same sort of killing spree there, using the help of another infatuated young woman. At the end of his homicidal spree, he killed her, too."

Kim was shaking all over now. "You're lying! I don't believe you!"

"We texted Garrett's picture to that girl's family. Her brother recognized Garrett as the doctor his sister had run off with. Her body was later found in a landfill," Finn told Marilyn's mother. "I'll spare you the gory details."

Kim Palmer looked at them with tear-filled eyes. She appeared haunted and lost. "What do I do now?"

"You cry. You pull yourself together. And you get Marilyn the best damn lawyer you can find," Nik answered, "because she's going to need one. *And*," she added, "you be grateful that your daughter didn't wind up being among all those other women who crossed that doctor's path." Finished, Nik turned toward Finn. "I need to get out of here."

"Yes, you do," he agreed, guiding her away from Kim Palmer's house.

He waited until he got Nik to his car before he said anything. In the driver's seat, he turned to look at her. "About that drink," he began, prepared to coax her if he had to. If he'd ever seen someone who looked as if they needed a drink, it was her.

He saw a sheen in her eyes and knew that she was doing her best to hold back tears. "Do you have anything to drink at your place?" she asked hoarsely.

Finn realized that he had never felt so very protective of anyone in his life. He smiled at Nik, then started up his car. "Funny you should ask."

He drove her away from Kim Palmer's house as quickly as he could, hoping distance would help her deal with what she was feeling.

Twenty minutes later, he unlocked his front door and brought Nik into his single-story house.

"What'll you have?" he asked, turning on the living-room light. "I've got vodka, rum, whiskey and—"

He never got to the "and" part because as he'd turned toward Nik to continue giving her a selection to choose from, Nik suddenly launched herself into his arms, her mouth immediately finding his.

"This is what I'll have," she told him, kissing Finn with an urgency that gave no indication it would be quenched anytime soon.

Clothes began to go flying, falling helter-skelter to the floor without notice. Nik's questing mouth was every-where. She was a parched woman lost in the desert and seeking water in order to save herself.

Finn was that watering hole.

And he was desperate to help.

They made love feverishly, using every single ounce of strength they could summon.

They made love not once but twice, until finally, too exhausted to even move an eyelash, they remained where they were, on the floor in his living room. The only thing Finn could manage to do was put his arms around Nik and hold her.

He held her until the first rays of daylight began to softly slip into the room.

"Better?" Finn finally asked when he felt her stirring against him.

He felt her lips forming a small smile against his chest. "I didn't mean to attack you like that," she said ruefully. "Sorry."

Nik tried to rise but Finn wanted to keep her where she was for a few moments longer.

"I'm not sorry," he told her.

He felt her warm breath move along his skin as she laughed softly. "I guess you could just think of that as a last hurrah," Nik said, attempting to make an excuse for her actions.

But Finn didn't understand. "Why would I think that?" he asked.

She was trying to distance herself and it hurt. "Well, because the case is over, it's solved, and you'll go back to your regular cases and I'll go back to insurance investigations and we won't see each other anymore."

The finality of that tasted bitter in her mouth.

Finn raised himself up on his elbow and searched her face. He could feel something die inside of him. "Is that what you want?"

"I thought that's what you wanted," she told him. "To have me go," she added, the words creating a sad, helpless feeling inside of her.

She wasn't going to cry, Nik silently insisted, but even now, she could feel something moist forming on her lashes.

"Lady," Finn informed her authoritatively, "you have no idea what I want. It certainly isn't what you just said."

Nik didn't want to hope. It was too awful if that hope didn't bear fruit. But she couldn't seem to help herself. "Oh?"

"Yeah, 'oh,'" he echoed.

"All right," she said slowly, feeling her stomach forming a hard, almost disabling knot inside her. But she knew she had to continue, knew she had to get Finn to explain what he meant—otherwise, she was going to go on nurturing this glimmer of hope for the rest of her natural life. "What do you want?"

"You," he said, looming over her. "I want you. For the rest of my life, I want you. I want to wake up to you, I want to go to sleep with you. And, just in case I haven't made myself clear, Kowalski," he told her, "*I want you*."

Laughter bubbled up within her chest. "You talk too much, Cavanaugh," she told him, pulling his mouth down to hers.

"Just trying to make myself clear," he murmured, drawing away from her long enough to say that one last thing before he completely gave himself up to making passionate love with the woman he planned to marry.

Very, very soon.

Because when you find the one your heart has been looking for since the very beginning, he saw no reason to wait.

* * * * *

*Don't forget previous titles in the
Cavanaugh Justice series:*

Cavanaugh's Missing Person
Cavanaugh Cowboy
Cavanaugh's Secret Delivery
Cavanaugh Vanguard
Cavanaugh Encounter

*Available now from
Harlequin Romantic Suspense!*

#2067 COLTON'S RESCUE MISSION
The Coltons of Roaring Springs • by Karen Whiddon

The sudden spark of attraction toward his brother's former fiancée, Vanessa Fisher, takes Remy Colton by surprise. Seth's addictions and emotional distress have gotten out of control. Will Remy's desire to protect Vanessa from his brother be his own downfall?

#2068 COLTON 911: FAMILY UNDER FIRE
Colton 911 • by Jane Godman

Four years ago, Alyssa Bartholomew left Everett Colton rather than see him in danger. Now, when their unexpected baby is threatened, the FBI agent is the only person who can keep her safe.

#2069 DETECTIVE ON THE HUNT
by Marilyn Pappano

Detective JJ Logan only came to Cedar Creek to figure out what happened to socialite Maura Evans, but as the mystery surrounding her deepens, local police officer Quint Foster finds himself hoping she'll stay a little longer—if they get out of the case alive!

#2070 EVIDENCE OF ATTRACTION
Bachelor Bodyguards • by Lisa Childs

To get CSI Wendy Thompson to destroy evidence, a killer threatens her and her parents' lives—forcing her to accept the protection of her crush, former vice cop turned bodyguard Hart Fisher.

Get 4 FREE REWARDS!

We'll send you 2 FREE Books
<u>plus</u> 2 FREE Mystery Gifts.

Harlequin® Romantic Suspense books feature heart-racing sensuality and the promise of a sweeping romance set against the backdrop of suspense.

FREE
Value Over
$20

"What the hell are you doing?" she asked as she glanced
nervously around.

The curtains swished at the front window of her
parents' house. Someone was watching them.

"I'm trying to do my damn job," Hart said through
gritted teeth as he very obviously faked a grin.

She'd refused to let him inside the house last night.
From the dark circles beneath his eyes, he must not have
slept at all. Too bad his daughter's babysitter had arrived
at the agency before they'd left. He wouldn't have been
able to take Wendy home if he'd had to take care of
Felicity.

But even though his babysitter had shown up, the little
girl still needed her father—especially since he had full
custody. Where was her mother?

"You need a safer job," she told him.

"I'm fine," he said, but his voice lowered even more to a growl of frustration. "It's my assignment that's a pain in the ass."

She smiled—just as artificially as he had. "Then you need another assignment."

He shook his head. "This is the one I have," he said. "So I'm going to make the best of it."

Then he did something she hadn't expected. He lowered his head until his mouth brushed across hers.

Her pulse began to race and she gasped.

And he kissed her again, lingering this time—his lips clinging to hers before he deepened the kiss even more. When he finally lifted his head, she gasped again—this time for breath.

"What the hell was that?" she asked.

He arched his head toward the front window of the house. "For our audience…"

"You're overacting," she said—because she had to remind herself that was all he was doing. Acting…

He wasn't really her boyfriend. He wasn't really attracted to her. He was only pretending.

Don't miss
Evidence of Attraction *by Lisa Childs*
available December 2019 wherever
Harlequin® Romantic Suspense
books and ebooks are sold.

Harlequin.com

HRSEXP1119

Need an adrenaline rush from nail-biting tales
(and irresistible males)?

Check out **Harlequin Intrigue®**,
Harlequin® Romantic Suspense and
Love Inspired® Suspense books!

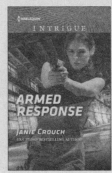  

New books available every month!

CONNECT WITH US AT:

Facebook.com/groups/HarlequinConnection

Facebook.com/HarlequinBooks

Twitter.com/HarlequinBooks

Instagram.com/HarlequinBooks

Pinterest.com/HarlequinBooks

ReaderService.com

**ROMANCE WHEN
YOU NEED IT**

SGENRE2018R